The Nightmare Frontier

The Nightmare Frontier

By Stephen Mark Rainey

Other Books by Stephen Mark Rainey

Novels:
Balak
The Lebo Coven
Dark Shadows: Dreams of the Dark (with Elizabeth Massie)
Blue Devil Island
The Nightmare Frontier
The House at Black Tooth Pond

Novels in *Elizabeth Massie's Ameri-Scares* series for Young Readers:
West Virginia: Lair of the Mothman
Michigan: The Dragon of Lake Superior
Ohio: Fear the Grassman!
New Hampshire: Ghosts From the Skies
Georgia: The Haunting of Tate's Mill

Novella:
The Gods of Moab

Collections:
Fugue Devil & Other Weird Horrors
The Last Trumpet
Other Gods
The Gaki & Other Hungry Spirits
Legends of the Night
Fugue Devil: Resurgence

Anthologies (edited):
Song of Cthulhu
Evermore (with James Robert Smith)
Deathrealms
Deathrealm: Spirits

Dark Shadows Audio Drama Scripts:
The Path of Fate
The Labyrinth of Souls
Blood Dance

Tay Ninh Province, South Vietnam
(War Zone C)
June 1967

Technically, it wasn't jungle. Its official military rating was "triple-canopied rain forest," which meant visibility through the trees and undergrowth exceeded thirty yards, at least in places. In the past hour, the platoon had hacked its way through more than a thousand yards of matted vines, creepers, thorns, and bamboo clusters—half again the limitation of "jungle" terrain. Still, even though sunlight penetrated the leafy tiers only sporadically, the temperature hovered around the hundreddegree mark, and at ninety-nine percent relative humidity, the air quickly left a man feeling as if he were drowning in hot bathwater. Moving little faster than the ants that marched to their own drumbeat, the thirty-nine Americans advanced single file through the brush, foregoing the standard parallel columns, which offered Charlie not one but two tantalizing groups of targets should he be in the mood to spring an ambush.

Since the First Infantry Division had been deployed, Charlie had been in the mood an awful lot.

On point, PFC Ryan Cortland was making decent time and actually seemed to have a cool head on his shoulders—doubtlessly because he was the FNG (fucking new guy) and hadn't learned yet that, out here, showing initiative more often led to a bad end than a promotion. Hell, though; if there were snipers in the bush, your odds were about the same whether you were the point man or Tail-End Charlie. Or anywhere in between.

The last time there were no snipers in the bush, Lieutenant Glen Martin had been Mister Glen Martin, sipping vodka and tonics on his back porch in Huntington. The VC always hit hard and then turned invisible with shocking suddenness, largely because they could pop in and out of concealed entrances of their tunnels, which formed an impressive, if ominous, network between Tay Ninh and Svay Rieng, Cambodia. Today, Martin's objective was to rout the vermin out of the ground and into his sights.

He had brought along his best tunnel rats for the job.

Cortland slowed his pace, and Martin moved forward, leading with his M-16. Softly he asked, "Smell something, private?"

The young man, his eyes brilliant amid black greasepaint, shrugged uncertainly. "Looks like a break ahead. Think I saw something moving."

Martin held up a fist, halting the column. A broad swath of daylight split the hardwood pillars some fifty yards ahead, and within it, a wisp of shadow swayed slowly back and forth—which he finally identified as a bunch of creepers caught in a breeze too feeble to penetrate the tree line. The air smelled of rotten citrus and sour loam, but it bore no trace of cordite, petroleum, or other human detritus. Of course, out here, that meant diddlysquat; if Charlie didn't want you to know he was around, you didn't know he was around. Simple as that.

Where the trees ended, Martin could see pale gray stone—either the face of a tall cliff or the wall of some hulking structure, though the latter seemed unlikely. He waggled one finger in the direction of the clearing, and the line started moving, slowly, only slightly louder than a band of Cherokees. As they neared the break, sure enough, Martin could make out the irregular outline of a massive stone edifice, overhung with vines and deeply stained from God knew how many years of exposure to the elements. No sound trickled from the building, and birds, insects, and other unseen noisemakers kept up a constant chatter in the distance.

Good sign, that.

From what he could see, the structure resembled nothing he had previously encountered in this country. Definitely not one of the ubiquitous Cham temples, which featured tiered, intricately sculpted walls, friezes, and porticos. This one was obviously ancient and built to last for ages, but its contours were simple, its ash-hued walls featureless, though severely pitted with age. Off to the left, he could see a row of thick gray pillars, maybe twenty feet high, apparently all that remained of a long, covered entranceway. Above the broken green canopy, a tall spire the color of old bone rose high into the sky, which lent the building the superficial appearance of a European cathedral.

A relic left by the French?

He paused to allow his second-in-command, Sergeant Matt Collins, to catch up to him, then whispered into the shorter man's grease-painted ear, "Send Sieber's squad to the left, Wiley's to the right to secure the entrance. For God's sake, watch out for traps."

Collins's eyes flashed, and he rushed to carry out the order. Martin then crept up beside the stocky, simian figure of Sergeant Samuel Barrow, his senior tunnel rat. Like Martin, Barrow was a West Virginian, but he came from some podunk town in the mountains that probably subsisted on coal mining. A vulgar, supremely ugly hillbilly, Barrow had damn near become a company legend for scurrying recklessly through tunnels, blasting everything fore and aft, burning Charlie out of his hive with the zeal of a crazed exterminator. Martin admitted to a grudging respect for the man because, like himself, Barrow was on his second tour of duty and—also like Martin—had never qualified for a Purple Heart.

"Sergeant," he said, immediately getting that quizzical, cockeyed gaze from Barrow that slightly unnerved him. "Ever seen a place like this before?"

Barrow shook his ungainly, oversized head. "Nawsir. But if

they's Charlie in there, we'll roust 'em out."

Martin nodded. His men had assumed attack formation expertly and stealthily; if they were going to take fire, it would come as soon as they were in the open.

Now he could now see a tall, rectangular doorway beneath a bizarrely tilted portico, so cattywampus it looked as if a strong wind might topple it. A narrow apron of rubble-choked, sharp-bladed grass girded the structure.

Just the place to find punji pits, toe-poppers, or other extremely nasty booby-traps.

Martin felt the presence of an enemy as plainly as the scorching sun on his shoulders. He glanced at Sergeant Collins, raised his right arm, and gave the signal to move.

Corporal Sieber's squad went first, fast and low, the leader's eyes on the ground, the rest scanning the tree line, the rubble around the building, the looming black entryway. They reached the first row of pillars and pressed close to them for cover, half their guns pointing at the trees, the other half at the building entrance. Martin's finger tightened on the trigger of his M-16, expecting to hear the lethal clatter of AK47s at any second; but even as Sergeant Wiley's squad rushed for the entrance, the forest remained eerily still.

Martin tapped Barrow on the shoulder and said, "Let's move, Sergeant." Then they were hauling pell-mell across the apron of knifelike grass, skirting waist-high blocks of stone rubble, Sieber's men closing up to form a cordon behind them. Martin screeched to a halt just shy of the weirdly angled portico, realizing its floor might be counterweighted to give way beneath them.

Holding back his troops, he thrust the butt of his M16 against the floor, which solidly deflected the blow. He took a tentative step forward, found the surface steady and unyielding, and with a few long strides, crossed the floor and slid up next to the yawning black rectangle.

The rest of the rats followed, several with heavy-duty flashlights in hand. The first pair leaped into the darkness, lights blazing, the second pair covering them with their M16s. Still no enemy fire.

As flashlight beams played wildly on gray stone walls, Martin stepped through the uncannily tall door, averting his eyes from the lights to keep from being temporarily blinded. The walls rose higher than the beams could reach, all bare stone, cracked in places, splotched with green-gray mold. The air reeked of mildew and something vaguely sulfurous. He counted six walls, all of varying widths, and two arched portals, both nearly as tall as the main doorway. No furnishings, no adornments—nothing to indicate that this place had been used by human beings for a very long time. However, the distinctive pressure at the back of his neck, a sure warning of an enemy presence nearby, grew more insistent.

He tapped the nearest man—PFC Cortland. "Private, let's have a look through one of those doors, shall we?"

Cortland nodded and crept to one of the archways, flashlight in his right hand, the muzzle of his M-16 balanced on his forearm. At Martin's signal, he crouched and thrust his flashlight through the opening. When the yellow-white beam fell upon the thing in alcove to his right, Martin's heart almost stopped.

For a disturbing second, he thought it was alive: a twenty-foot-tall wormlike beast rising from a broad, bulbous base, numerous whip-like tails curling around it, with multiple rows of needle-like spines that ran the length of its body. Atop a gnarled, spindly stalk that protruded from the base, a bright, cyclopean, sapphire eye glared at him with the disconcerting illusion of sentience. When he took a few steps toward it, the glittering eye appeared to follow him.

"God awmighty." The low whisper came from behind him, and he glanced back to see Sergeant Samuel Barrow leaning in to study the grotesque figure. "That is one ugly motherfucker."

"I can't claim to be an expert on local culture," Martin said, "but this looks like a whole lot of nothing I've ever seen anywhere."

Mesmerized, Barrow knelt to peer at the brilliant, egg-sized stone. "How much would you say that's worth, Lieutenant?"

"Doesn't matter, since it's not going anywhere, Sergeant."

Barrow snorted. "Just askin'."

Martin was about to order Barrow to move on when the first blast of gunfire rang from beyond the chamber. He automatically ducked and swiveled, just in time to see the strobing flashes of machinegun fire in the anteroom, the reports shattering the silence of the enclosed space like the clashing of deafening cymbals. He scrambled toward the towering archway just as the body of PFC Guiliano hurtled past him like a broken marionette and struck the floor with a moist, sickening thud. A long, arrow-like shaft protruded from the young man's neck, and it dawned on him then that the gunfire had come only from M16s.

Through the ringing in his ears, he made out Sergeant Collins shouting, "Hold your fire! Hold your fire!"

Confusion reigned as the men, deprived of their targets, whirled uncertainly. Martin clambered through the portal and grabbed Collins by the shoulder. "What the hell happened?"

"The bastards are in here! They just appeared out of nowhere and cut loose with—something. Arrows, blowguns, something. Quiet as hell. But they were here all along."

A few of Sieber's men had rushed in from outside, but Collins held the rest of them back. "Stay put. If there are more outside, we don't want them getting in here."

Then, from the adjacent portal, a deep thrumming sound, like a heavy engine warming up, reverberated from the building's depths. Martin peered through the arched opening and for a second glimpsed a distant flicker of light—a reflection perhaps—as something large but indistinct began moving slowly toward them.

"Don't know what that is, sir," Collins said, "but I'll make book it ain't about to wish us good day."

"Let's pull back and pin them inside," he said. "We'll see how this big rock candy bastard holds up to a couple of thousand-pounders." He nodded suggestively at the ceiling.

"You heard the man!" Collins sang out. "Fall back to our original positions. Squad order. Move it, move it!"

Martin glanced around and realized Sergeant Barrow had never emerged from the secondary chamber. He thrust his head back through the opening, realizing too late how careless he had just been; he felt surprised when nothing streaked out of the darkness to spear him. Beyond Guiliano's prone, twisted body, he could discern the errant sergeant's back. Barrow was kneeling as if in prayer before the tall, monstrous-looking statue in the alcove.

"Sergeant, let's move. *Now!*"

"Just coming, sir," came the low, gruff voice. The figure straightened and ambled unconcernedly into the dim light that shone through the archway. "No worries, Lieutenant. Everything's under control."

"Good. You can carry Guiliano's body out of there. Make it fast, Barrow; I reckon we've got ten seconds before anyone left inside this place ends up in a few more pieces than he's accustomed to."

Like a gorilla lifting a sack of bananas, Barrow hoisted the dead man to his shoulders and lumbered through the door. With a mocking leer, he growled, "Come on, Lieutenant, time's a-wasting."

Martin saw a discarded flashlight on the floor, picked it up, and on a whim, shone it into the dark room Barrow had just vacated. As the deep, pulsing beats of the approaching engine bore down upon him with increasing intensity, he stood peering at the thing he had come to think of as the demon god, and his anger began to seethe.

The giant, sapphire-hued stone—the god's eye—was gone.

Now, he was forced to turn and face the heavily thrumming apparatus—for machine it must be—which at any moment would burst from the dark opening into the anteroom. *Something* was moving slowly up the passage, just beyond the range of his beam: an erratically writhing shape, still indistinct but larger than a man, issuing deep thudding and chugging noises like a locomotive.

He felt a sudden tug on his bicep and whipped his head around to see Sergeant Collins glaring at him in warning. "Come on, Lieutenant. Standing your ground don't look like the best plan today."

Before he could react, he felt a bone-numbing impact and found himself hurtling awkwardly through the tall portal, into the blistering sunlight. He landed heavily on his back, his breath exploding through his mouth, his helmet clanking sharply against a stone in the tall sawgrass. Without pausing to catch his breath, ignoring the God-awful pain at the back of his head, he struggled to his feet, just in time to see an obviously wounded Sergeant Collins crawling through the doorway toward him.

At that moment, his eyes began playing tricks on him. They *had* to be, because the serpentine cables that sprang like grappling hooks out of the darkness, encircled Collins's body, and dragged him back inside, precisely resembled the spiny appendages of the sculpted demon god in the alcove. Collins cried out in pain and disbelief as his hands scrabbled desperately but vainly at the rough stone floor; then his body vanished into the rectangular black maw. The long, mortal wail that rang mournfully out of the darkness was silenced a moment later by a sharp, wet ripping sound.

Gunfire erupted around him, and half a second later, two of his men yanked the pins on a pair of grenades. The cry went up—"Fire in the hole!"—and Martin lowered his head as the pineapples sailed into the abyss beyond the door. Three seconds later, with a gut-wrenching *boom,* a huge blossom of orange flame roared from the opening, sending a hail of prickling shards over the crouching men. Then the tilted portico groaned like a dying elephant and slowly toppled, throwing up a thick cloud of gray dust, which quickly cloaked the structure. Inside the building, something—the ceiling of the anteroom, perhaps—collapsed heavily, sending a tremor through the ground beneath Martin's feet.

As the smoke and dust dissipated on the hot breeze, he saw that rubble now completely choked the building's entrance. Only the upper third of the twenty-foot portal remained exposed, dribbling a pale, thin streamer of smoke and dust.

"Imagine that—with just a coupla pineapples," came Barrow's voice, and Martin turned to glare at the smug-looking sergeant. A coating of grime rendered his simian features barely recognizable.

"Seems to me," Martin said, almost surprised by his own vehemence, "I made mention a while back that what we found in that place was to stay there."

Barrow scowled incredulously at him and waved a hand at the destruction. "Don't tell me, *sir,* that with all this, you're gonna get riled over a friggin' trinket?"

"It's not the trinket," Martin said, his voice icy. "It's when I tell you something, you better listen and listen good. You've known that since day one, and you'd better keep that in your head from here on out. Am I perfectly clear, Sergeant Barrow?"

Slack-jawed, Barrow slowly nodded. Martin gave him a final glare. "Your selfishness could have cost somebody his life. Now get your ass together; we've still got a job to do here."

If Barrow intended to respond, he never got the chance. Like black lightning, something coiled around his legs, ripped them quickly out from under him, and began dragging him toward the smoking ruin. With a cold thrill of dread, Martin saw that a long, spiny tendril the color of gunmetal had snared Barrow and was now retracting into the partially blocked opening. He bolted after the writhing figure, raised his M-16 in one hand, and emptied half a clip into the black mouth, from which several more spiked cables whipped forth like living, thrashing barbed wire.

Now one of the appendages slithered down the rubble toward him, its tip rhythmically tapping the ground like the questing tongue of a snake. He drew to a halt and quickly backed out of harm's way, his eyes lifting to meet Barrow's last regretful gaze. One of the sergeant's hands slid into his shirt, dug for a second, and then emerged holding a small green bundle, which he wound up and hurled into the air. As the package landed with a thud right at Martin's feet, Barrow disappeared without so much as a grunt or groan into the leering black gullet.

Martin scooped up the canvas ammo pouch, knowing what he would find inside, and stuffed it into a deep thigh pocket. He unhooked a grenade, yanked the pin, and heaved it with all his strength into the opening. Then he spun and hauled at top speed away from the advancing arms of the enemy, calling as he ran for the platoon to fall back to the tree line. Around him, soldiers scurried for cover, and then the world exploded again. The shock wave washed over his back like a fiery sirocco.

By the time he reached the cover of a huge teak tree, the world had fallen eerily silent. One of his hands dipped into his thigh pocket and withdrew the ammo pouch that Barrow had tossed to him. He held it up discreetly, lifted the flap, and inspected the glittering shape that hid within.

The egg-shaped jewel seemed to radiate its own light—a brilliant electric blue generated deep within its cold, crystalline heart. Captivatingly beautiful, he thought; it had certainly captivated Sergeant Barrow. Martin knew that, back home, Barrow had two little boys, one of which had been born just before he had left for his first tour of duty.

As of today, they had no father.

PFC Cortland ambled up to him, sweat pouring down his youthful face. Martin stashed the stone back in his pocket and made himself forget it existed. Cortland shook his head wearily.

"Charlie's gotten damned clever, ain't he, sir?"

Martin nodded ruefully, his eyes locked on the towering house of deadly secrets. In fifteen minutes, on his order, a flight of Thuds would arrive to knock the place down like a house of cards.

"Yeah, private. Mighty damned clever indeed."

#

Day One

Chapter 1

Driving on the interstate, the casual traveler rarely engages two synapses reflecting on what lies beyond the forests of billboards, traffic signs, food and fuel plazas, viaducts, floodlights, and orange barrels, the prevalence of which would suggest that civilization's mantle extends well into those remote, sparsely populated corners of the United States that many have forgotten still exist. Even when dusty prairies, broad rivers, rolling hills, or forested mountains dominate the vistas surrounding our asphalt and concrete conduits, there is always the sense that little truly changes from one place to another. When one exits onto an unfamiliar side road, seldom will his confidence of locating an Exxon, a McDonald's, and perhaps a WalMart be shaken for very long. And when one's adult perceptions have been shaped almost exclusively by the urban sprawl along the western shores of Lake Michigan, the expectation of a vast human footprint on any given locale comes all the more honestly.

It was the odd, almost overwhelming sense of isolation, rather than the gravity of his current undertaking, that dominated Russell Copeland's musings as his city-bred Lexus bounded roller coaster–like up, down, and around the narrow, winding thread of West Virginia 201—a highway in name only, its surface so pitted and potholed that his car's recent alignment had been shot to hell after less than five miles. He met traffic only infrequently, which was fortunate, since avoiding a disastrous sideswipe meant veering so far to the right that he risked plummeting down steep, rocky embankments or plowing into close-pressing trees whose roots had actually burrowed up through the asphalt. The shadows beneath the dense canopies of oak, walnut, sycamore, and pine seemed less the product of obstructed sunlight than sovereign, burgeoning masses of darkness that teemed with unseen life, the sounds of which occasionally gusted in through his open windows. At least the early spring air smelled earthy and sweet, and certainly cleaner than the cloying, almost sickly odor that permeated the forest preserves around Chicago.

So far, the West Virginia experience felt nothing like a homecoming, even though, as a boy, he had lived very near here, at the edge of a now-defunct dolomite quarry. His dad, a stone-processing company executive, had earned a respectable salary for his day, so his family fared much better than the majority of the local population, whose existence could be described politely as modest (or more bluntly as squalid). Still, Byston County's sole private school had provided young Russell with a more than solid education, and when it came time to choose his calling, he'd fled as far from rural West Virginia as possible, into a field that ensured a permanent escape from these desolate, gloomy backwoods. His specialty was electronics and, for the last half-dozen years, he'd worked as a high-end IT system designer, contracting primarily with various government agencies, all of which involved high security clearance. The field excited him, and the money wasn't bad.

Until recently, he had actually been happy.

Until his final blowout with the lunatic Megan…

Judging from the unsightly hovels, decrepit-looking gas stations (some of which still bore the trademarks of oil companies that no longer existed), and slovenly commercial establishments, little had changed overtly since his final escape from Silver Ridge.

Still, the years had effected certain alterations on the socio-economic landscape; most of the quarries were closed, the coalmines cleaned up, the forests largely protected from ravaging by timber companies. Over time, the locals had slowly shifted from one brand of poverty to another—though they nowadays suffered in relatively good health, since Medicaid offered the nonworking poor marginally better benefits than the working poor had ever known.

A stark reminder of how far he was from home, in the thirty miles since Elkins, he had not passed a single familiar fast-food restaurant; only a couple of nondescript burger joints and a diminutive shack called The Chicken House, whose sputtering neon sign boasted that their birds were fed on nothing but the finest yellow corn. Somehow, he didn't think he was sold.

Even when he drove into the town proper, he found few recent commercial developments, and not a single residential subdivision jammed with expensive, clapboard shoeboxes like the ones that mushroomed on virtually every spare acre from Illinois to Ohio. As seemed fitting, the tiny downtown sprang from a 1940s-vintage postcard, every business locally owned and bearing the name of its proprietor. The bank and the department store belonged to the Bullards, the hardware store to the Kolodnys, the garage to the Hobarts, and the pharmacy to the Wamplers. There was also a church (Baptist, naturally), a post office, a courthouse, and a fire station, none of which exhibited the first sign of life on this late Sunday afternoon. Having long ago closed the book on this part of his past, he had only the vaguest recollections of any of these places, and in his memory, they needed considerably less paint and fewer replacement windows.

At the next intersection, Greenhill Road, he turned left and drove another mile or so, now passing small but well-kept houses with very green, immaculately trimmed yards, flagstone walkways, and expensive cars out front—obviously the seat of whatever wealth remained in the community. Knowing he must be nearing his destination, he checked the house numbers against his scribbled directions. Around a curve, past a neat, stone-walled arboretum, and there it was, tucked into a grove of lush white pines, barely visible through the boughs: his sister Lynette's house. His mind finally snapped back to his reason for being here, and he slowed the Lexus to a crawl, a token gesture of respect for the dead, before turning into the driveway.

Lynette's house blended pleasantly into its surroundings; small, but well-kept and comfortable-looking. Like many of the nearby homes, it resembled a miniature Tudor, with a pair of gables, half-timberings, and a tall, brick chimney, though an incongruous screened-in porch jutted awkwardly from the left side of the house. To the right, just beyond the cluster of evergreens, a similar house pressed so close to the property line that a breezeway could have easily connected the two. He parked behind Lynette's silver Grand Am, slid out of the driver's seat to the sound of joints creaking, and paused for a moment to summon his nerve before venturing toward the door.

It opened just as he reached for the doorbell, and a slouching figure materialized out of the shadows, dimly seen eyes regarding him curiously. After a moment, Lynette Lawson heaved a sigh, drew herself up, and patted her disheveled blonde hair almost back into place.

"I'm so glad it's you. I wasn't sure you were ever going to get here."

Except for the obvious signs of grief, his sister had hardly changed in the seven years since he had last seen her—at their own mother's funeral. Copeland opened his arms and she fell into his embrace, her body so slight that he hesitated to hug her firmly. However, her slim arms were well-toned, and she gave him a surprisingly strong squeeze before releasing him.

"Long drive," he said. "How you holding up?"

"Just barely." She started to usher him inside, then paused and said, "Wanna bring in your bags?"

"Later." He followed her into a cool, deeply shadowed foyer that smelled of lilies and cigarette smoke. "Visitors all gone, I take it?"

"Yeah. They've been coming and going all day. I have enough food to last a month."

She led him into the living room, the windows of which faced the wall of pines. Flowers of all varieties occupied every corner of the room, their vibrant colors brightening the naturally dim chamber. But their sweet, heady aroma seemed to remind Lynette of her pain, for her shoulders slumped again, and her eyes melted into a shining pool of tears. From an ornate cherry table that had belonged to their parents, she lifted a framed portrait, gazed longingly at it for several moments, and finally handed it to him.

It was a fairly recent photo, for Rodney Lawson had been only eleven years old at the time of his death. The smiling, blue-eyed, sandy-haired lad closely resembled his mother—and even his Uncle Russ to a slight degree. In his Little League uniform, with a bat propped on his shoulder, he was the picture of carefree innocence but for a faraway, almost haunted look in his eyes. At the time the portrait was made, he was still grieving for his father, who had been killed in Iraq the previous year.

With her husband and now her only son gone, Lynette was entirely alone.

Copeland had met Rodney only once, when he was four; of course, he felt terrible about the boy's untimely death, but the grief that came pouring out now was entirely for his sister. He took her in his arms again and held her, as if he could shelter her from any further blows that life saw fit to deliver. "I'm so sorry," he whispered. "I know how much you loved him."

Lynette's gray eyes slowly rose to meet his. "The funeral is at eleven tomorrow morning. Closed casket. He was...oh God." She broke down then, and he felt her legs give way. He held her tenderly and let her weep for several minutes; when she finally regained her composure, he led her to the couch and gently lowered her to a sitting position. She took several deep breaths and offered him a faint smile. "Thank you."

He sat down and slid an arm around her shoulders. Hesitantly, he asked, "Have the police...?"

She shook her head. "No. They took his body to Charleston to... autopsy. They have no idea who—or what—could have killed him."

"You're the one who found him?"

She nodded. "Out on Yew Line Road, a couple of miles from

here. He was so late, I went looking for him, and I saw his bike, and he was lying there, just off the road. He was...oh God, oh God." Tears started to flow again, but she wiped them away in frustration. "All I've done is cry. I'm spent, Russ, I'm just wiped out."

"I know." He squeezed her shoulder reassuringly and then fell silent. Though hardly lacking compassion, finding consoling words had never been his strong suit. "I'm sure you've had a long, miserable day," he finally said. "You should probably get some sleep. Don't worry about me, I can manage just fine. We'll have plenty of time later."

"How long can you stay?"

"A week, at least. Maybe ten days. I want you to count on me for anything you need."

"I will," she said gratefully. Some of her energy seemed to snap back, and she stood up with an abashed frown. "What am I thinking? You've been driving all day; you're exhausted too. What is it, ten hours?"

"More like twelve. But I'm fine, really."

"You need a drink, something to eat. Don't worry, I don't have to fix anything. The fridge is bursting at the seams."

"I'm sure I wouldn't mind a drink."

"Still Johnnie Walker on the rocks?"

"Yeah."

She went to a small sideboard, stocked for the benefit of her apparently plentiful callers, dropped a couple of cubes into a tumbler, and poured him a generous measure from a crystal decanter. She swirled the ice in the glass before handing it to him. "It's the good stuff. Enjoy."

"You're still not drinking?"

"Not for ten years. Not when Roger died. And not now."

"That's good."

She gestured at the sideboard. "Feel free to have at it whenever you want. It doesn't bother me for people to drink around me."

"You're still smoking, though."

She nodded. "Guess you can't miss the smell, can you?"

"Not to mention an ash tray in every corner."

With a weak smile, she motioned for him to follow and led him into a small kitchen, as abundant with flowers as it was with food. Sure enough, the refrigerator practically overflowed with meats, casseroles, vegetable trays, cakes, and other assorted dishes—all very simple, very southern, he thought. He selected a couple of pieces of fried chicken (briefly wondering if this bird had been fed on the finest yellow corn) and some coleslaw, figuring that this and the scotch would hold him for the night. Lynette sat with him at the table and sipped bottled water, though she ate nothing and said little as he worked on his supper. Her eyes were far away, and he knew that, for the moment, his presence barely registered.

Only when he had finished and carried his plate to the sink did she look him in the eye again. When she did, her expression nearly chilled him. Behind her sadness, he saw a disturbing mélange of anger and terror.

"When I found Rodney," she said slowly, "I thought he must have been hit by a car and dragged. His body was so terribly mangled, his arms and legs almost gone. But then I saw it wasn't like a car accident. He had been burned. And it looked like some animal had...gnawed on him."

He sucked in a sharp breath. "Maybe dogs or something, after he was dead."

She shook her head. "That's what the coroner thought at first, but then he concluded the wounds had been made while Rodney was still alive." Her voice trailed away and she stared vacantly into space for a time, her tears exhausted. Finally, she said, "The bite marks did not come from a dog. Or a wildcat. Or a bear. Or anything else that lives around here. No one knows what it could have been."

"So, it wasn't a person who killed him."

"We don't know for sure. The burns. What could have caused the burns? Everyone's baffled."

"Are the state police involved?"

She shook her head. "The sheriff has no interest in calling them in unless…"

"Unless something else happens?"

"Pretty much."

Copeland downed the last of his scotch, and Lynette started to take his glass to get him another, but he waved her away. "You're shot, my dear. Get some rest. I'll fetch my bag, unpack, and hold the fort. Tomorrow's not going to be easy."

"I know. The wake last night was bad enough." She shot him a questioning look. "Oh, by the way. I didn't ask you to be a pallbearer since you and Rodney never really knew each other. I've got some adults he knew well from school and from church. I hope you don't feel slighted or anything."

"No, not at all. It's better this way."

She nodded, satisfied. "There's a room for you upstairs. Get your bags, and I'll take you up."

When he went back out to the car, the sun had fallen beyond the steep mountainside that pressed close to the back of the house and the air had grown noticeably cooler. He had to admit that Lynette lived in a beautiful place, for he had never a seen a violet sky so clear. A light, clean breeze whispered through the trees that surrounded the house. No sounds of traffic infringed on the quiet evening; only soft, musical birdsongs and the melancholy chirping of crickets from the woods. For a brief moment, his mind zoomed back to his nearly forgotten childhood, when he could take for granted sweet, peaceful nights such as this in his mom and dad's comfortable, country home. So different from his present suburban dwelling, which, even though separated from the worst of city bustle and clamor, scarcely served as a retreat from the rigors of metropolitan life.

And since he and crazy Megan had split up a couple of years ago, "home" felt too big and too empty, required too much effort to maintain, and bit too deeply into his finances. He had been threatening to downsize his domicile for a long time but simply hadn't; inertia, he supposed. After this trip, he would buckle down and deal with the situation.

But now was not the time to think about his personal issues; not with the tragedy that had befallen his sister, leaving a host of unanswered questions. In comparison, his own troubles were trifling. He removed his two suitcases from the trunk and started toward the front door, only to pause in mid-stride as the world around him suddenly stopped.

For several uncomfortable moments, he wondered if he had lost his hearing, for the birds, the insects, the breeze, all had gone abruptly silent as if cut off by a switch. Then a rustling sound crept from the bushes that lined the porch on the left side of the house—an animal, no doubt, but something larger than a squirrel or rabbit or a raccoon. A dog, perhaps. Then he recalled his sister's remark about *something* having gnawed on her son's body, and an urgent, unfamiliar sense of paranoia suddenly compelled him to hurry back to the safety of the indoors. When he pushed his way through the front door, he was already chiding himself for having succumbed to a ridiculous, childish, and inappropriate impulse, but at the same time, he realized how far out of his element he felt in this remote quarter, which he had left by design so many years before.

However, the atmosphere of impending threat remained even when he again stood inside the little foyer with the door securely closed. The stillness seemed strangely exaggerated, overbearing, and even recognizing that he was far safer here than on any given Chicago street failed to dispel his anxiety. Only when the grandmother clock in the living room began to chime eight o'clock did his surroundings seem to return to normal. He realized he was holding his breath.

"Anything wrong?"

Lynette stood in the kitchen doorway, eyeing him with concern. He absently shook his head and lifted one of his bags. "Wanna show me where to stow these?"

She gestured for him to follow and headed up the stairs. At the top, she turned right and led him to a small bedroom with two windows, one that faced the dark pines at the northern end of the house, the other facing the night-shrouded back yard. The décor was neutral, so he knew this had not been Rodney's room, for which he felt a moment of sincere relief.

"Well, make yourself at home. The booze and anything in the kitchen are yours for the taking. There's clean towels and stuff in the bathroom—second door down on the right. If you're okay, I'm going to try to get some sleep. Anything else you need?"

"Not a thing," he said. "You sleep. I'll probably crash before long." He gave her another hug and kissed her on the forehead. She smiled weakly, said goodnight, and softly closed the door behind her.

The window hung open, admitting a pleasantly cool draft. Copeland opened his bags and began stowing his clothes in empty dresser drawers and in the closet. Outside, birds and insects chattered blithely, and he now found some reassurance in their energetic voices. He made up his mind to forget his momentary attack of paranoia; the whole thing seemed stupid anyway.

Still, when for one brief moment the crickets ceased to chirp, he stiffened involuntarily.

As he put away the last of his clothes, he noticed a light snap on outside his window. Through a gap in the evergreen boughs that pressed close to the house, he saw an illuminated window of the adjacent house, and someone moving inside. At first, he paid the figure scant attention, but when he realized it was a woman—a very attractive one, at that—he felt compelled take a longer look.

She was a slim, well-proportioned brunette, her hair barely shoulder-length, her face angular, her eyes dark and narrow. She also appeared to be putting clothes in drawers, perhaps having finished a load of laundry. She wore jeans and a light-colored sweater. Thank God she fully dressed; the young woman was probably so accustomed to the room across the property line being empty that the prospect of someone glimpsing her from it never occurred to her. If she should look up, though, she would quickly notice his curious eyes. Copeland was hardly prone to voyeurism, but under the circumstances, he felt in little hurry to draw the curtains. Finally, though, with a little sigh, he moved away from the window, hoping it was in time to salvage at least a shred of his decency.

Still, he felt a little thrill at the unexpected "encounter." He could not deny the fact that, since Megan had ripped out a fair chunk of his soul and pulverized it with a jackhammer, loneliness had been a profound, worrisome bedfellow. Okay. So what if he did meet this woman? He lived 700 miles away and had no interest in a mere fling. For all he knew, she was married, with a redneck husband who would as happily kick his ass to China as shake him by the hand.

Before he undressed, he closed the curtains. And as he began to get out of his clothes, he gave himself a thorough mental flogging for having not only seriously contemplated getting acquainted with this woman, but also for making the unrealistic—and possibly disastrous—assumption that, if they did meet, she would be single and willing to give him more than a passing glance.

Foolishness, he thought and decided that, before he took off his pants, he would go downstairs and pour himself a nightcap. That, at least, was an emotional investment he could still afford to make.

#

Day Two

Chapter 2

Copeland awoke to a faint sound tickling his eardrums, not at all unpleasant, even appealing, since the dreams he was leaving behind had been forays into dark, troubling territory—most having to do with his bitter divorce from the wacko Megan. Warm rays of early morning sunlight sifted through the branches of the white pines to shimmer on the bedspread, just missing his face. The soft, melodic chiming of bells, perhaps from the church he had passed yesterday, drifted in through the open window, as mellow and relaxing as a woman's fingers caressing his brow. For several minutes, he lay basking in the satisfying warmth of his blanket and the gentle music on the cool breeze, until he realized that, more than likely, the bells were tolling for his sister's lost son.

After reluctantly dragging himself out from the covers, the first thing he did was go to the window and peer through the foliage at the house next door. Hardly unexpectedly, he saw nothing and no one in the now-darkened window, but after the little thrill of glimpsing Lynette's neighbor the night before, he felt a little pang of disappointment. Then, as he started to turn away, he noticed someone moving beyond the neighboring house, so he stood fast and craned his neck hopefully.

Alas, it wasn't her. The big tree largely obscured his view, but through a small opening in the branches, he could see a squat figure, standing belligerently in the middle of the road, heedless of any traffic that might come around the curve. It was a white man, mid-forties, stringy-looking black hair, heavy brow, tattered jeans, dirty denim jacket. Sure enough, he seemed to be glaring intently at the house next door, which made Copeland's hackles rise. Even if he couldn't claim to know Lynette's attractive neighbor, he always trusted his instincts—and right now they told him that this was some local redneck aiming to make trouble for someone who didn't deserve it.

He dressed quickly and tiptoed down the stairs, in case Lynette was still asleep. At the bottom, he heard her moving in the kitchen, but rather than detour to greet her first, he went directly outside and up the driveway to the road, figuring that by making himself visible, he might discourage the interloper from doing something he would regret. But by the time he reached a point where he could see around the trees, the unkempt man had vanished.

"Taking in the air?" Lynette asked as he stepped back inside. He gave her a noncommittal grunt and a good-morning hug. "Coffee's ready," she said. "I assume you want a cup."

"Gimme."

She poured him a large mug from the steaming pot—an ancient, stainless-steel percolator with a long, curved spout—and asked if he wanted breakfast. He declined, generally accustomed to having his first meal around noon. For the moment, Lynette appeared to be in relatively good spirits, though he doubted she could sustain them for very long.

Sure enough, as the morning crept by and she went upstairs to dress for the funeral, she fell deeper and deeper into gloom. By ten o'clock, she would not even utter a word; she just sat and smoked cigarette after cigarette. Now more than ever, Copeland wanted to comfort her, but in apparent proportion to her grief, the means to ease her pain eluded him. Finally, he took away her smokes and held her for a while, rocking her gently back and forth the way their dad had when she was small. He wasn't entirely sure she was even aware of his presence.

A few minutes before they were due to depart, the doorbell chimed, and Copeland left Lynette on the living room couch and went to answer it. When he opened the door, he barely kept his jaw from hitting the floor, and his cheeks began to warm before the woman from next door even spoke a word.

"Hello," she said, offering him a pleasant but rather sad smile. She was dressed for the funeral and held a small black purse in one hand. "I'm Debra Harrington. You must be Lynette's brother."

He nodded and took her extended hand, hoping she didn't notice his face flushing. "Russ Copeland. Please come in."

"Thanks. I live next door. We're supposed to ride together, I believe."

"Ah. Lynette didn't mention it. She's not doing so well, I'm afraid."

"She loved that boy so much," the young woman said with a distressed shake of her head, heading for the living room as if she knew just where to find his sister. "We've known each other a long time. We both teach at the high school."

He nodded, withholding his surprise, and watched silently as Debra gave Lynette's shoulder an affectionate squeeze. "Hey, honey. It's me. I guess we're all about ready to go?"

Lynette looked up at her friend and nodded. "Time to say goodbye?" she whispered.

"Yes."

No sooner had she spoken than another knock came at the door, and Copeland opened it to reveal a tall, balding man wearing a crisp, black suit and a somber, sympathetic face. The limousine was parked in the driveway behind Copeland's Lexus.

"Lynette Lawson?" the man asked in a low, mellifluous voice.

"One moment."

Copeland went back to his sister and offered her his hand. She gripped it tightly as he led her toward the door; and he could feel her trembling. Debra took her other hand to offer extra support.

"Take her on to the limo," he told Debra. "I'll lock up behind us."

"Sure."

They rode in silence to the church, which was not the one he had passed on the way in, but the Cheat Mountain Church of Christ, which lay in the opposite direction. The small, white building nestled in a wooded grove at the base of a steep ridge, and Copeland could see a few gravestones peeking out from the trees on the far side of the tiny parking lot. One grave was open and surrounded by a cordon of white cloth. A small crowd had already gathered at the front of the building, and the minister stood at the door, greeting the mourners as they made their way inside.

Copeland and Debra assisted Lynette as she got out of the limo, a bit shaky, but she maintained herself without faltering. The minister, a middle-aged, rotund, bespectacled fellow named Reverend Lee, greeted them warmly and personally led them to the pews at the front of the sanctuary, directly before the casket, which was closed and—most distressingly—little more than half the standard size. Before taking her seat, Lynette went to the casket, leaned over it, and softly wept for several minutes. Copeland and Debra remained a respectful step behind her, but close enough to catch her in case she suddenly went faint.

As they turned to take their seats, Copeland froze, rather rudely jolting his sister. He mumbled an apology and assisted her into the pew, but as Debra started to sit down, he touched her shoulder and whispered in her ear, "Take a look at the back pew and tell me if you know that man."

When Debra looked around, her dark brown eyes widened briefly and, unless Copeland was very much mistaken, her face lost some of its color. But when her eyes turned back to his, she appeared unshaken. "He's familiar. Why do you ask?"

"I saw him out in front of your house this morning. He doesn't strike me as a particularly fine human specimen."

He hadn't meant to speak quite so candidly, but there it was. He almost expected her to give him a reproving glare, but she merely shrugged. "No, he doesn't look like much, does he?"

Then she touched the back of his hand, a subtle but clear signal of gratitude for his concern, and a pleasurable tremor passed through his body. Trivial though the gesture might be, he couldn't help but feel that something had passed between them; perhaps the beginning of a bond, however tenuous. Then guilt for his self-centeredness, so inappropriate under the circumstances, nudged him briefly, and he took his seat next to Lynette, who reached for his hand and squeezed it, as if he were the rock she needed to cling to. Better he should be one now than allow his attention to wander; but before bringing his focus back to the sad affair before him, he glanced quickly back at the shabbily dressed, conspicuously out-of-place mourner and found the man's black, unblinking eyes staring, not at Debra, but at him.

#

The service was a poignant, if brief, tribute to Rodney Lawson, delivered eloquently by Reverend Lee, who had obviously known the boy well. There was no shortage of tears, but for her part, Lynette held up well enough, her spirit bolstered by the pastor's message of hope for both the departed and those left behind. After his eulogy, he directed the mourners to the cemetery on the hillside, and as the small crowd gathered, four men bore the small casket to the grave.

Copeland took the opportunity to search the faces for the strange interloper, but he had seemingly vanished. On at least a couple of occasions, Debra also surreptitiously scanned the crowd, and when she determined that the object of her search was no longer present, her demeanor relaxed noticeably. She remained close to Lynette as they stood at the graveside and took her arm when Reverend Lee stepped forward to say his final words before the earth claimed Rodney's body.

"Father, please look with compassion upon the mother of your servant, Rodney Allen Lawson, and support her in this time of deep personal loss. To you, Lynette, I say rejoice in the knowledge that your beloved son is now in arms of our heavenly father, where he shall know eternal peace and joy, looking forward to the day when he is permanently reunited with his loved ones. And now his body is consigned to the earth whence it sprang, until that day when corruption shall be no more, and all who are one in Christ shall rise and walk in the new Jerusalem. Lord, we humbly pray for your blessing, in the name of your son, Jesus Christ. Amen."

Lynette's tears had begun to flow anew, and Copeland slid a supportive arm around her waist, hoping now that this business would end quickly so they could get out of here; the assembly of caring friends was important, but maintaining her composure in front of them was wearing her out. He had always hated funerals, and having to endure the interment of a child who had barely lived at all was particularly excruciating—especially in view of the effect it had on those closest to the boy.

The four pallbearers had laid the casket onto the lowering device—a stretcher suspended from a steel frame above the open grave—and now, one of the men pulled a lever at one end, and Rodney Lawson's remains slowly descended into the dark pit without fanfare; no heavenly chorus, no wails of anguish, no cries of rapture. Then the preacher turned and slowly, solemnly made his way back to the church, signaling that the service had ended.

The caretaker would seal the dead within the earth after the mourners had left.

Finally, a few voices rose to a soft murmur, and people began to migrate slowly away from the gravesite. Lynette continued to stare into the dark opening, but her tears had all dried.

"Be at rest, my dear boy," she finally said. "I love you so much." Then, gently removing Copeland's hand from her arm, she turned and slowly walked back toward the church building, her gait steady, her expression sober. Several people came forward to speak to her.

One of them, an older, white-haired man with tanned leather skin and a hawk nose, stepped up and extended a hand to Copeland. "You're Russell, aren't you?"

"Yes, I am."

"I doubt you remember me. I used to play golf with your dad, back in the dark ages. I'm Glen Martin."

"Ah, yes, I think I recall. Good to see you."

Martin gave Lynette a concerned glance. "Your sister's had such a rough time. First Roger, and now her boy. It's good you could be here for her."

"I hope I can be of help."

"I'm the school principal, by the way, and I'm sure she's going to need some time away. She's one of the most dedicated teachers I know, and I don't want her to worry about her job."

"I appreciate that. I know it will ease her mind."

"Nice meeting you. Or I should say seeing you again. Must've been nearly thirty years ago."

"I have gotten a little bigger, haven't I?"

Martin smiled. "I should say so. Take care, now."

Lynette was speaking softly to an elderly woman, so the principal turned his attention to Debra. The two of them stepped out of Copeland's earshot and spoke in hushed tones; a couple of times, Debra glanced his way, her expression unreadable. But something about the way they huddled together gave Copeland the distinct impression that secrets were passing between them.

"Excuse me—are you Russ?"

Copeland turned to regard a man about his age, with curly, bronze hair just turning silver at the temples. His eyes were narrow and violet blue, his nose long and straight, his chin goateed.

"I'll be damned. Candle! Candle McAllister!"

"You're good. Very good."

"How could I forget that hair of yours?"

"Lynette said you'd be coming."

Copeland clasped his old friend's hand. As kids, hardly anyone knew McAllister's Christian name was Doug.

"Byston Hill's most degenerate degenerate. You're still living here?"

"They didn't dare set me loose on the world." McAllister's face darkened. "I'm very sorry about your sister's boy. So tragic, young as he was."

"Thanks. You and Lynette friends?"

"She and my wife, really. That's her over there. Carolyn." He pointed to an attractive, slim blonde engaged in conversation with another woman. "I heard you gave up on marriage a while back."

"Didn't have much choice in the matter. But believe me, I prefer it this way."

"I guess that's good." McAllister smiled wryly. "How long you gonna be here?"

"Maybe a week." He glanced half-discreetly over the other's shoulder and saw that Debra and Martin were still talking. "Depends on how Lynette gets along."

"I know you'll be busy, but if you get any free time, give me a call and let's have a drink. I wasn't the only degenerate at Byston Hill, if I remember right. We should catch up and see who has fallen the farthest."

Copeland cut a thin smile. "At least they let me leave town. So, what's your lot in life?"

"I own the Toro dealership in town. You would have passed it on your way in."

"Didn't notice."

"Need a mower?"

"Nope. Doesn't everyone in this town own goats?"

McAllister grinned. "Damn, it's good to see you after all these years. Pity about the circumstances."

He swatted his old friend's shoulder. "I'll call."

"I hope so."

Debra and Martin parted just as McAllister went to rejoin his wife. The aging principal stepped over to offer his condolences to Lynette, and Debra remained where she stood, her eyes subtly wandering through the crowd. Copeland pretended to stroll casually to her side.

"I gather a lot of these people are from the school."

She nodded, inspecting the nearby trees before turning to face him. "Lynette's very popular. She's an excellent teacher."

"What do you teach?"

"Social studies."

"Never my strongest subject."

"You didn't go to the public schools here, did you?"

"Nope. Byston Hill, up near Elkins. Lynette too, as I'm sure you know."

"The local schools have made great strides since we were kids. Even with our limited budgets, we've got great programs and faculties. My dad has worked wonders here. If I had kids, I wouldn't think twice about sending them to the public schools."

"Your dad is Glen Martin?"

She nodded and raised an eyebrow. "Oh, you didn't know?"

"No one bothered to mention it. Hell, I never even knew he had a daughter." He chuckled wryly and started to make a wise remark about nepotism, but then thought better of it. "So. Since your last name is different, I gather that you're married."

She smiled wistfully. "Tried it for a while. It didn't work out."

"Likewise."

"So I'm told." She then gave him a long, thoughtful look. "You asked me about that man this morning. You said he was outside my house?"

"Yes."

"His name is Levi Barrow. His son, Malachi, is in my class. Neither of them is very good news."

"I got that impression."

"I had some trouble with Malachi last week. What am I saying? I've had trouble with that boy every day of every week."

"You think his father is on the warpath?"

She shrugged. "Wouldn't surprise me. He dotes on that kid as if he were God's gift. As far as he's concerned, Malachi's never done anything wrong in his life, and all his problems are everyone else's fault."

"You think the man's dangerous?"

After a long pause, she said, "I doubt it."

"You don't sound very sure."

"Let's put it this way. He's never killed anyone, at least that I know of. But everyone around here avoids the Barrows like plague. They live out on Yew Line Road, a few miles out of town. They make moonshine and grow pot for their livelihood. Those are their respectable endeavors. Levi's been known to get into fights from time to time."

"Yew Line Road...that's where Rodney was killed, wasn't it?"

Debra nodded.

"You don't think there's any connection, do you?"

"Neither Lynette nor Rodney ever had any trouble with them. They're a strange brood, though. Three men and the boy, all under one roof. There's Levi, his brother Joshua, and their grandfather Amos. Their father, Samuel, got killed in Vietnam. Levi's wife—maybe Malachi's mother, maybe not—died several years ago, supposedly of cancer."

"Supposedly?"

"When she died, they just up and buried her. Didn't notify the police, hospital, anyone. The sheriff threatened to charge them with a host of crimes, turn it over to the state, maybe the feds. But not one thing ever came of it. You think any 'reputable' family could have gotten away with something like that?"

"They sound charming. If Levi Barrow were hanging around my house, I might just decide to give the sheriff a ring."

Debra rolled her eyes. "He's a distant relative of theirs, which is the only reason they aren't all in prison. You know, if you look at the crime statistics for this county, you'd think there isn't any. That doesn't mean we don't have our share. Somehow, it just never manages to find its way into the record."

"Interesting. For a lot with Biblical names, the Barrows seem anything but saintly."

"Levi likes to boast that the family is related to Clyde Barrow—you know, the male half of Bonnie and Clyde. That may be rubbish, or it may not. Who knows? In a way, I feel sorry for Malachi, coming from that background. The kids call him 'Malarkey,' and some of the older ones have beaten him pretty severely. Make no mistake, though. He's a bully, a liar, and a thief, so he comes by trouble honestly. Given the choice between showing him sympathy or the way to juvenile detention, I'd go with detention any day."

Before his brain had fully engaged, Copeland heard from his own lips, "Well, if Mr. Barrow comes around looking for trouble, give me a call. He may not be so brazen when he's up against someone other than a single woman."

Debra gazed at him coolly, but then a tiny glimmer of humor appeared in her eyes. "I'm not asking for anyone's help, Mr. Copeland. I can handle my own affairs."

"I didn't mean to imply you couldn't. I've just never taken kindly to...people like that."

Now her smile was a little warmer. "You sound as if you've known your share."

"Maybe not quite like the Barrows. But I've dealt with some very ugly people in my time. I admit I get some satisfaction when I see them reap what they've sowed."

A hand touched his shoulder, and he turned to see Lynette looking at him with weary eyes. "Catching up on Silver Ridge gossip?"

He smiled at her. "Just a social studies lesson. Your friend is a good teacher."

Debra rolled her eyes again and turned to Lynette. "Are you ready to go home?"

She nodded. "Yes. They're having lunch in the social hall, but I don't think anyone will be offended if I skip it."

"I'm sure they won't."

They started back toward the limousine, where the driver stood dutifully. He opened the door for them and then slid behind the wheel once they were all in.

As the car started off, Copeland glanced at Debra, whose attention was all on Lynette now. The woman really was quite attractive, especially her eyes. They were narrow and dark brown, yet at the same time very bright, as if lit from within by an energetic flame. She was several years younger than he, probably early thirties. He enjoyed her frank manner of speaking and the youthful lilt of her voice; but she also had a measured, sagacious demeanor, probably a result of having taught children for a long time.

He felt glad yet leery of the fact that she was single, for it meant that the only thing to stop him pursuing her was his own good sense.

As they drove away from the church, on a lark, he glanced back through the rear glass and was only slightly surprised to see an unkempt, stringy-haired figure wearing denim jeans and jacket step out from a stand of trees to watch after the retreating vehicle.

Again, Levi Barrow seemed to focus specifically on him rather than Debra. And though he could not pinpoint any rational basis for it, he felt a soul-deep tremor of fear, as if he had been marked for something awful; perhaps the same fate that his nephew Rodney, for whatever reason, had tragically—and horribly—suffered.

#

Chapter 3

Hard to accept that Rodney was gone, laid underground until the end of forever. God rest your soul, bud, and all that.

Zack Baird had never been to a funeral before Rodney Lawson's, and he hoped it was the last, for he could not have imagined a more depressing, tearful event. He had nearly bawled like a baby, and crying in public was not something his friends should ever see. Fortunately, most of them had been sitting behind him, so he doubted they could have glimpsed the tears that had leaked down his cheeks.

On the good side, he could not complain about school being called off for the memorial service, and since it was a beautiful afternoon, going riding on his bike seemed just the thing to turn the whole day around. He had called Sammy and Chuck, but their parents wouldn't let them leave the house. Since Rodney's death, his own mom and dad had forbidden him to ride up the mountain, but unlike his friends', his parents had to return to work after the funeral; he could easily be back home watching TV and looking bored by the time they got in from work.

But damn! Rodney would never be out here again, hauling ass through the woods and hitting the jump ramps they had built off Yew Line Road. For a "little kid," Rodney had sure held his own with the best of the thirteen- and fourteen-year-olds. He could ride faster than any of them, and he performed stunts that none of the others could hope to match. Old Sammy was even hoping he could talk Ms. Lawson into giving him Rodney's bike, though Zack had warned him not to go begging too soon; all they needed was a pissed-off math teacher with a long memory waiting for them when they got old enough to go to high school.

Yew Line Road was a long, very steep and winding road that went up into the mountains, but numerous trails through the woods shaved off much of the distance. Still, many stretches of trail were so steep that he had to push his bike, and the late April sun had turned the afternoon quite warm; by the time he reached Greasy Bend—a long curve so named because it was hard to negotiate without slipping over the edge—sweat had begun to sting his eyes and dampen his Tshirt. Anyway, this was almost as far as he could go before reaching Barrow land, upon which no soul dared trespass. Barbed wire blocked the trail at the property line, and the boys had once seen old Joshua Barrow standing near the barricade, brandishing his shotgun and looking as if he *wanted* to use it on them. They always halted well short of that boundary before beginning the long, exhilarating ride back down through the woods.

As he started up and around Greasy Bend, Zack felt, before he saw, that something seemed different about the place. Beneath the freshly bloomed trees, little sunlight reached the trail, but he knew the ridge as well as his own driveway. As many times as he had ridden the curve, he should not have had to draw up short to avoid running into a huge, rough-barked tree that grew right in the middle of the trail. Nor should he have found his bike sliding out from under him as seemingly solid earth gave way to a pit roughly the size and shape of a shallow grave, swallowing him before he realized what was happening.

He automatically let go of the handlebars and threw out his hands to break his fall, just in time to keep his head from striking the rocky edge of the opening. As the bike went tumbling away, he landed with a heavy thud, and his breath whooshed out of his lungs. For second, the lights went out, and he was afraid he had gone blind. Finally, the trees, lit by murky daylight, swam back into focus.

"Shit!" he gasped as he struggled to his feet. The walls of the pit were cold and slick, but with an effort, he managed to reach an exposed tree root and gradually pull himself up to firmer ground. The first thing he saw was his new pants covered with mud and the knees ripped. Jeez, that wasn't good! At least he had escaped being injured. The clothes he might be able to explain away to his mom, but if he had gotten hurt, he could say goodbye forever to riding on the mountain. The second thing was that his bike lay thirty feet or more down the hill, and getting to it—not to mention back up to the trail again—posed a pretty hairy problem.

But how had he managed to blunder into a tree and then fall into a pit? He had come this way only a few days ago. *No way* could a huge tree like that have grown in such a short time!

He glanced up the trail in the direction of the Barrow property. The whole place seemed wrong somehow. *All* the trees seemed too tall, too lush, even though foliage had started popping out in earnest over the last few days. And the curve, up near the top—it was supposed to bend to the right, not to the left! Could he have somehow strayed onto some side path that was similar, but not identical to the main one? How could he? He and Sammy and Chuck rode here all the time, rain or shine, heat of summer or bleak midwinter; he knew every inch of this trail, every fork, every twist and turn.

Well, whatever, he had to retrieve his bike. He just hoped it hadn't been damaged going over the edge like that. With a sigh of reluctant resolve, he started down the sheer hillside, using the smaller tree trunks as handholds and making short, controlled slides into the larger boles to keep from careening to the bottom and ending up a pile of broken bones. With some relief, he saw that his bike looked okay; no bent handlebars, and the chain wasn't broken.

When he reached it, he carefully lifted it from the ground and brushed off the clinging dirt and leaves. So far, so good. But now came the real bitch—getting back up to the trail with his burden. The bike was light, but not *that* light.

Then he made his biggest mistake: glancing down the hill into the deep woods. His breath froze in his lungs because, only a few moments ago, the bottom had been perhaps sixty or seventy feet below; not hundreds and hundreds, as it now appeared. And there was supposed to be a small clearing down there where daylight always shined—not a thick knot of tar-black foliage that swallowed every ray of sunlight that filtered through the canopy.

"Jee-zus!" he whispered, utterly disbelieving and, for the first time in his twelve years, afraid that the world might *not* be a stable, familiar place. That a child really *could* suffer an awful, unthinkable death—a fact that Rodney Lawson's funeral had almost, but not totally, driven home. Rodney had been found not far from here. Was *this* what he had seen in his last moments—a world turned topsy-turvy right before his eyes?

Then, somewhere above, he heard a loud, very strange clicking sound, almost like somebody smacking a number of sticks together at once. A heavy rustling crept down from the trail, its source just beyond his range of vision, but obviously getting nearer. He craned his neck, trying to detect a trace of movement, some sign of an animal or—God forbid—a human being making its way toward him. So far, *nada*.

"Hello?" he called, immediately wishing he had not. If someone was up there, it would almost certainly be one of the Barrows, and a member of that lowlife clan was the last person anyone would want to meet out here. For all he knew, one of them could have even killed Rodney.

Click-click-clack, click-click-clack.

The sounds grew steadily louder and more agitated, almost but not quite insect-like. The rustling, too, became more violent; but he felt certain that no human was behind it. Not a steady, regular pace like something on two feet, but an erratic and rapid shuffling. Maybe an injured fox or a coon? If it was just a critter, he probably didn't have anything to worry about—not from it, anyway. His main concern now was how to get off this bizarre, once-familiar mountainside, both with his bicycle and in one piece.

The rustling stopped on the trail just above, and Zack realized that the woods had fallen deathly silent, leaving the atmosphere heavy and horrible, its weight pressing insistently upon him. This felt like one of his nightmares, in which terror seeped like infection from every aspect of his surroundings—the dark trees, the patchwork sky, the cold earth beneath his feet.

Then the rustling began anew, and something lurched over the edge of the trail and started toward him beneath the thick underbrush—something he couldn't see, something that raced toward him like a fast-moving snake, thrashing and clicking with palpable rage. He had only seconds before it reached him, so in that panicked instant, he opted for the only plan his terrified brain could concoct: he shoved his bike straight down the hill and leaped onto its seat, praying he could keep it upright and put enough distance between him and his pursuer to get out of this tight spot alive.

Down he went, bounding into the seemingly bottomless chasm at dizzying, insane speed, somehow maintaining control, veering in and out of the trees without even thinking of the consequences should he crash. Limbs slashed at his face, threatening to dislodge him, but his fingers clutched the handlebars with desperate strength, and his feet worked the pedals automatically, hitting and releasing the brakes at strategic moments to keep from smashing into a tree or tangling himself in undergrowth. He couldn't even think of looking back to see if he had lost his enraged shadow; one wrong move and he would end up plastered against a huge trunk or dashed to pieces on the rocks that occasionally jutted from the ground. Every now and then, he thought he detected a faint clicking sound behind him, but he mostly heard only the rush of wind in his ears as his bike carried him farther and farther from the trail—the one thing out here that looked even halfway familiar.

As he rode on, the light grew constantly dimmer, and tears began to stream from his eyes, blurring the trees that flashed out of the darkness like onrushing columns of troops. He knew he needed to slow down before the bike got away from him, but if he did, that *thing* would catch him and butcher him, as it had his friend. The thought sent cold, tingling tendrils into his groin. Trapped between terrors fore and aft, he kept going, always descending, farther and farther into the deepening, seemingly endless gloom.

Finally, he jammed on the brakes, twisted the handlebars, and dug one foot into the ground, which didn't quite stop him but slowed his progress enough to take stock of the situation. A few seconds later, he heard a loud, distinctive *click-click-clack, click-click-clack*, more distant than before but undeniably still behind him.

With a cry, he shoved his weight onto the pedals, and down he went again, deeper into the great gulf, his eyes no longer registering the obstacles that lay in front of him, his mind no longer an even remotely rational thing.

#

Chapter 4

"Will you be all right if I leave you alone for a while?"

"Of course I will," Lynette said, giving Copeland a look that said she was tired of being coddled. "The house is a mess after all the company. I've got plenty of work to do."

"You know I'll be happy to take care of anything you need."

She shook her head. "It'll give me something to occupy my mind. I'm serious. Sitting around here doing nothing is the worst thing for me. Where are you off to?"

"I thought I'd drive through town, maybe visit the old neighborhood. I barely remember what it looks like."

"Well, whatever you might remember, it's not the same anymore. It's mostly Hispanics now. Nothing against them, except that they cram all their relatives into every house, and then the neighborhood goes to seed. It's a shame."

"Everybody's gotta live somewhere."

"I guess. I forget you're from Chicago. English-speaking WASPs like you are probably a minority."

"Pretty much."

"Well, have fun. For God's sake, don't worry about me. I'll be fine."

"Okay then."

Copeland patted his pocket to make sure he had his keys and went out the front door into the bright afternoon. Lynette was right—keeping herself busy was the best thing she could do. She had taken a nap after the funeral and now seemed almost a changed person. The service had provided her with some sense of closure, at least spiritually, for her faith in God was firm. But he also knew that as long as her son's murder remained unsolved, the peace she felt was transitory; she needed to know that whoever or whatever had killed Rodney was not still out there. He was not about to tell her that, rather than pay a visit to the old neighborhood, he intended to drive out to Yew Line Road to take a closer look at the scene of her son's death. Not that he expected to uncover dramatic evidence the police had somehow overlooked, but he did feel drawn to explore, to view firsthand the site where Rodney had died.

As he pressed his remote key button to unlock the door, he noticed Debra Harrington collecting the mail from her box at the end of her driveway. She looked like a young, dark-haired Eva Marie Saint, he decided. He gave her a little wave, expecting that to be the end of it; but instead of walking back toward her house, she detoured toward him.

"Afternoon," he said as she approached, his pulse increasing a tad. "Anything for me?"

She thumbed through the envelopes. "Are you Resident?"

"No."

"Then you're out of luck. Going out and about?"

"Thought I'd take a drive, see what I've been missing over the last two and a half decades."

She raised an eyebrow. "Is that all?"

"Isn't that enough?"

"How's Lynette?"

"Much improved—at least until something triggers her

memories. Then she may fall to pieces again. But for now, I think she's all right."

Debra nodded. "She's going to be fragile for some time."

"I'm glad you two are close. She'll be very lonely once things calm down."

"It takes time for such a loss to sink in. The pain dulls, but the emptiness doesn't change." She gave him another appraising look. "I'd guess you're going out to see where Rodney got killed. Am I right?"

"You're quick."

She shrugged. "It's what I would do."

On a whim, he decided to chance it. "I don't suppose you'd care to ride along?"

"Why would I?"

"Because you would hate to see me get hopelessly lost out there. Anyway, you'd make a better guide than my failing memory."

She glanced at her watch, at her house, and then at him. She shrugged. "Why not? Let me put the mail away and lock up."

As she headed for her door, he slid into the driver's seat, smiling to himself at the prospect of her company. The more he saw of her, the more he appreciated that wry little gleam in her eyes, her way of addressing him so familiarly while remaining aloof. And, he thought, as he watched her disappear into her house, her walk really wasn't half-bad.

At any rate, he could see why she and Lynette would have hit it off. They were both intelligent, near the same age, and bore a hundred or so of the same burdens, at least during the school year.

She reappeared moments later and walked toward him with her eyes on the ground; only when she had opened the door and slid into the passenger seat did she lift her head and give him a somber smile. "You know how to get to Yew Line Road?"

"I think so. Just not sure what to look for once I do."

"I can show you. Rodney and his friends have been riding their bikes out that way ever since they could get up on two wheels. This town has always been so safe; no one's ever given a second thought to letting their kids ride around on their own. This is such a far cry from the big city."

"It certainly is that," Copeland said as he backed out of the driveway and headed north on Greenhill toward Cheat Mountain Road, the same route they had taken to the church. "I used to enjoy riding my bike too, but I never went out to Yew Line. It's a long way off, and I never cared for the uphill part."

"There's a lot of that. But I've seen those kids ride. They'd push their bikes up the Matterhorn if they could speed back down. I'm sure those trails are a thrill."

"I take it you grew up around here?"

"I did, but until recently, I've been living in Charleston. My ex-husband's hometown."

"How come he's an ex—if you don't mind me asking?"

"He did a lot of traveling for business. Turned out he was one of those men who need a woman in every port of call. After a while he did a lot more traveling than business, if you get my meaning."

"I'm glad you're not bitter."

"Like hell I'm not." She smiled ruefully. "Anyway, after we split up, I couldn't stand the idea of staying in the city. Never liked it there anyway, so I came back here. Dad helped me get a job at the school."

"Thank God for Dad," he said, again failing to think very far ahead.

Without defensiveness, she said, "I'm a hell of a teacher. I have to tell you, the schools here are one up on Charleston's. How shall I put it? They suck."

He chuckled. "I'm sure you did the right thing. Anyway, I'm certainly glad you're here now." When she raised an eyebrow, he added, "For Lynette's sake."

"Ah."

Ahead, Cheat Mountain Road veered to the left, and he soon saw the familiar church on the right. A short distance beyond it, another left turn bore them onto Yew Line, which immediately began to climb and wind into very dense forest. With the windows down, the temperature felt as if it had plummeted ten degrees.

"Real wilderness," he said, noting the thick oaks, maples,

poplars, and sycamores, which pressed so close to the road that low-hanging branches swept the roof of his car. "Back home, the biggest hills we have are the bridges over the expressways. I've always preferred the city to the country, but I have to admit it's beautiful out here."

"I never cared for the city. I guess this place has spoiled me. I'm sure Charleston is nothing compared to Chicago, but as far as I'm concerned, it's got too many people, it's too hard to breathe, and too much of life is wasted trying to get from one place to another. In this town, there's never been a traffic jam that lasted more than two minutes."

He nodded in understanding. "To think I once lived around here. Of course, I spent all my school days up at Byston Hill, and when I was a kid, our neighborhood was 'exclusive.' I have very few memories of the town in general."

"From your perspective, that's probably just as well. Don't you ever get out of Chicago?"

"I do a lot of traveling, but it's almost always to other cities. The most 'country' I've experienced in the last few years is the Wisconsin Dells, and it gets so crowded you need an appointment to see the trees."

"No chance of that here."

After a minute or so of silence, Copeland said, "How far is it?"

"Not far. Just before we get to the Barrow property."

"Ah, the Barrows. You know, you made a good show, but I get the feeling that Levi Barrow showing up this morning upset you."

Debra looked uncomfortable. "He's what we politely call white trash. As I said, I can handle any problems with him."

"You know, at least twice, he seems to have shown a special curiosity about me. What would you make of that?"

"If he's seen you with me, he's probably sizing you up, to gauge whether you might get involved if he confronts me about his son."

"What if I said I would?"

She shrugged, her eyes betraying a hint of exasperation. Then she pointed to the road ahead. "Slow down. Right up here."

Copeland braked and pulled off to the right. It was a long, fairly straight stretch of road, with tightly packed deciduous trees on both sides. Ahead in the distance, the road disappeared around a curve to the left; there, the trees changed abruptly to very tall, very dark pines. He shut off the engine, got out, and in his most chivalrous fashion, went around and opened Debra's door for her. She stepped out and pointed to the knee-high grass in front of the car. "He was right over there. Lynette brought me out here the other day and showed me. It was all I could do to get her to leave. I suppose she feels close to him here."

He nodded, taking a long look at his surroundings. To his right, the land declined sharply a short distance from the road; to the left, it rose just as quickly. Apart from the road, the woods appeared unbroken as far as his eye could see in every direction. A few birds sang melancholy dirges, but otherwise, silence covered everything; no distant rumble of cars, no thunder of airplanes, no other sounds of identifiably human origin. It seemed almost eerie. An hour or more remained until sunset, but shadows had already begun to swallow the land. He doubted he would care to be out here alone after dark.

No markings remained in the grass where Rodney's body had lain, although depressed patches here and there indicated where the investigators had done their work. Still, a strange sadness seemed to linger in the air, as if the forest itself retained some memory of the unknown, fatal event. Serene and peaceful, yet somehow foreboding, he thought, looking up at the tulip poplars that gathered profusely around the site.

Debra pointed down the hill into the woods. "The trails the kids ride on are just down there."

Copeland was looking up the road again, northward. "How far from here do the Barrows live?"

"Half a mile, maybe."

"You sure Rodney never had trouble with them? Something he might not have talked to his mother about?"

"If so, I'm certainly not aware of it. Anything's possible, of course."

"And the sheriff's not investigating them?"

"Not at all, as far as I know."

"That's almost enough to make one curious."

Debra stepped up to him, her expression grave. "Russ, don't even think about confronting any of them. I said that, to my knowledge, they've never killed anyone, but that doesn't mean you want to cross them. Especially not you, a city boy. You could still end up... damaged."

"Don't worry," he said with a reassuring smile. "I'm not thinking of doing anything foolish. The sheriff won't break my arms if I talk to *him*, will he?"

"Not if you catch him on a good day. But even then, you'll never convince him to look askance at the Barrows."

"If it comes down to it, the sheriff isn't the only law enforcement in the state." He started back toward the car. "Well, I guess this is what I came out here for. Now I've seen the place."

"And?"

"Well, I'm glad I did. I mean, the kid was my nephew, and this was where he breathed his last. I guess it gives me some sense of perspective. Do I feel any closer to him? I don't know."

She nodded sympathetically. "I suppose for some it's natural to want to see the place where tragedy occurred when the victim is one of your family. I don't know that I would, though."

Still inclined to display more than his customary gallantry, he again held the door for her as she got back in the car. But once he pulled onto the road, rather than head back toward town, he continued north on Yew Line, which earned him a particularly hard stare.

"You're going this way. I told you not to go this way."

"Strictly for a look-see," he said with a humorless smile. "This is a public road, right?"

"I don't know what you expect to find, other than a rundown house."

"You know, I didn't see a vehicle anywhere around your place this morning. Does Levi Barrow drive?"

"Yeah. It's not likely he would have walked that far."

Tall pines now rose on either side of the road, which snaked up and over the ridge. As he crested the rise and started down again, in the distance on the left, just where the trees broke, he saw a sagging, two-story wood-frame house with a half-toppled brick chimney. An ancient, rust-encrusted Chevy pickup truck sat in the driveway, and just beyond the house, in a field of tall grass, the remnants of an old barn stood like a monument to the gods of negligence and decay. "No Trespassing" and "Keep Out" signs sprouted in profusion all around the house.

"Don't slow down," Debra said, eyeing the house warily. "You're slowing down. Would you please not slow down? Dammit, Russ."

He gave her a sidelong glance, just this side of derisive. "Don't get excited. Just looking at the lay of the land."

"You're as bad as my kids," she sighed. "If you were in school, I'd keep you after."

"Don't let my age stop you."

Debra didn't reply, for her eyes had shifted to focus intently on the field beyond the house. She suddenly put a hand on his knee. "Slow down. Slow down!"

"You're kidding."

"There's something out there," she said, peering out his window and leaning so far over that she shoved him against the door. He had slowed the car to a crawl, and even he had not intended to be so conspicuous as they passed the Barrow dwelling. He tried to follow her gaze, but he saw nothing unusual in the field or amid the pine forest beyond.

"What is it?"

She slid back into her seat and shook her head. "I don't know. For a second there, I would swear I saw some kind of tall building. Something that was never there before. But once we got to where I could get a clear view of it, it was gone."

"Well…I didn't see anything like that."

Debra's face had gone chalky. *Something* out there had rattled her. "Trick of the light. Mirage, I guess," she said, obviously unable to accept her own explanation. "Whatever. It couldn't be what I thought it was."

"Okay," he said, swinging the car off to the side of the road and making a hard U-turn, "I guess that's enough. We're heading home."

As they passed Barrow manor again, Debra could not take her eyes off the field. This time, Copeland gave the house a more thorough scan and saw, to his dismay, that someone now appeared to be watching them from one of the front windows. Levi Barrow had had ample opportunity to view his car in Lynette's driveway, and he might well recognize it now. Nothing he could do about that, he thought as the road began to rise, carrying them back into the tall black pines. However, it might be prudent to take a few extra security measures once he got back to his sister's.

And for Debra to do the same.

"I do not like coming out this way," she finally said, giving him a stinging glare.

"Yeah, I get that. How much land do the Barrows own, do you know?"

"I don't know for sure; a lot, though. Not just here, they own plenty of land in the county."

"Judging from the signs, they're pretty protective...Jesus God!"

The kid on the bike flashed out of the trees and onto the road so fast that Copeland had to stand on the brakes to avoid running over him. The car started to fishtail, and only the fact that it was on a straight stretch rather than one of the hairpin curves kept it from careening off the road. By reflex, his right arm had extended to keep Debra from pitching forward, and as the car straightened out, he discovered to his chagrin that his hand had made less-than-subtle contact with her breasts. He quickly drew it away.

"Sorry about that. What the hell does that kid think he's doing?"

Debra, oblivious to the intimate contact, pointed to the speeding figure on the bike. "That looks like Zack Baird. One of Rodney's friends."

Copeland started after the retreating cyclist, still numb from the shock of very nearly killing him. The boy must be doing fifty miles an hour, he thought. Even going downhill, he had to hit the accelerator to catch up.

"Something's wrong with him," he said, watching the young man's feet pumping the pedals furiously, his upper body hunched over the handlebars. "He looks like he's in a panic."

"Be careful," Debra said. "I don't think he's aware of anything around him."

As they slowly closed the distance, Debra leaned out the window and called, "Zack! Hold up! We're here to help you!"

At first, Zack paid the car behind him no mind whatsoever. Copeland maintained a safe tailing distance, in case the kid hit the brakes or turned unexpectedly, but the way his bike was hugging the center line, an oncoming car would surely take him out. Finally, though, Zack glanced back, as if registering the Lexus for the first time, and he slowed down, eventually coming to a stop on the side of the road—fortunately on a section straight enough for Copeland to pull over without posing a danger to traffic. But as soon as Zack stopped his bicycle, he began to waver unsteadily, only to collapse in an awkward heap.

In an instant, Debra bolted out the door to kneel over the boy. "Zack!" she said, placing a hand on one of his cheeks. "Zack, what's wrong?"

As Copeland joined her, she looked up at him with wide, alarmed eyes. "My God, what's happened to him?"

The kid's face was frozen in a contorted rictus, his eyes bulging like white marbles, his tongue lolling out of his mouth. His breath whooshed in and out in short, rapid bursts, and his fingers clenched and unclenched in an involuntary rhythm. The scream that tried to burst from his lungs remained stifled behind a trauma-induced wall.

"This kid needs a doctor," Copeland said, his mind snapping back to the Barrow house and Debra's insistence that she had glimpsed something wrong, however fleetingly, on the property. "He's in severe shock. He doesn't look injured, does he?"

"No," she said, hurriedly checking over the boy's arms and legs. "What on earth could have done this?"

"The same thing that killed Rodney, I expect."

"We don't know that," Debra objected, but her eyes indicated she believed exactly the same thing.

"I don't believe in coincidences like this," he said, kneeling and placing his hands underneath Zack's shoulders and lower back. "Let's get him out of here." He lifted the boy with little difficulty and carried him to the car; Debra opened the back door for him and Copeland gingerly laid Zack on the seat.

"What about his bike?"

"It'll fit in the back." He unlocked the trunk, picked up the fallen bicycle, and was just maneuvering it inside when Debra tapped him on the shoulder.

"Look back there."

Copeland turned and peered in the direction she was pointing. For a moment, he saw nothing; then he realized that a patch of tall grass at the edge of the road appeared to be burning. Small flickers of orange light flashed in and out of the grass like roiling flames, but no smoke rose from the spot. After another few seconds, he could see that, no, it wasn't a fire, but some kind of object—something that glowed and pulsated with the brilliance of fiery coals.

It was moving toward them. Rapidly.

Copeland's first instinct was to go investigate, but Debra took hold of his arm and said in a quavering whisper, "Russ, I think that's what Zack was running from."

The image of the boy's terror-contorted face—and the sudden memory of Lynette telling him that Rodney had been burned—was all he needed to change his mind. He shoved the bike into the trunk and slammed it shut, but the handlebars kept the top from closing all the way. "Screw it," he said, left the trunk open, and got back behind the wheel. Debra was in the back seat with Zack in an instant, and as he started the car, he glanced at the side mirror to see if the thing was still behind him. It was. And it appeared to be moving faster now, though it remained indistinct behind the veil of grass. Throwing the Lexus into gear, Copeland hit the gas, and before he knew it, the car was pushing sixty.

Debra cradled Zack's head in her lap. "He's frigid. And I'm still shaking."

"Is the hospital still out on Hawthorne Road? That's a long way from here."

"Yes. But Zack lives much closer. Let's get him home to his parents. Legally, it's the better thing to do. Anyway, they'll need to know what happened."

"I wish *I* knew what happened."

"I tell you this—we may have saved this boy's life. I don't know what that was back there, but it sure *looked* like it was deliberately coming after him—or us."

"Direct me to his house, and if we have to, we can go with them to the hospital. Agreed?"

She nodded. "All right. We'll take a left on Cheat Mountain, and then it's just a short distance. I hope they're home. Zack's brother Tom is in my class; he should be there, at least."

Following Debra's directions, Copeland drove at high speed to the Baird house, where they found, to his relief, two cars in the gravel driveway and lights on in the windows. Darkness was falling quickly now, and the temperature had dropped to sub-comfortable. He parked behind a weathered white Oldsmobile Cutlass, got out, and went to the door while Debra remained in the back seat with Zack.

He knocked hard several times before the curtains of the adjacent window fluttered to reveal someone peeking out. Finally, the door opened just a crack. "May I help you?" came a coarse female voice.

"Are you Mrs. Baird? My name is Russ Copeland. I'm Rodney Lawson's uncle. Ms. Harrington and I found Zack up on Yew Line Road. He needs a doctor."

The door flew wide to reveal a short, tawny-haired woman in her mid-thirties. Her face went pale at the sight of Debra cradling her son's head. "Oh, my God!" the woman cried, and tears immediately glistened in her eyes. "What have you done to my boy? What have you done to him?"

She ran quickly to the car, fell to her knees, and gently wrapped her arms around her son's head, her chest heaving with sobs. Copeland said softly, "Mrs. Baird, we found him this way.

You need to get him to the hospital."

To his surprise, the woman turned to him and glared furiously. Then she spat, "Mister, if you've done anything to hurt my Zack, I'll shoot you. I'll shoot you in the fucking head."

#

Chapter 5

"Never let it be said that country folk are friendlier than city folk," Copeland said, tipping his glass of scotch of his lips. "I've had warmer welcomes in the projects."

Debra nodded in agreement, pouring herself a snifter of brandy from the decanter on Lynette's sideboard. "To say she was distraught is an understatement. But I doubt she would have actually done anything rash."

The grizzled, rather portly sheriff stared at Copeland with poorly concealed disdain. "Emma Baird's a bit high-strung at the best of times, but under the circumstances, it's easy to understand why she might overreact. You're not wanting to swear out a complaint against her, are you?"

"Good lord no," Copeland said. "Not against her. But we did feel it was best to advise you of the situation. That boy might have died if we hadn't found him. If nothing else, a car might have run over him."

Sheriff Grayson's expression softened a little. "Well, you did the right thing. His mama got him to the hospital straight away and word is he'll be all right. I'll be able to talk to him in the morning, and maybe then we'll find out what's going on."

Lynette was sitting on the couch, her face a pale mask of apprehension. "Whatever killed Rodney is still out there. Sheriff, you'll have to keep people away from that road."

"Well, ma'am, I can put out an advisory and increase patrols on Yew Line, but I can't just close down the road."

"I guess that would put undue hardship on the Barrows, wouldn't it?" Copeland said, giving his drink another liberal taste. Debra threw him a sharp glance.

"What was it you say you saw?" Grayson growled irritably. "Something 'low to the ground and lit up like it was on fire'? That doesn't sound like any of the Barrows to me, Mr. Copeland."

"No, but a brutal killing—plus one narrowly avoided—so close to their property might warrant a little looking around. Just my opinion."

"You don't know for a fact that the boy was ever in real danger. He was out of his head, that's all we know. Maybe in the morning, I'll find out something new."

"I hope so," Debra said in a placating tone. "Unless you have any objections, tomorrow I'll ask my father—Principal Martin— to broadcast to the school that Yew Line Road, and especially the woods out there, ought to be avoided. Other than Malachi Barrow, no students live out that way."

Grayson put on his most thoughtful face, but it quickly slipped into an ambivalent scowl. "Well, if you feel it'll do some good, I'm all for it, but in my experience, you tell kids not to do something, that's exactly what they'll do."

"With Rodney dead, that may not be an issue." Realizing she might have spoken too bluntly, Debra cast an abashed look at Lynette, who gave no sign of being affronted.

"Who's to say the Barrows might not have seen something odd up there," Copeland said, determined to press the issue. "I don't see the harm in asking. Do you?" He felt sorely tempted to mention Levi Barrow's recent, unwelcome visitations, but as Debra had warned him, Grayson left nothing to the imagination when it came to that family. For all practical purposes, it was untouchable.

"Tell you what, Mr. Copeland. I'll ride out that way and see what I can see. And I'll warn Amos and them that they might want to be extra vigilant for a few days—just to be safe. Would that meet with your approval, sir?"

"Well, it is a nice way of showing you care."

Grayson sighed crossly and then glanced at Lynette. "Mr. Copeland, I feel badly for your sister—and Mrs. Baird too. I sure don't want anyone else to have to go through such an ordeal. If something is wrong around here, I intend to sort it out."

Copeland nodded, aware that he had pushed the sheriff about as far as he could. "Well. I'm glad Zack Baird is going to recover. Maybe he'll offer you some useful information."

"I appreciate what you did for him. I know his mama does too. She just didn't quite grasp what was going on at the time."

"I understand."

"Then I'll bid you folks a good evening. You have my number."

"Thank you, Sheriff,"

Lynette said with a polite smile, but Copeland could see that it was forced. He walked with the older man to the door and saw him out without saying a word. Then he rejoined the two women in the living room.

"I get the feeling he's out of his league if he has to do anything more than write speeding tickets."

Debra gazed at him, half amused. "You barely pulled your punches."

"Just wanted to see his reaction. What does it take to get the state police involved here?"

"Either the sheriff or the county district attorney has to call them in," Debra told him. "One's about as likely as the other."

"Is the D.A. another Barrow cousin twice removed?"

"Drinking buddy."

Copeland raised his glass of scotch. "What a shock."

Debra smiled wryly, finished her brandy, and said to Lynette. "Tomorrow is going to be a long, stressful day. I'd better say goodnight too."

Lynette rose and gave her friend a quick hug. "Thanks for coming over. You probably did save that kid's life today."

Debra shook her head wearily. "If only we knew what was out there. Or whether that thing we saw was really after him at all. I keep going over and over it, and I just can't figure it out."

Copeland downed the last of his drink. "I hope our illustrious protector and servant is as good as his word and no one else comes to harm."

Both Lynette and Debra went silent for a moment, sobered by the thought. Then, with a weak smile, Debra started for the door.

"I'll walk with you," Copeland said.

"It's a hundred feet at most, and I do it all by my lonesome most every night," she said.

He shook his head. "I really think I might better, under the circumstances."

She sighed with mock exasperation. "Come along then, if it'll make you feel useful."

"Back in a few," he said to Lynette, then headed out into the cool night with Debra. Clouds had sneaked in during the past few hours and smothered the moon, leaving the landscape drenched in heavy darkness. As he walked beside the attractive young woman, he could not deny a vague but persistent feeling of nervousness; whether it was due to her exhilarating presence or something else altogether, he wasn't sure.

"You were very cool in a bad situation back there," he said. "I've seen people panic under less dire circumstances."

"Functioning under pressure is second nature." She offered him a wry smile. "Look at what I have to do every day."

"Tough, is it?"

"Sometimes."

As they passed the thick pines that separated the houses, Copeland could not help but peer into the impenetrable shadows beneath them. "What was it you thought you saw at the Barrow place? A building, you said?"

She stopped in front of her door and gazed at the featureless sky for a moment. "I don't know. I saw *something*. I wish I could explain it. For maybe two seconds, it looked like there was a big stone tower or something. Tall as can be—even higher than the mountains. I've tried attributing it to a reflection on the windows, a cloud, smoke...anything. It's just so plainly impossible. But I've got two very good eyes, and I'm not willing to write it off as hallucination."

"Whatever that was chasing Zack, that was no hallucination. And it *was* after him."

"I think you're right."

"Thanks for coming with me today. I really appreciate it."

She offered him a wan smile. "Now, I'm not so sure I should have."

"You were right where you supposed to be at the time. At least for that kid's sake."

She unlocked her door, then turned and gave him a long, appraising look. "That's not bad. Not bad at all. Well, Russ. I guess I'll be seeing you."

"I guess you will."

She left him with another smile, this one warmer, and closed herself inside. He remained where he stood for a moment, taking in the brief, aromatic draft that had escaped before the door swung shut.

One lovely lady.

He started back across the yard for Lynette's front door, but as he passed what he had come to think of as the great pine barrier, on a whim, he detoured around the side of her house and made his way to the small back yard. Despite the darkness, something—perhaps the simple desire to acquaint himself with his surroundings—drew him to explore. As he carefully picked his steps, he began to make out the shape of the steep, densely wooded ridge that pressed claustrophobically close to the left side of the house. To the right, beyond Debra's fenced back yard, the land opened up, and he vaguely discerned a broad meadow that stretched toward another long ridge, perhaps two miles distant. The Barrow house lay somewhere beyond that rambling hump, he knew. Not a single light intruded upon the nighttime landscape, which appeared as desolate and primeval as when Indians were the only ones who could have beheld it.

No, he was mistaken. Atop the ridge, he detected a brief flicker; probably a car out on Yew Line Road. But a moment later, he saw it again, slowly creeping through the darkness, and he realized it was too dim, too irregular to be a moving vehicle. For perhaps five minutes, it meandered across the ebony backdrop, sometimes winking out for a few seconds, only to reappear somewhere else on the ridge. It was obviously not traveling on the road. Finally, it disappeared, as if swallowed by the dense forest. Quite unexpectedly, Copeland found himself heaving a sigh of relief. The atmosphere out here felt outright eerie.

When he went back indoors, he found Lynette sitting at the kitchen table and smoking a cigarette. She gave him a sardonic smile. "Been kissing on Debra all this time?"

He felt his face flushing. "I was just out looking around the house."

"For what?"

"Anything unusual."

"And did you find anything?"

His immediate inclination was to mention the light on the ridge, but then he thought better of it. "Just a very dark night. Thought I might see some stars, but it's gotten cloudy."

"You like her, don't you?"

He shrugged. "She's okay."

"You act like a smitten schoolboy around her."

"I can't help it. She's a teacher."

"So am I."

"Remind me to bring you an apple."

#

Lynette had retired early, and Copeland sat in his room with his laptop, going over some email from the office. No major problems there, at least; he could ill-afford headaches on both the personal and professional fronts.

Now and again, his eyes wandered toward the window that faced Debra's house, but he saw no sign of life beyond the pine barrier. Lynette had readily noticed his attraction to her friend, and he very much hoped he'd exhibited more class than a lovesick adolescent. He had not interacted closely with a woman, other than the insane ex-wife, since before their marriage, and the requisite social skills had grown rustier than he liked to admit.

Though the night air was chilly, he preferred the windows open, mainly because of the cigarette smell that saturated the house. The upper floor stayed warm anyway, so the breeze that swept in felt clean and refreshing. He had just closed up his laptop when he heard a soft *creak-thump* from somewhere below—the outside kitchen door, it sounded like. Lynette? he wondered. He set his computer aside, went to the window, and peered into the darkness, but with the nightstand lamp on, he could see nothing outside.

"Lynette?" he called softly, but received no answer. He went out to the hall, to her door, and gently knocked; when she did not respond, he opened it, only to find the room pitch dark. He felt for the overhead light switch, found it, and flipped it up. Her bed was turned down but empty.

Not yet alarmed but curious and concerned, he hurried down to the main floor, through the kitchen, and out the back door, onto the small terrace that faced the yard. At first, he saw nothing, but as his eyes began to adjust, he made out a pale, willowy shape moving slowly toward the distant black hump that melded subtly with the starless sky. He started after her at a clip, heedless of any obstacles that might hide beyond the relative safety of the yard.

To his left, the trees that hemmed the lower slope of the ridge leaned over him as if curious about the stranger in their midst, their gnarled limbs grazing his head and shoulders, sometimes threatening his eyes. Once he passed the property line, holes, rocks, roots, and branches lurked in the knee-high grass and weeds, constantly threatening to trip him. He had no idea if Lynette regularly sleepwalked, but she was certainly risking life and limb venturing out here like this.

When he saw that he was beginning to gain on the pale figure ahead, he called, "Lynette!"

At first, she gave no sign of hearing him, but eventually she stopped and turned toward him; he could almost make out her features in the darkness. She was wearing only her light, silky nightgown, and she wrapped her arms around her torso as if feeling the chill for the first time.

As he strode to her side, she again turned to face the distant ridge.

"I heard Rodney calling me," she said softly.

"You've been dreaming," he said, placing a gentle hand on her shoulder. "This is no place for you to be."

She didn't look at him but continued to gaze into the distance. "No, I had to come. I heard his voice. He called me 'Mama.'"

"It must have seemed very real."

She finally turned to look at him, and the sorrow in her eyes nearly broke his heart. "I thought it was him," she whispered. Then she turned and started back toward the house, her gait faltering as she tried to navigate the rough ground. He took her arm to steady her.

A low breeze had begun to sweep across the meadow from the north; even through his clothes, the cold bit into his flesh. But he didn't dare push her any faster on her bare feet. He would have offered to carry her but for fear of tripping and injuring the both of them.

"Have you sleepwalked before?" he asked.

She shook her head. "Not that I know of."

The lights ahead shone like welcoming beacons, and when they finally reached the soft, freshly mowed grass, Lynette released an audible sigh of relief, now treading very gingerly. He led the way to the door and opened it for her, feeling a momentary twinge of sympathetic pain when he saw that her right foot left a thin smear of blood on the stone step.

"Let me get that cleaned up for you."

She waved him away. "It's nothing. I'll take care of it upstairs. Lord, I can't believe this. I could have been hurt a lot worse. Or you could have."

"You're stressed all to pieces, my dear. I wouldn't worry too much about this."

She looked him squarely in the eye. "I heard Rodney calling

me so clearly. Hard to believe it was a dream. But it had to be, didn't it?"

He nodded.

She sighed and glanced at her foot. "Well, I'm going to clean this and go back to bed. Do me a favor and make sure all the doors are dead-bolted, will you?"

"You sure you don't want me to give you a hand?"

"I'm fine. I'll see you in the morning."

"Goodnight, then."

Lynette disappeared through the door to the hall, and Copeland went to the back door to close and lock it. Before doing so, he leaned out and gazed into the darkness, listening more than looking. From the nearby ridge, the wind whispered like a low, masculine voice mouthing nonsensical words; and then some of the trees began to creak and moan weirdly—a high-pitched, dissonant accompaniment to the deeper, throaty wind-sound.

Its plaintive voice cried, "Maaa-maaaaa..."

If that sound had wended its way into Lynette's subconscious, small wonder it had upset her. Even to his waking mind, the rough screeching took on a disturbing, all-too-human quality, and he was grateful no one was around to see him when he closed and bolted the door with more than necessary haste, then made his way upstairs to his room and closed the windows with far more force than necessary.

#

Day Three

Chapter 6

Sheriff Mike Grayson could claim kinship with the Barrows by way of a great uncle on his mother's side who had married Amos's paternal aunt some eighty years back, and even though he was not a blood relative, he had generally found favor with the current Barrow clan, who took a particularly dim view of outsiders. Still, the fact that he represented the law made no more difference to them than if he were a plumber or an unemployable halfwit; in their eyes, the law existed only when it suited them.

Grayson parked his aging but still hardy Ford Crown Vic, which packed a specially modified 4.9-liter, 244-horsepower V-8 under its hood, just behind Levi's dent-ridden, rust-stained, 1980s vintage Chevy four-by-four. He clambered out, sauntered past the three stark red-and-white, hand-painted "Keep Out" signs that welcomed one to the property, and stepped up to the sagging front porch, where he rapped solidly on the crooked, wormy door.

When it groaned open, the stench of stale urine and mothballs wafted out, followed by a knobby, oversized head, which slowly swiveled on a stalk-like neck to reveal a pair of tiny, marble-like eyes that wallowed in deep black cavities. "Mr. Mike," rolled a guttural voice from thick lips that didn't quite close over a single protruding incisor. "Whatcha know?"

"Morning, Joshua. Where's Amos?"

"Where he allus is."

The brutish-looking figure held the door open and Grayson stepped into the gloom of a dank, sparsely furnished living room, its floor covered by a rug so ancient and tattered that every step he took unraveled a few more threads. How anyone could live like this had mystified him from day one, but he knew better than to even think of exhibiting manners that the family might in any way construe as rude.

With a hesitant clearing of his throat, he turned to face his distant cousin. "I have a question for you, Joshua, maybe two. You know that a boy got killed out this way a few days ago, right?"

"That teacher's lil boy, right, right. I seen him around before."

Grayson narrowed his eyes. "How much before?"

"A while back, on that bicycle of his, him and them boys that ride down in the woods."

"Now, they've never given you any trouble, have they?"

"Nah, they ain't given us no trouble. Not after they seen me and my gun that time."

"Scared 'em, did you?"

Joshua's tiny eyes gleamed. "Mr. Mike, I just know you ain't askin' if we done somethin' to 'em."

Grayson replied with an exaggerated shake of his head. "I just want to make sure everything's all right up this way. You see, we don't know what killed that young fellow, and I'd hate for you to be exposed to anything...dangerous. You know?"

Joshua gave a grotesque snicker. "Nah, nah, nothing dangerous around here. If they was, you can be sure we'd know about it."

"You don't mind if I say good morning to Amos, do you? Been a long while since I've seen him."

"Nah, you go right on up. He'll be happy you come to say hey."

Grayson went out to the hall and started up the creaky wooden stairs that led to the second floor, aware that Joshua's eyes followed him as he climbed; not that he would expect any different, for Joshua always displayed curiosity—*not* suspicion—about him because he was a lawman. Today, though, Grayson felt a bit more on edge, perhaps because this was not a social call. Lynette Lawson's brother—that Copeland fellow—had made some unkind and far too perceptive remarks about the goings-on in the community; as a city man, he seemed the sort who just might have the wherewithal to involve outside agencies in what ought to be Grayson's sole jurisdiction.

Amos Barrow would frown on such intrusions—and consequently on Grayson, for failing to nip the problem in the bud.

At the end of the hall, only murky, dust-flecked light shone through a half-open door. Grayson approached it slowly, almost reverently, for the senior Barrow vehemently disliked surprises.

Just before he reached the door, a slow, sonorous voice rumbled from within. "Would that be Mr. Mike I hear come to call?"

Grayson stepped into a dim chamber with a single window, which admitted a few sickly sunbeams through grimy, translucent curtains. Strange, abstract-looking ceramic sculptures that almost resembled sea animals—with fins, stalks, scales, barbs, and other less-than-attractive attributes—rested atop almost every surface of the room. Amos had always displayed a crude artistic talent, often sculpting odd-looking, distorted representations of people, animals, and objects. But these particular pieces were new—and strangely repulsive, as if the mind that conceived them had become fixated on the grotesque.

"I s'pose you've come to talk about that lil dead boy," the deep voice said. "Did Joshua offer you a glass of tea?"

"No, but that's quite all right. And yes, that young boy is somewhat on my mind."

"Well, have a sit, if you're gonna talk, talk. Don't need to be pacing up and down."

Grayson offered him a respectful nod and settled himself in a warped wooden chair across from the family patriarch. Amos Barrow had looked old when Grayson was just a boy, and he had barely changed after all these years. His body was an immense, corpulent mass that spilled over his once-plush wing chair, but his arm muscles still rippled with quiescent power, and his legs looked strong enough to launch the enormous body from its chair with ease. A huge, football-shaped head nestled in the folds of flesh atop his broad shoulders, and the salt-and-pepper hair was close-cropped except at the forehead, where a tall, gray, damn-near comical plume jutted upward from the skull. Milky blue eyes peered quizzically at him from behind thick, circular lenses in gold wire-rimmed frames. His billowing, dingy overalls were obviously handmade.

"You looking a lil tired and edgy," Amos said, ending the sentence with a deep *hroom* in his throat. "Guess you got a lot on your plate these days."

Grayson nodded, noticing that Amos's left hand had settled protectively on a luminous, sapphire-blue stone about the size and shape of an egg, which rested on a metal stand atop the circular table next to his chair. The lighting must have shifted just then, he thought, because the gleaming surface of the object began to pulsate in curious fashion. He felt Amos's eyes studying his, so he met the old man's gaze and said, "Sad business that boy being killed out this way. There's some that think it was an animal that did it, and some think it must have been a crazy man."

"Folks do terrible things to each other, don't they? And it's all the worse when it's a young'un."

"There was another little fellow ended up in the hospital yesterday evening. He had an...experience...in just about the same place. Right out here on Yew Line Road."

"Do tell."

"I spoke to him and his mama this morning. He seems to not remember a thing that happened, except that he was scared out of his mind and trying to run away."

"Them kids ought not to go traipsing through these woods and such. Just cause there's people living around here don't mean there ain't still bears and what not. You know, Levi shot him a bear not far from here just a few weeks back."

Grayson shook his head. "I don't think he was running from any bear, least that's the impression he gave me. And a couple of other folks—not kids—say they saw something too, but they don't know what it was."

"How does somebody not know what they seen?"

"Well, they claimed they never got a good look at it. But anyway, what about you and your boys? I don't suppose y'all have seen anything that'd make you up and take notice?"

The pale eyes behind the spectacles held a jovial sparkle. "Well, I'm not sure what you mean, Mr. Mike, but I ain't seen a thing around here but what I've a perfect right to see."

Grayson cracked a little smile. "You're sharp, as usual. Frankly, though, from all accounts, I think we're looking for some kind of animal. And whatever it is, I'd have to consider it dangerous. I know your boys like to get out and wander on your land, and if they were to happen on something, and it took after them the way it took after these kids...well...it could be a bad situation. Now, your grandsons listen to you, so I hope you'll insist that they take extra care. Especially for Malachi's sake."

"You're mighty kind to be thinking about us."

"You know I've always got your best interests at heart."

Amos's huge head nodded. His hand absently caressed the blue gem. "How is Janie?"

"She's all right. Had some kidney stones a while back, you know, but we think all that's passed, if you take my meaning."

"Your job. Is it a heavy burden for you?"

"My job? I been at it so long, I wouldn't know nothing otherwise."

Amos's thick lips spread in a knowing smile. "You know, Mr. Mike, there comes a time that a man has to pause and evaluate where he is, what he's doing. I reckon someone like you, who often sees the worst in people, has to take stock right often."

"Well, I do the best I can. I like to think I do some good. I sleep well at night, if that's what you're getting at."

"Yep, yep. But I s'pose when you're upholding something you believe in, it puts a strain on you when those close to you believe something different. I'm wondering if what I'm talking about is why I'm seein' that strain in your eyes, Mr. Mike."

Grayson stiffened, not certain what Amos was talking about,

but leery of where he might be leading. "I don't follow you."

"I'm talking about making choices, and our reasons for making the choices we do. You always done right by us because we're kin, and you know I've always been right fond of you. Much as you uphold your beliefs, your law, your kinship with this family has always taken its rightful place—at the head of the table, so to speak. Wouldn't you agree?"

He nodded, now feeling distinctly nervous. Amos was not one to mince words, but neither was he prone to speaking openly about subjects that brought the issue of the law between them. Grayson knew well enough that the Barrows lived as they saw fit; and most often, the less he knew about their affairs the better. He could more comfortably see nothing when he did not know what to look for.

"As I said," Amos continued, "sometimes we have to make hard choices, and when it comes to it, we hope we make the right ones. All I'm saying, Mr. Mike, is that I must trust you to do the right thing when the time comes."

More and more bewildered, Grayson found himself shifting nervously. "Amos, I've always done right by you and I don't intend to change anything now. Without you being more specific, though, I can't rightly understand all you're saying."

He desperately did *not* want Amos to be more specific.

The old man's hand again caressed the odd stone, which definitely appeared to radiate its own light. Outside, a cloud had passed over the sun, but in the deepening gloom, the sapphire shimmering grew brighter.

Then, to his surprise, Amos leaned close to the gemstone, one ear cocked, as if he were somehow listening, all the while studying Grayson's face thoughtfully. At last, he settled back in his chair and closed his eyes, indicating that their meeting was over.

"Thank you for stopping by, Mr. Mike. You've been good kin," the slow, deep voice said. Then Amos was asleep, his massive chest heaving slowly, his lips slightly parted.

Grayson could barely bring himself to rise from his chair. Amos, in his own way, had actually threatened him, he was certain of it. *Jesus*. Even when Grayson had confronted the family following Dottie Barrow's death, he had never considered himself in danger. Levi and Joshua had made it clear they would "set him straight" if necessary, but at the time, his gravest peril seemed to be an exile from their confidence—an admittedly unattractive prospect. But all that had been made right, forgiven and forgotten.

Now, though, Grayson had come to question Amos and found himself being questioned; to what end, he feared to guess. If the family was somehow involved in that boy's death, how could he turn a blind eye?

No. He wouldn't. Not anymore. *He* was the law here, and it was time he started acting like it. Whatever his kinfolk's plans, he could never condone killing, especially if kids were involved.

He left Amos's room, shuffled down the stairs, and found Joshua standing at the front door gazing at the mid-afternoon sky. He forced himself to meet Joshua's penetrating stare with one of his own.

"Granddaddy gone to sleep?"

"Yeah, he's resting. But we had a nice talk."

"He's sleeping a lot these days. Reckon it comes with getting older."

Grayson nodded. "By the way, what's that bluish stone he's got up there with him? It's unusual, ain't it?"

Joshua's eyes brightened. "It is kinda special, yeah. An heirloom, you might say."

"Never seen it before."

"He's always kept it in a safe place, least till lately. Nowadays he seems to have taken a shine to it." He snickered at his own wit.

"Is Levi around?"

"He's out yonder somewheres," Joshua pointed to the meadow that bordered the road. "He's just wandering, you know how he enjoys that."

"Remember what I told you—it could be dangerous to wander alone, even on your own land. I still don't know what's out there."

"Right, right, I'll mention that to him. I 'spect he's fine, though. He'll take care of anything that bothers him, you can be sure of that. Hey, you know what?" Joshua leaned in close. "I think Levi's got his eye on somebody. Wouldn't that be somethin' if he got him a new mom for Malachi?"

Grayson dropped his jaw, then tried to close it without looking too startled. "Who's he interested in?"

"Can't say. If he wants you to know, he'll tell you. I just mention it in case you see him around town."

"Well, that's most interesting."

"I guess you'll be getting on back to work then, huh?"

"Yeah, back to work." He clapped Joshua solidly on the shoulder. "You take care of your granddad, now. Like you said, he's getting up there. And you and Levi be watchful."

"We'll do that."

"See you later."

Grayson started toward his car, but Joshua called after him. "Granddaddy gave you some good advice, din't he? I hope you got it in your head to mind him."

He didn't turn, but a stab of fear nearly stopped him in his tracks. He forced himself to continue on to his car and merely waved a hand in acknowledgement.

He had just reached the end of the driveway when a yellow school bus rounded the curve from the direction of town. Its flashing lights came on, and it pulled to a stop just in front of the house. Its final passenger, Malachi Barrow, stepped off the bus, crossed the road, and headed toward the sheriff's vehicle with an inquiring expression. Grayson leaned out the window and gave the teenager a taut smile.

"Afternoon, Malachi. Doing all right?"

"Hey, Mr. Mike. Whatcha doing out here?"

By even the most generous standard, Malachi could not be considered anything other than ugly. He was tall and lanky, with a bony, oversized head that resembled his uncle Joshua's more than his father's. But like Levi's, his black hair was long and stringy, and his violet eyes gleamed oddly beneath a single, coarse eyebrow.

"I came to see your great-grandfather and your uncle. I guess your dad's not home."

"Daddy's got his business and all. You been talkin' to Great Granddaddy, I s'pose."

Grayson almost trembled under Malachi's knowing gaze. "We had an interesting visit."

Malachi snickered, its harsh sound remarkably similar to his uncle's. "I reckon he's still fond of you."

"I should hope so," he said, trying to hide his increasing apprehension. "Hey, Malachi, you knew that young Lawson boy, didn't you?"

The bright eyes darkened. "I reckon I did. You still looking for what killed him, I 'spect."

Grayson hardened his expression. "Yeah, I am. I guess you don't know anything about that."

"I know he's dead, sure enough. Ain't that something?"

"Let me guess. You didn't like him very much?"

Malachi's eyes flickered toward the house, and Grayson saw movement behind one of the windows. Abruptly Malachi said, "Well, I gotta go now, Mr. Mike. I'm gonna say goodbye, awright?"

"Maybe we'll get to talk later."

"I reckon. Goodbye, Mr. Mike. Goodbye." Malachi started toward the house, and Grayson pulled out of the driveway and accelerated up the road toward town, now more anxious than ever to get away from the Barrow property. He threw a last glance in the rearview mirror, only to see Malachi standing by the front door, waving after him, his homely face five miles long.

Grayson could no longer suppress the shudder he had been holding back, for *something* was very different about the family he had known for so long. They had always considered themselves above the law, this much was true, and they went about their business with little or no regard for others. Hell, Grayson had personally kept their names out of every controlled substances investigation in the county for the last twenty years. They had never posed an active, physical threat to anyone who didn't meddle in their affairs; now, though, Grayson wasn't so sure. Above all, he was positive that his favored status had somehow become tenuous, hinging on his decision to side with the family in whatever matter they had instigated. He dreaded the possibility that they might be responsible for the violence that had come to Silver Ridge, for if they were, he could no longer deny the sight of his aging but still discerning eyes.

And the Barrows knew this—even Malachi, for there could be no mistaking in the boy's long, regret-laden wave the clear intimation of absolute finality.

#

Chapter 7

Thad Smallwood had never enjoyed the drive into Silver Ridge from the Midland Brewery Distribution Center in Clarksburg, even though once every two weeks it provided him with a respite from the bane of his existence—traffic grinding to a screeching halt on what ought to be wide-open road. There was no Interstate to Silver Ridge, just a few of the worst two-lane roads in the state, and despite the picturesque mountain scenery, something about the surrounding countryside always seemed desolate and oppressive. The folks at the few Silver Ridge stores where he unloaded showed every bit as much prejudice toward a black man as the poorly educated clods of the much deeper south; unlike at most of the bigger stops, they never offered him a decent meal or even so much as a soda or cup of coffee.

Today, the road seemed even less hospitable than usual. Route 201 had needed maintenance for years, but now Smallwood's Sterling Acterra bounced and jolted mercilessly over hidden bumps and potholes, which forced him to hold back even on the rare straight stretches. It could only be his imagination, but as he drew nearer to the town limits, the curves seemed far more acute than they should have, the dips and inclines longer and steeper than ever before. Beneath the towering trees, a deep darkness smothered the highway, but sporadic mid-afternoon sunbeams cut through the canopy like gleaming blades, briefly blinding him with their brilliance.

In his twelve years of professional driving, Smallwood didn't think he'd ever been so uncomfortable.

Odd; by now he should have come upon the Chicken House, which was the only place around to get decent home cooking; and, somehow, he had missed seeing Buck Wagner's Texaco, which had to have been a couple of miles back. And the eons-old billboard for the Skylark Motel ("We're here for YOUR comfort!")—had it been taken down since last month? No way he could have passed it by.

The road veered sharply to the left, which somehow didn't seem proper, but he braked normally to go into the hairpin curve. Then his foot jammed the pedal to the floor because, a shockingly short distance ahead, the road became a narrow dirt path that vanished into an otherwise solid wall of towering pine trees.

"Jesus God-a-mighty!" he exploded as the truck shivered and shook to a sliding halt, only a few feet shy of smashing into vast boles that could not possibly stand where they now stood. A cloud of hot, fetid dust billowed up, swirled around the cab, and completely obscured his view for a long minute, during which time torrents of sweat began to stream down his forehead to sting his disbelieving eyes.

His mind zoomed back over the last several minutes of his trip. He had not made any unusual turns or detoured due to construction. His eyes had never left the road, and by every indication, he had followed the exact same route he had taken once every two weeks for the last ten months. His truck was not equipped with a GPS system, but his sense of direction was faultless; he had ceased needing a map to this locale by the end of his first haul here.

So, where the hell was he—and how did he get here?

The only thing to do was back up the truck, find a place to turn around, and drive until he found a familiar landmark. He *must* have somehow taken a wrong fork, regardless of how certain he had been of his route. He couldn't worry about that now, though, for negotiating this narrow, winding road in reverse would take all his concentration; hazardous as hell, but under the circumstances, necessary. He was just about to shift into reverse when a distant, electric blue flash in the woods ahead captured his attention. He leaned forward and peered into the distant shadows, hoping to catch another glimpse of it. A second later, he did. And again a few seconds after that.

He shut off the engine, shoved the door open, and dropped to the ground, landing on dry but yielding gray-brown loam. As he stepped toward the trees, he scanned the shadows for the source of the light—which flashed again, evidently a long way off, somewhere down the narrow path in front of the truck. When he glanced up, he realized that these trees were surely the tallest he had ever seen—their tops so high they actually seemed to reach the clouds! The sight of them sent his head reeling, so he turned his eyes back to the path, his heart racing with apprehension, his feet reluctant to take the first step into the silent darkness of the woods.

It was damned quiet out here. Not the first birdcall or insect chirp or sigh of the wind; only the soft crunch of his feet on the earth as he strode forward and penetrated the veil of shadow beneath the awful black pines. He stifled the urge to call out because his voice had no business intruding on this eerie, silent cavern of wood, and though his heart implored him to turn around and get back in the truck, the flashing blue light mesmerized him, beckoned him like a ghostly hand through the artificial night. So, he trudged on, glancing around constantly, warily, half-expecting *something* to materialize out of the darkness, or some subtle vibration to shatter the overpowering absence of sound. And as he drew near to the source of the light, he finally broke into a run, recognizing but not quite accepting what he was seeing.

It was a dogshit brown Ford Crown Victoria bearing the insignia of the Byston County Sheriff's Department, its blue lights flashing erratically, the driver's door hanging suggestively open. The car was empty, its engine off, though when Smallwood peeked cautiously inside, he found the keys in the ignition. The hood still felt warm.

So here the car sat, tucked in among the densely packed pines with no visible means of ingress. It could not have passed between the trees from the direction he had walked, nor any other that he could determine. By all indications, the vehicle must have been *dropped* here—yet it bore no sign of damage, and above it, not a tree limb appeared bent or broken. Besides, these pines rose hundreds of feet above his head, and in the lush evergreen canopy, he saw no significant breaks.

Somehow, it seemed, the forest had spontaneously grown *around* the car.

Now he could not help himself. Before he fully realized what he was doing, his mouth had opened and his voice was echoing with shocking, terrifying volume through the incredible forest: "Hello! Is there anybody here?"

Now, a sharp, staccato clicking, almost insect-like, burst from the darkness around him. He frantically scanned the shadows for the source of the sound, but he saw nothing. When he looked left, the rapid *click-click-clack, click-click-clack* seemed to come from the right; when he looked behind, it came from the front. Some distance farther down the trail, bright daylight gleamed through a break in the trees, and thinking it the most likely direction the car's occupant might have gone, he started jogging toward it. To his relief, as he put some distance between himself and the sheriff's vehicle, the bizarre sounds began to abate.

Though his mind had yet to grasp the nature of his predicament, he stalwartly clung to the belief that the world itself had not changed, for that was impossible; he simply didn't have enough information to process what had happened. But the moment he set foot in the open space between the great trees, his last bastion of rationality crumbled and dispersed on the four winds like so much dust; his breath caught in his lungs, and his body nearly collapsed beneath its own weight.

Miles and miles distant, beyond a series of mist-shrouded ridges, a stone tower ascended to the heavens like a monolithic needle, dwarfing a multitude of block-like structures, immense in their own right, which gathered at its base. Taller than any manmade edifice, the thing bore a strangely *organic* aspect, as if it had thrust itself out of the ground and reached toward the sun, seeking to pluck it from the sky. The dimly glowing, oblong objects that drifted in the air around it, diminutive in comparison, had to be bigger than whales to be visible from such a distance.

Smallwood heard a rustling sound behind him and, fighting back nausea, dazedly swiveled around. Of the shocking images his eyes had just beheld, the one now standing before him was surely the most incongruous: a disheveled-looking white man with long, greasy hair, dressed in tattered denim, regarding Smallwood with hostile, deep violet eyes. His lips slowly spread in a shark-like smile to reveal a mouthful of crooked yellow teeth. He was obviously not the driver of the sheriff's car.

"Whatcha say, nigger?"

For a second, Smallwood stared in disbelief, as rooted to the earth as one of the giant pines. But the words served to anchor the chaos in his mind, and like a low flame, fury began to displace his terror. Then, before he even realized what he was doing, he leaped forward with a cry and began to pound the smaller man with his fists. With every blow he landed, his dread diminished ever so slightly.

"You son of a bitch," he growled. "You wanna know what I say? This is what I say." He smashed his fist straight into the man's nose, and his hand came away bloody. "What the hell's the matter with you?"

The smaller man staggered slightly but maintained his footing; and then, shrugging off the punches as if a child had delivered them, he rose to his full height and offered Smallwood another mocking smile. "That kinda attitude ain't gonna get you nowhere, boy."

Before Smallwood could even consider a reply, the clicking sounds again rose all around him, and now he could see signs of movement in the underbrush between the trees. Here and there, flecks of light appeared in the shadows, and a strong acidic odor, like the smell of ants he had crushed in his fingers as a child, rushed to his nostrils, bringing water to his eyes. He backed away from the strange white man, trying to orient himself so he could make a break for his truck.

As the *click-click-clack* noises grew louder amid the trees, behind him, from the direction of the tower, a deeper, heavier sound rose, as if in response to the others. Like the pounding of drums, the noise grew stronger, more tangible, vibrating through the ground with such force that he felt it in his shins. The sunlight dimmed, as if a cloud had passed overhead, but a small, timid voice inside assured him that the sky was cloudless; and with a cry of near-mindless panic, he suddenly bolted and ran at breakneck speed into the trees, back in the direction of his truck.

Behind him, the chattering noises rose in volume and pitch. And mixed in with them, the distinct sound of human laughter: the cruel mirth of the man who had called him "nigger." Soon, Smallwood could no longer hear laughing, human or otherwise; only his own shrill cries as he dashed along the path toward his truck, which seemed as remote as the safe, comfortable life he had left behind in a world that no longer existed.

#

Chapter 8

The blended aroma of fresh produce, seafood, tangy spices, pine oil cleaner, and old sweat transported Copeland back almost thirty years, to a place in his memory that would have remained sealed if the unique and apparently timeless smell of Cooper and Rankin's Supermarket had not unexpectedly unlocked it. The store's interior had probably been remodeled a time or two since the 1980s, but one would never know to look at it. He could almost be an adolescent again, walking in to buy some groceries for his mom and dad—or to sneak a peak at some of the magazines they used to keep behind a special partition in the far corner of the store.

Lynette needed a few items that well-wishers from Rodney's wake had not provided, so he had volunteered to go shopping for her. For the better part of the day, she had been writing thank-you notes and signing legal documents, holding up admirably, but still a few days short of being up to sort through Rodney's room and personal belongings. Not to be insensitive, but he hoped she might manage it while he was still around to help her.

From the moment he had awakened this morning, it was

Debra Harrington who had dominated his thoughts; not just her nascent influence on his emotions but also her strange "vision" at the Barrows' place the previous afternoon. That, together with the bizarre events of the past couple of days—among which he counted the weird light he had seen on the ridge and maybe even Lynette's sleepwalking—added up to a disturbing, unfathomable mystery that still nagged at him. That each inexplicable occurrence tied in with the others he could not doubt, yet the prospects of piecing together such a puzzle seemed bleak when each disparate fragment defied comprehension.

Again and again, in his judgment, the clues led to the doorstep of Barrow manor. The idea that such a degenerate clan might be at the center of some heinous but simple intrigue hardly seemed a stretch, but this community's recent tribulations were far from simple. Unfortunately, the strongest evidence against the Barrow family was his intuition, and on reflection, he could not ignore the possibility that their worst offense might be the fact they offended his every sensibility. But each time he considered offering them the benefit of the doubt, the image of Levi Barrow's cunning, staring eyes—or the shocked face of Zack Baird as he fled from the Barrow property with the devil at his heels—removed all doubt from his mind.

He had just picked up some soap and a package of razors when he felt a tap on his shoulder. Turning, he saw a stooped, grizzled octogenarian clutching a wooden walking stick and regarding him curiously from behind Coke-bottle glasses. "'Scuse me, sir. You live around here?"

"Not really, no."

The old man sighed. "That figures. You look like you got some sense about you."

"Do you need help?"

"Me and my boy are trying to get to Elkins, and we can't get no good directions from these people. I was hoping maybe you could do better."

"Maybe I can. You take a right out of here. Go about a mile and get on 201 South. Then it's about fifteen miles to U.S. 250 West, and that takes you straight there."

"That's exactly what the fellow down at the gas station and that woman over there at the register said. But we already done that, and we just ended up on some back road that damn near took us over the edge of a cliff."

Copeland frowned. Perhaps the man had happened upon the old dolomite quarry, except that it lay five miles in the opposite direction. "I'm sure they have maps here. Maybe a map would help."

"I got one. And it don't show this town but for a little black dot in a big green blob."

He chuckled. "Can't say I'm surprised. Well, I wish I could be of more help."

"Oy," the man grumbled with a vexed shake of his head. "Thanks anyway." As he ambled toward the front of the store, he struck the floor with the tip of his cane a bit harder than necessary.

Copeland couldn't help but feel sorry for the man, though he wondered whether such a frail old thing ought to be behind a wheel, especially on these treacherous mountain roads. If the rest of the world were lucky, his son would be driving.

Paper towels. Lynette had wanted some paper towels. He had already passed the paper goods, his mind on other things, so he headed back that way, going over his mental list in case anything else had slipped his mind.

As he strolled by the checkout aisles, it occurred to him that an inordinate number of people were waiting in line—damn near as bad as the Dominick's back home.

No wonder. Only one lane was open.

The middle-aged woman at the register was saying to an irate-looking young man, "Sorry, sir, I'm the only one here. Our other two checkers didn't show up this morning. It's not like them at all."

Copeland had just grabbed a couple of rolls of paper towels when a little vibration began at the back of his neck. The kind of thing that happened when something was wrong that he couldn't quite pinpoint—such as when enough separate, seemingly insignificant events converged to create a single, remarkable one.

But what?

He stood in line for ten minutes, barely containing his

impatience, his discomfort exacerbated by a squalling child in the arms of an oblivious woman in front of him. One more reminder to thank God that he and the lunatic Megan had never considered having children.

When he had finally finished with the store and returned to his car, he found himself inexplicably dwelling on the old man's inability to make his way to U.S. 250—a procedure that required a single right turn onto 201, which was reasonably well-marked, and staying on it for a quarter hour. On a whim, rather than returning directly to Lynette's, he headed toward the highway instead. When he came to the turn, there was the sign, plain as day, identifying the road as West Virginia Highway 201. Hardly perplexing so far.

Just for good measure, he turned right, away from town—the way he had come in other day. Unsure why any of this particularly mattered to him, he took special note of the intersections he passed, none of which seemed problematic. The old man had just gotten confused; nothing difficult to understand about that, either. Still, he drove for another five miles before deciding to turn back toward Lynette's; she would be waiting for her groceries and probably already wondering what was keeping him.

Seeing an opening on the right where he could turn around, he pulled in and found himself face to face with The Chicken House. Though it was almost the dinner hour, only a single car occupied the parking lot. Well, maybe those yellow corn-fed birds weren't all they were cracked up to be. As he swung around and started to pull back out onto the highway, he looked left, looked right...and kept looking, suddenly doubting his eyesight.

His fingers tightened on the wheel as an electric thrill of terror and disbelief arced down his spine. Where moments ago a long, curving stretch of highway had descended into a thickly wooded vale, a vast open space had opened in the earth, filled with pale, slowly swirling mist, tendrils of which began to worm slowly up the road like the questing arms of a monstrous sea anemone.

Beyond the great miasma, something very tall and very dark rose into the sky, but he could not make out any details through the ghostly veil. One trembling hand reached for the door handle, found it, and tugged; his body weight forced the door open, and he slid out of the seat, clutching the doorframe in case his knees gave way beneath him.

When he swiveled his head to peer back at the fog-choked emptiness, it had vanished.

Highway 201 had reappeared, snaking into a valley of oaks and hickories as it had for countless years. No trace of mist crept along the road, and only a distant, tree-crowned mountaintop rose above the landscape like an ancient, green-robed monarch.

He took a few halting steps onto the cracked asphalt of the highway and stood there, dumbfounded, heedless of any vehicles that might bear down on him, thinking he now knew why young Zack Baird's eyes had been frozen wide with shock.

After a full five minutes of nothing happening, he began to breathe a little easier. But in that time, not a single car had passed in either direction.

The lost old man. The grocery checkers who had not shown up for work. Debra swearing she had seen a building that could not possibly exist.

It was one thing to doubt his own perceptions. It was another to know that others had borne witness to something incredible, even if they did not realize it.

As surely as he stood here, that unknown something had killed his nephew and driven another young boy out of his mind.

This *had* to be a hell of a lot bigger than the Barrows.

He turned and walked back toward the Chicken House, bypassed his car, and pushed his way in through the glass front door of the little building. It was hot inside, and the odor of grease hung like a dirty fog in the air. The half-dozen tables were all empty, and no one stood behind the counter.

"Hello! Anyone here?"

After a moment, an elderly man wearing a white apron ambled out to the register, the eyes behind his thick glasses not on Copeland but on the window.

"Sorry," the old fellow rasped. "Didn't want to stand out front, not the way things are going around here."

Copeland leaned close to the man's face. "What do you mean by that?"

The man pointed out the window. "That fog that keeps coming around every so often. When it does, the road goes dead for a pretty good while. You the first person to come round in 'bout an hour or so."

"When did it start?"

"Late this morning. At first, I thought it was just some weather. Then I saw them trees didn't seem to be where they was supposed to be anymore. That, sir, just ain't right. And then my help didn't show up, which got me a bit worried."

"Have you seen anyone drive in or out of that fog?"

"A few went in earlier today. Then it's like they just not there anymore. And not one thing's come out. Mind you, it ain't always there. But it seems to be happening more often now than at first."

"Have you called anyone? The sheriff? Family?"

"Can't. The phone's out."

Copeland started to reach for his cell, but then he remembered that, since there was no service out here, he hadn't bothered to bring it with him. "I don't know what's going on," he said softly, turning to peer out the window at the road. "But I think it might be better if you closed up and went home."

"Thought of that too, 'cept I live down down yonder," he said, pointing southward, "and I ain't much liking the idea of heading straight into something I don't know nothing about."

"Why don't you head back into town? I don't think I'd stay here if I were you."

"Don't know where I'd go."

"Maybe the sheriff's office for starters?" he said, painfully aware that Mr. Grayson would be about as receptive as a brick to such an outrageous story. Who could blame him? Regardless, this *had* to be turned over to some authority, and around here, Sheriff Grayson was it. "At best, this road should be closed."

"That where you going?"

He thought for a minute. Sheriff Grayson would have a harder time discounting the statements of two witnesses than one, but having earned the sheriff's disdain during their previous encounter, he doubted his chances of making a convincing case. No…there was a better way. He knew a few influential people in Washington who trusted his judgment, and they were in strategic positions to get things moving officially—as if he had any idea of what to get moving.

"No," he said at last. "I know some government people who will want to hear what I have to tell them."

The old man seemed to consider the idea for a time. Then he opened the register, took out the cash drawer, turned, and disappeared into the back. When he finally reappeared, he said, "Okay, I'm officially closed."

"What's your name?" Copeland asked as they headed out to the parking lot.

"Billy Hart," the man said, pausing to lock the door behind him. "Been running this place for the last twenty-some years, and I ain't never seen anything so peculiar in all my life."

"I don't imagine anyone has," Copeland said softly. "Russ Copeland. Pleased to meet you."

"You're not local."

"Not exactly."

"Well, good luck, Mr. Copeland. Hope you can get through to your people."

"Yeah. So do I."

As he got behind the wheel, Copeland's hands trembled, his mind's eye fixed on that misty chasm, which had appeared where every logical circuit in his brain assured him none could exist. It was too absurd to accept. Still, he wasn't ready to write off his own sanity quite yet. Something in the air, maybe; a chemical or biological agent capable of inducing hallucinations.

What other explanation could there be?

But Rodney had not been killed by any hallucination.

As he turned north on the highway, he kept his eye on the rearview mirror, half dreading, half hoping to actually witness a transition, something that might offer a clue about what was really happening.

His gut told him he needed to get back to Lynette.

When they reached the business district, having encountered no other traffic, Hart turned off toward the sheriff's office, and Copeland continued straight to Lynette's house, more than recklessly disregarding the 25 mile per hour speed limit. Strange old bird, he thought; Hart seemed to take what he had seen in stride, despite being so close to the event. The old fellow might even make the more credible witness, since he seemed lucid enough and might be less prone to impatience with a Doubting Thomas—which the sheriff would surely be.

A new thought now occurred to him. He had assumed that this phenomenon was confined to the vicinity of Silver Ridge; but what if it went well beyond that? All the more reason to contact someone outside the area. Ed Stratton at Homeland Security? Why not? Might as well start at the top.

Once he pulled into Lynette's driveway, the first thing he did was walk around the house to observe the distant ridge where he had seen the strange light, his intuition suggesting that if these phenomena were related, then manifestations in one place might be reflected in another. At present, nothing seemed amiss. The late afternoon sun burnished the tree-crowned hillsides with gold, and a few birds sang longingly to each other in the nearby woods.

The fact that everything seemed perfectly normal troubled him all the more.

"Looking for something?"

The voice felt like a velvet glove on his tense nerves, and he turned to see Debra and Lynette coming around the house to greet him. Debra's brown eyes were curious, her face a shade paler than usual. But she gave him a tiny smile.

"I think I just found it."

"We saw you pull in. You look like you've seen worse than a ghost."

What should he say? Debra was the one person who might understand, but it seemed unfair to add to Lynette's burdens. On the other hand, keeping her in the dark was neither fair nor practical. If he intended to report his experiences to Ed Stratton or anyone else, he might better get some practice explaining it.

He finally said, "Whatever happened to Rodney appears to be the tip of an iceberg. And the berg is getting bigger."

Debra's eyes narrowed. "As I was just telling Lynette...a quarter of the school was absent today. No notes, no calls from parents. And Dad couldn't reach a single one of them by phone."

"Damnation. Well. You recall what you saw yesterday, out by the Barrows'?"

"No way I could forget that."

"I saw something just as impossible." He described his vision of the fog-shrouded chasm, and the fact that Billy Hart had also witnessed it. As she listened, Debra stared broodingly at the distant sunset.

"You didn't believe me yesterday. What do you think now?"

"There's more. Something's happening to people. At first, I didn't put it all together. But that lost old man at Cooper's, the missing employees there and at the Chicken House, hardly any cars on the road—and all those kids out of school. No way these could all be coincidence."

"God forbid anyone else should end up like Rodney," Lynette whispered.

Debra nodded, her face losing another shade. "Or Zack Baird, for that matter."

"Assuming old Mr. Hart made his report to the sheriff, I shouldn't be surprised if we hear from him again." He looked at Lynette. "Sorry to bear bad tidings. I know you don't need any more stress."

"But there *is* more." Her eyelids fluttered with apprehension. "You knew I had sleepwalked the other night. I had pretty much written it off as nerves...anxiety...something."

"What?"

She turned to Debra. "I saw a thing just like what you described. Out by the ridge—last night, after Russ had come to get me. When I got back inside, I looked out the window, and there it was, just for a few seconds—this tall tower that looked like it was made of black stone. And it had a kind of glow about it."

"And then?"

"Then…just like you said. It suddenly wasn't there anymore. What was I supposed to think? I couldn't believe I had dreamed it. Now, I'm not so sure I was dreaming when I heard Rodney calling me, either."

For a minute or so, no one spoke. Finally, Debra heaved a sigh and looked at Copeland. "So what do you do when you've run out of logical explanations?"

He shook his head. "I've never run out of them before."

"Logical or not," Lynette said, "there must be a reason for what's happening. Rodney died for some *reason*. And I want to know what it is."

"Lynette, you know I work with people in the government. I'm going to make a few calls this evening. Not they'll have any immediate answers, but I'm far more inclined to put the ball in their court than look to your sheriff here for a solution."

"Wise choice."

Satisfied that, for the moment, the world wasn't coming apart beneath their feet, they started walking toward the front of the house, though Copeland glanced back several times at the ridge. As they reached the front yard, he detected a faint vibration at the back of his ear, and when he halted and listened, he recognized it as the distant sound of music.

It was a chorus of voices rising in a dark melody, slow and lyrical, reminiscent of Bach, perhaps, though he did not recognize the piece. Then a chorus of heavy baritones and tremulous sopranos joined in like the voices of restless spirits, rising harmoniously to weave a haunting, melancholy dirge. A deep, unidentified thudding sound punctuated the rhythm.

"Is that coming from the church?"

Lynette nodded. "Sounds like it. You can sometimes hear the music when conditions are right. But there's no service tonight, not that I'm aware of."

"It's a rather odd, uh, hymn. Or whatever it is."

Debra cocked her head and listened. "Yes, the rhythm is peculiar. The time signatures keep changing. Listen—that's 11/8…

now 6/8...now 7/4."

Copeland raised an eyebrow. "You're very well-versed in music."

"I used to sing in the church choir."

Lynette continued staring into the distance beyond Debra's house. "If the choir was doing a program—or even practicing for one—I'd know about it. Yes, very odd indeed."

"On the current order of magnitude, I'm not sure I'd rate it all that highly," he said.

However, as they made their way to the front yard, Copeland noticed that music began to assume a completely different character. The choir's voices rose in sharp dissonance, the rhythm faltered, and the devastated melody become a cacophony of long, frenzied, nonsensical cries that pealed raucously and endlessly to the heavens. Then another, heavy, unidentifiable sound—almost like the rumble of an approaching train—joined the chorale.

He knew then that he had spoken too soon, for this perverse chorus sounded positively unearthly.

Very definitely on par with the rest of these recent bizarre events.

#

Chapter 9

The dark-toned choral music that drifted from the church took Loretta Gleasman by surprise because, as far as she knew, the building was empty. Earlier, Reverend Lee and Irma Rodgers, the church secretary, had been there to do whatever it was that church staffers did, but they had left at least two hours ago. Loretta gently set the chicken she was stuffing down on the counter and went to the window, which overlooked the lonely white building across Cheat Mountain Road. No cars visible in the parking lot, the doors and windows all closed. The odd-sounding anthem couldn't be a recording, she thought; it was too full, too resonant, to be anything but live singers. But good lord, whatever they were singing, it wasn't any traditional church music. In fact, the words weren't even English—just disjointed strings of guttural, barely human-sounding barks and moans that made no sense to her.

Behind the litany of nonsense, some kind of heavy percussion rose like a sporadic pounding of thunder, powerful enough to rattle the windowpanes. Loretta heard all kinds of noise when the choir practiced on Thursday nights, but never anything like this. It had better not become commonplace, she thought, or she would have to speak to the reverend. Church or no church, they had no right to disturb the neighborhood's peace. Since she'd turned forty, unpleasant rackets set her nerves on edge far more quickly than in the old days, and the last thing she needed was a church choir competing with hip-hop-blasting neighborhood cruisers for the royal crown of obnoxiousness.

Corky, an orange tabby of exceptional girth who enjoyed nothing better than yowling about his empty stomach, cast a thoughtful eye at the chicken as Loretta went to the sink to wash the grease from her hands. "This has nothing to do with you, so you can just take yourself right out of here," she said sternly, and he gave her his most potent scowl of disdain. She picked up the baking tray, carried it to the oven, cat close at her heels, and promptly placed dinner out of harm's way. Corky gazed at her, still perturbed, but kept his yowling to himself, which was rare for a thwarted cat. "Don't fret; I'll feed you before Daddy gets home. And he's a soft touch, so you can con him for more."

Denied the prospect of an early dinner, Corky's attention turned to the window, which he regarded pensively for a full minute. Then his eyes widened, his ears flattened, and he turned and raced out of the kitchen.

"That's what I say too," Loretta grumbled. She went to the little den and flipped on the television, but the persistent low thumping of percussion overpowered the voice of the broadly smiling weather woman on Channel Six News. A few bands of distortion rolled up the screen, and for a startling moment, the wailing chant seemed to emanate from the TV speakers. Well, so much for that. She turned off the box, went straight out the front door, and headed across Cheat Mountain Road (without bothering to look both ways, which out here was a waste of energy). The music was unnaturally loud, the number of voices prodigious. Without a single car in the church lot, how on earth had the performers gotten here? Some of the members who lived nearby often walked to services, but no way could all these singers have hoofed it unless they had met at a nearby house first. But why? Some kind of special event?

As she made her way toward the building's main entrance, she paused and grimaced as something swept briefly over her body: a noisome breeze, a disagreeable tingle of electricity. The sensation passed, but a feeling of clamminess lingered, not unlike the chicken grease she had washed off before leaving. Shuddering, she went up the short flight of steps to the door, now strangely nervous, half-afraid she had made a mistake leaving her home. But why? The singing was weird, but it was just music.

Very loud, very bizarre, very spooky music.

She tried the door handle, and, sure enough, it was unlocked. Pushing her way into the narthex, she stepped into a thick sea of gloom, as if a thunderhead had gathered inside the building. Here, the throbbing music assailed her nerves like a battering ram, and its tempo increased as she took a few steps toward the darkened sanctuary. She could tell before she passed through the looming archway that something here was very, very wrong.

There were no singers inside the chamber.

No choir in the loft beyond the empty pulpit. No parishioners in the pews on either side of the crimson-carpeted aisle. No trace of the mouths issuing these swirling vocal strains, which plainly originated in the shadowy spaces around her. It *must* be a recording, she thought, yet the sheer power of the melancholy harmonies and sinister-sounding drumbeats solidly refuted the notion. Her legs quivered as she took a few more steps down the aisle, her disbelieving eyes roving, her mind aching for some logical explanation. But every line she cast in search of one came back empty.

Somehow, the late afternoon sunlight failed to penetrate the stained-glass windows; all appeared as black as pitch and peered down at her like huge, vacant eyes. She had never been in the sanctuary when it wasn't full of people, and now it seemed a starkly different place: huge, overpowering, as forbidding as a vast, subterranean chamber in which unseen eyes studied her with palpable hostile intent. Yet curiosity—or something—rooted her there, as if she anticipated the commencement of some spectacle she didn't dare miss.

A hint of a deep chugging sound, in counterpoint to the rhythm of the chorale, broke through her hypnosis and drew her attention to something that was just beginning to take form on the ivory-hued wall high above the choir loft: a huge shadow, distinct and well defined, yet totally unrecognizable—uncast by any light source she could discern. A slowly shifting black spider with long, crooked legs, becoming more and more solid with every passing second, as if it materialized out of the bare plaster. The discordant locomotive sound intensified, a ghostly train inexorably closing on her.

Loretta had stopped walking when the chugging sound began, and now she shifted into reverse, still just shy of panic. This was an event, inexplicable and frightening—but something surely profound, perhaps even an act of God. This was *his* house, after all. Still, as the huge, awful-looking shape on the wall expanded and solidified, she could never in this lifetime accept it as anything even remotely divine.

As the otherworldly wailing and the unmusical chugging built toward a chaotic crescendo, the sanctuary fell suddenly, shockingly silent. A sharp ringing lingered in her ears like a needle in her auditory canal, and for several seconds she felt dizzy. Some moments later, she realized that the shape on the wall had vanished.

The late afternoon sunlight that now warmed the colorful stained-glass windows had transformed the great chamber into an ordinary, welcoming place of worship. Then, somewhere nearby, a door creaked sharply, and Loretta felt a thrill of terror more intense than during the height of the spectacular phenomenon. When slow footsteps began to echo through the great hall, panic at last exerted its hold, and she turned and bolted for the exit, her every instinct warning her to flee now or die. She shoved her way through the double wooden doors, sprinted across the parking lot, and into the road, too terrified even to think of pausing for traffic.

She did not feel the jarring thud of impact with the grille of the oncoming vehicle. Her body sailed into the air and slammed to the pavement like a slab of old meat tossed by a careless butcher. Consciousness remained just long enough for her to realize that neither of her erratically jerking arms had any business bending in so many directions.

The driver of the ancient, rust-coated Chevy four-by-four slid out of the cab with an annoyed frown, and his small black eyes briefly regarded the broken body. Then, with a dismissive snort, he turned and strode toward the front door of the church, unwilling to abide even a brief diversion from the business that had brought him here in the first place.

#

Chapter 10

After dialing a half-dozen numbers with no result, Copeland had about decided he would be better off pouring himself a double shot of Johnnie Walker Black, joining Lynette and Debra on the screened porch, and drowning everything in his mind even remotely related to current events in Silver Ridge. The dial tone sounded normal, but each time he entered a number, the receiver went dead. Under normal circumstances, his cell was useless until he got closer to Elkins, and he had no intention of going out to that dark road. He put away the phone in disgust, went downstairs to the living room, and flipped on the television. The network news came on, but the picture appeared snowy and the sound came out garbled—which for all he knew might be normal here, since Lynette had no direct TV connection. He had to wonder how Rodney had ever entertained himself without 300 channels of crap to choose from. He tried the available six and found similar reception on each, but as near as he could tell, the news from the outside world revolved only around commonplace events. He was just about to shut off the tube when a new, flickering image on the screen captured his attention and actually caused him to gasp.

The sound from the speakers rose to a shrill, unintelligible muddle of noise, which infuriated him now because, before his eyes, he saw the unbelievable, monolithic tower he had earlier encountered out on the highway. Though warped, the image of the gigantic stone construct stood out in stark relief against a garish backdrop of arcing lightning and scrolling color bars, its upper reaches twisting and writhing serpent-like in the grip of video distortion. In the foreground, a strange shape appeared to crawl across a wildly shifting landscape toward the camera—something pale and shimmering, moving with an undulating, worm-like rhythm, vaguely suggestive of a limbless man. Copeland involuntarily drew back, a cold, sick feeling in his stomach. Then the picture faded into a swirling, crackling field of colorful video snow, and with a frustrated curse, he switched off the television.

His regular daily routine involved extensive communication, electronic or otherwise, and here he was, essentially cut off from everything and everyone beyond the town limits. Since afternoon, a low, simmering fear had begun to erode even his firmest bulwarks of denial, and now, after viewing this disturbing image, his nerves felt raw. The increasingly dramatic evidence of an insidious deliberation behind all that was happening clashed at every point with his natural inclination to believe in a logical, even if improbable, explanation. Yet his initial hypothesis of a widespread hallucinogenic agent now struck him as more outlandish than accepting these events at face value.

Until now, the only things that truly frightened him were serious illness, homelessness, and terrorism—not necessarily in that order. In the course of two days, all that had changed.

With hands on the verge of trembling, he poured himself a scotch from the decanter on Lynette's sideboard, went to the kitchen for some ice, and made his way to the screened porch where Debra and his sister sat in tense silence, their eyes on the distant ridge to the northwest. A bloody sun had settled above the long, wooded hump, lending it the appearance of a huge, charred animal carcass. Both women appeared mesmerized by the hazy, haunted-looking vista, and Copeland's thoughts turned to that debased family whose domain lay beyond it—whose role in all that was happening he still firmly believed to be significant. Debra *must* know more about Levi Barrow's interest in her than she let on, he thought. As the object of his unwanted attention, she likely faced the gravest personal danger of all.

"Lynette, is the picture on your television usually half-scrambled?"

She shook her head without looking at him. "No. It's quite clear. Why?"

He nodded to himself, unsurprised. "I've seen that tower again," he said, and both women's attention now turned to him. He described the scene on the television. "The odd thing was that it didn't look like a story on the news. It seemed more like a closed-circuit image."

Lynette shuddered visibly. "I had thought it was a nightmare. I wish to God it was."

Before he could say anything else, the rumble of tires on the road drew their eyes to the front of the house; a moment later, a white Buick LeSabre cruised slowly into view, obviously intending to stop. At first, Copeland did not recognize the driver, but then he realized it was Debra's father, Glen Martin. The Buick rolled past Lynette's house and pulled into the driveway next door.

Debra rose from her seat and gave Lynette a gentle pat on the shoulder. "I'll come back in a little while," she said. "I doubt Dad will be here very long." As she left, she turned briefly and gave Copeland a warm smile. Suddenly, nothing seemed quite as bleak as it had moments before.

"I'm worried about her," Lynette said, somewhat to his surprise. "She doesn't let on, but with everything that's happening here, it's Levi Barrow she's most afraid of."

He nodded. "I'm sure there's more to his interest in her than getting bent out of shape over his kid."

"That's just his excuse. He's stalking her, Russ. The other day was not the first time he's come around. But if she goes to the sheriff, he'll find a way to make it appear her fault."

"As witnesses, we could make that difficult for him."

Lynette shook her head. "It wouldn't make any difference. But there is one other possibility. Her father. The Barrows apparently hold him in some regard."

Copeland raised an eyebrow. "Why would that be?"

"Years ago, Major Martin and Levi's father served together in the army. There is some tie between them."

"Major Martin, is it?"

"Everyone's called him that for years. It fits."

"Well, in my book, stalking a man's daughter is no gesture of respect. If you're saying that we should alert him to what's going on, I agree with you. You work with him; how well do you know him?"

"Pretty well. He's soft-spoken, but very firm. I know for a fact he's not the kind of man to take such an offense lying down."

"Well, there you are. You want me to try to catch him on his way out? Or would that upset Debra?"

"She'd never talk to him about it on her own, and she might shoot me for going behind her back. But I'm worried, Russ. I consider her safety the most important thing." She went silent for a moment. "Our relationship can be patched, if it comes down to it. The alternative might not be so easy."

"I have less to lose, relationship-wise, than you do. If she's going to be angry, let her be angry with me. I can talk to him."

She half snickered. "Very noble of you, dear brother, but I know them both much better than you. No, I'll talk to him in my own way. Besides, given how you feel about her, I would hate to see a blowout between you so early in the game."

"What do you know how I feel? I've known the woman for two days."

"You have that same look in your eyes you had when you were fifteen. Amy Carlisle, wasn't it? And when you first met your ex, Megan. You're hardly a closed book, Mr. Copeland."

He couldn't keep from chuckling, but then he said in a somber tone, "All that's well and good, but compared to what we've all seen in the last twenty-four hours, I'm not sure our personal feelings mean very much. Who knows what's going to happen by tomorrow? And I can't even make a phone call out of town."

"You're right, of course," she said with a sigh, her eyes turning briefly inward to focus on the memories of her son. "But whatever's happening, it can't put a stop to our lives. We can't just throw up our hands and surrender to something we don't understand. At least Levi Barrow I understand. He's an immoral, potentially violent, dangerously clever piece of walking garbage. Lord forgive me, but if he were to get run over by truck, I'd give the driver a hug."

"Let's put it this way," he said. "As long as I'm here, he will live to regret any trouble he causes. But let me tell you—and not because of Levi Barrow—I'm on the verge of getting us in the car and seeing what happens on the road. Nothing ventured, nothing gained, and all that."

For the first time, Lynette's eyes widened with obvious fear. "No. Don't you even think of doing that. After what you said you saw out there…and what I *know* I saw…it sounds like suicide."

"We have no way of knowing that."

"Russ, for now, we're all still here. If anything, I think we should try to get people in town together, to find out what others have seen, what they might know. We could get the people at the church together. In times of trouble, they are the ones I want on my side. It would at least be a positive step. A better one than some ill-conceived attempt to run away."

Copeland pondered the idea and found that he liked it. "All right. I'm inclined to agree with you. Anyway, I would never run out on you. You know that."

She nodded. "As a community, we might be able to keep something like what happened to Rodney from happening to anyone else."

"A worthy goal," he said. Then, as he downed the last of his scotch, he heard a car engine start; a moment later, Glen Martin's Buick backed out of Debra's driveway and turned in the direction of town. It had just passed beyond the neighboring trees when Copeland heard a low, clattering rumble, which gradually grew louder. After a few seconds, a familiar-looking, rusted red Chevy pickup drove past, evidently in slow pursuit of Major Martin.

"Jesus Christ," Copeland muttered. Without another word, he set his glass down on the table next to Lynette and rushed outside, heading for Debra's house. When he reached her door, he knocked sharply, then slowly pushed it open and called her name.

She did not answer, so he stepped inside, briefly listening to the hollow silence of her house, taking in its sweet, cedar-like smell, its warm, distinctly feminine ambiance. To the right, an archway opened to a cozy living room; to the left, another arch revealed a quaintly furnished dining room, its dark, hardwood table and China cabinet abundantly arrayed with silver. A beige carpeted stairway led to the second floor, and he started up, guessing he would find her in an upstairs bedroom. Halfway up, he called, "Debra?"

He finally heard a movement—a low creak of springs—and what sounded like a little sigh. Finally, her voice drifted down the upstairs hall: "Is that you, Russ?"

"Yes. Are you all right?"

At the top of the stairs, through an open door, he saw her framed against the dimly glowing sheer drapes of the window, sitting desultorily on her bed. "I'm all right."

"Sorry for barging in, but...I had to talk to you."

She looked up as he stepped inside, and her eyes were red. "What's the matter?"

"As your father left, Levi Barrow came down the road, apparently following him. Debra, I know that he's stalking you. Tell me what you know about that man."

She turned her eyes to the ceiling, obviously distraught. "God. Dad came here afraid for *me*."

"Because of Levi?"

She nodded. "He even said I should come back and stay with him and Mom, but I didn't want to go. What was I thinking? I should have considered the possibility that *they* could be in danger." She reached for the phone on the nightstand at the head of the bed, put it to her ear, and then held it out to Russ. "The phone is dead. I should have just listened to Dad." She disgustedly dropped the receiver back into its cradle.

He sat down beside her; she did not move away from him.

"Debra, I want you to tell me what's going on. You obviously know more than you have let on. You told me you didn't think Levi Barrow was dangerous. But that has apparently changed."

Her face turned grim. "I know one thing. If he threatens my parents in any way, Levi is the one who'd better watch out. Dad doesn't take kindly to bullshit, even from the Barrows."

"I understand your dad and Levi's were in the army together. What about that?"

Debra shook her head. "I don't really know much. Only that Samuel Barrow was killed in Vietnam and Dad helped the family out afterward—financially, I guess. He's never said as much, but I've always thought he must have felt responsible in some way. When I was a child, he went back to Vietnam a few times, even after he retired from the military. Ever since, the Barrows have always treated him with some deference, more so than most. But things have changed in the last year or so, at least with Levi. He's intentionally antagonized my father. And as you saw, he's been trying to...get close to me." She stiffened noticeably.

"So, it *is* more than him getting bent out of shape over some perceived 'mistreatment' of his kid."

She nodded. "What galls me is that Levi apparently put Malachi up to provoking me, just so he would have an excuse to 'meet' with me. Dad managed to get that much out of Malachi during the last episode at school—right before Rodney's death. Before you came. I guess Dad has been keeping tabs on the Barrows for all these years. I think he's been worried that something like this might happen."

"Your dad's a shrewd man. I wonder what really happened between him and Samuel Barrow. Did they know each other before the war?"

"Not that I'm aware of."

"Your mom and dad aren't originally from here, are they?"

She shook her head. "Huntington."

"So, your dad came here, to the Barrows' hometown, *after* Samuel was killed. Interesting."

"All this happened before I was born. Until recently, none of this meant anything to me at all."

"There's some connection between this and what's happening around here. I'm sure of it." Copeland bit his lip. "Do you think you could get your dad to open up on the subject?"

She shrugged. "He's more than close-mouthed about his past. If he hadn't been so worried about me, he wouldn't have even told me as much as he did about Levi."

"Communication in your family seems to be on a need-to-know basis. Pardon my bluntness."

"No, you're quite right. Don't misunderstand, I love my family. My dad can just be a very headstrong man."

"Then you come by it honestly," he said with a little smile. "Maybe I should talk to him."

"You wouldn't get anywhere. But maybe under these circumstances he'll be more willing to share things with me." She glanced at her watch and saw that it was going on six o'clock. "I'm tempted to head over to Mom and Dad's right now to make sure everything's all right. This has me all tied up in knots."

Copeland thought for a moment. "Debra, I may be completely off-base here. But I half suspect that Levi may be trying to goad you into doing just that. I'm sure he knows your dad can take care of himself. It wouldn't surprise me if he hopes to get you out there alone."

"I think you might be stretching a bit."

"I don't. For what it's worth, Lynette wanted to talk to your father—to alert him to what Levi Barrow has been doing. Look. The phone's not working. It's getting dark. My opinion is that we should all stay together tonight. If anything happens…I think we're all safer together."

"I'm just next door. It's not as if we're miles apart."

"Listen to me. Lynette's got an idea—and I think it's a good one—that we get together with people in town and share information. Watch out for each other. Face it; however hard it is to believe, we're being cut off from the rest of the world. I don't know how or why, but it's happening. Hell, for my money, your father is the first person we should go to. If nothing else, he knows the story behind the Barrows. If he needs any convincing, you're the one to do it. It only makes sense."

She thought for a moment, eyes still dubious. "It does make sense. But pressing my father on something that is obviously very personal to him would be a mistake."

"You know, teacher, now you're stretching. I think you've become used to having things your way, and now you're being contrary just for the sake of it."

"I am not."

"You are too."

"I am not."

He took a chance, reached for her hand, and held it gently. "Debra, at the very least, come back to Lynette's, and let's all stay together until we can figure out what's going on and what we can do about it. I don't believe it's safe for us to be separated. Especially for you."

"That worried, huh?"

He nodded. "The situation is bad enough as it is, and with Levi Barrow thrown into the equation…yes, I am that worried."

She gazed into his eyes, gauging his earnestness. She looked tired and shaken, and he thought she had might have been crying after her father's visit. But the cool gleam in her eyes indicated that her inner strength had hardly begun to be tested. Finally, she nodded and said, "All right. We stay together. After all…it makes the most sense."

He lifted her hand to his lips and kissed her fingers. "I guess you know that over the past couple of days I've rather come to like you. I don't want anything to happen to you."

She placed her other hand over Copeland's. Her smile was weak but sincere. "Thank you, Russ. I guess you're okay too. Mostly. Sort of."

"We'd better get back. All right?"

"If we're having a sleepover party, I need to grab a few things. Give me a minute."

They rose, and he went downstairs to wait for her. A pleasant warmth coursed through his body, but an aching, icy lump lingered in his stomach. A growing suspicion that new dangers lurked in the coming night eclipsed any satisfaction from his bonding with Debra. After Billy Hart had reported the mist-shrouded chasm appearing where a highway should have been, he had more than half-expected the sheriff to call on him. Maybe enough people had experienced the bizarre phenomena today to force him to investigate—and hopefully find a way to contact someone who could shed some light on the situation.

"I'm ready," Debra called. He turned to see her coming down the stairs carrying a small black overnight bag. "I hope Lynette has popcorn."

The mention of food reminded Copeland that he hadn't eaten anything since early morning. "Before we do anything or go anywhere," he said, "a few rations would do us good." She agreed with a nod, and as they headed back to Lynette's, she walked close at his side, seemingly relieved, in spite of all she had said, that she would not be spending the night alone. After stepping in through the front door, he took her bag and placed it on the floor next to Lynette's umbrella stand. "I'll take that upstairs for you in a little bit."

"If your heart is set on lifting my burdens for me, I've got some furniture at my house that needs to be carried upstairs."

"Later, perhaps," Copeland said with a laugh. He called for Lynette but received no answer. They went through the kitchen to the porch and found it empty. Then he noticed a faint, unfamiliar smell—something very unpleasant, reminding him of the formic acid smell that ants gave off.

"Russ! Russ, look!"

He turned to see Debra pointing to the little alcove off the kitchen where the back door opened to the backyard terrace.

The door hung shattered on its frame, apparently broken in from outside. Something had completely shredded its lower half, and as he leaned down to take a closer look, he saw distinct, black scorch marks on the wood. He immediately recalled the manner of Rodney's death and the glowing thing that had pursued Zack Baird down the mountain road the previous day.

"Jesus God," he whispered. He turned and ran up the stairs, calling Lynette's name. He found all the rooms empty, and up here, he could not smell the weird, acidic odor. Rushing back downstairs, he again called, "Lynette!"

Debra's eyes blazed with dread as she came out of the living room. "She's not on this floor. She's not here."

"Oh God, oh God," he moaned. "How long was I gone? Ten minutes?"

Debra went out the front door and rushed around to the back yard, shrilly calling for Lynette. Copeland was behind her in an instant, his eyes scanning the trees, the steep hillside at the south end of the house, the long meadow that led to Yew Line Ridge. Shaking violently, he went to the ruined door to examine it from the outside. On the bricked terrace, he found a glistening splatter of red.

"There," Debra said grimly, pointing to the grass at the edge of the terrace. "More blood. All the way into the trees."

Trying to deny the certainty of what the blood trail meant, he followed it until it vanished amid the oaks, sycamores, and pines that looked down on the house from the almost vertical hillside. Beneath the dense boughs, the shadows loomed thick and heavy, unbroken by even a stray beam of dying sunlight. He saw and heard nothing in that deep darkness; not a cricket chirping, not a mourning dove singing, not a squirrel rustling in the leaves.

Then, far in the distance, something went *click-click-clack, click-click-clack*. Then it, too, fell silent and did not come again.

The fiery rim of the sun finally sank behind the ridge in the west. As night spread over the land like a frigid, nightmarish cloak, Copeland dropped to his knees and wailed his anguish to the forest, while Debra wrapped her arms around herself and wept a river of tears, as if they could somehow wash away the awful trail of blood at her feet.

#

Chapter 11

"I don't know what it was, and I'm sure it doesn't mean anything."

Elise Martin huffed a sigh of frustration. "I tell you, Glen, people could hear it all over town. Most bizarre thing in the world, it was."

"Well, *I* didn't hear anything."

She had never seen her husband so frazzled; not that she could really blame him with all that was going on in town the last few days. Ever since Rodney Lawson's funeral, Glen had come and gone constantly, and he had not slept in at least seventy-two hours. His normally impassive face had gone taut with worry, and his eyes constantly batted back and forth as if searching for something hiding in the shadows. Today, he had spent the after-school hours visiting with Debra—but he claimed to have heard none of the weird music, which had echoed through the entire town late in the afternoon. *Everyone* had heard the sounds, and some said it came from the old church on Cheat Mountain Road, which was close to their daughter's house. How could he *not* have heard such a racket?

Glen never lied to her, but now she suspected…something.

Why? What possible reason could he have for not being honest with her?

Most tragically, not long after the sounds had ceased, Ike Gleasman had come home from work to find his nonplused cat sitting in the front yard watching his house—just across the road from the church—burn to the ground. No one could find a trace of Mrs. Gleasman, and according to Billie Wilkins, the firemen feared she had been inside when the house went up. Because the phones weren't working, the firefighters hadn't even gotten there until the blaze had grown far beyond their control.

"Debra's all right?" she asked.

"She's fine. I asked her to come stay with us, but you know her; she didn't want to do the sensible thing. Stubborn girl."

"Wonder where she gets that from?"

"Your side of the family. Your mother."

Elise snorted. "Okay."

She had prepared only a small dinner, leftover roast beef, corn, and fried okra, but Glen didn't want to eat. Without paying her any mind, he went upstairs and began making noise, moving things around, and Lord knew what. When he came back down, he had his car keys in hand again.

"Where to this time?"

"I'm going by a few students' houses. Too many of them were out today. With no phones, I want to check up on them."

"I didn't know that was in your job description."

He sighed. "Honey, in case you haven't noticed, there's trouble going on in this town. I'm just looking to help as best I can, all right?"

"Seems to me there's more to it than that."

He gave her a long, wistful look, and she knew she had hit on something. However, nothing she could say now would drag any answers out of him. If he intended to reveal anything, he would do it on his terms, in his own good time.

"I'll be back soon. Try not to worry."

"If I worry, it's your fault."

He gave her a brief hug and kissed her on the forehead. "We'll talk later. I promise. Right now, I have to do what I have to do. All right?"

She shook her head in frustration. "You've always been tightlipped, but never mysterious. You're going to drive me out of my head like this."

"Not for very much longer." Then he turned and went out the back door. She heard the car start, and off he went again.

"Why doesn't he just retire?" she asked the wall and sat down to eat her dinner by herself. He *could* have retired already, but he seemed intent on working until he was physically unable. She admired his energy, his strength of will, and his sharpness of mind, but she was getting tired of having to share him with his job after all these years. It was high time they spent their days together as they wished, without obligations that by right should have passed to the younger generation.

Outside, a loud, rattling engine briefly caught her attention. Lately, she had been hearing it frequently, and she wondered who would drive such a detestable noisemaker through their quiet neighborhood. No one had moved in, no one was having contract work done, and no one had friends or family who drove clunkers coming and going at all hours. Glen had successfully lobbied to make it against the law for these young people to go cruising with their music so loud it shook the walls, and as far as she was concerned, the same ordinance ought to apply to trucks that needed a new muffler, if not a whole new engine.

She had just finished her sparse dinner and carried her plate to the sink when something outside prompted her to stop in her tracks: a low rustling; nothing more than the sound a small animal might make moving through the bushes beneath the kitchen window. But for some reason—no doubt because of the strange goings-on of the last couple of days—the noise set her nerves on edge, and her heart began to beat faster than usual. She brushed the curtains aside and peered out the window into the dark back yard, but without the floodlights on, she could not see a thing. In the brightly lit window, however, she would be clearly visible to any spying eyes, human or otherwise, so she closed the curtains, uncertain whether to go through the house and lock all the doors and windows or to berate herself for being silly.

Click-click-clack…click-click-clack.

It sounded like the rapping of drumsticks on sheet metal, not loud, but very nearby.

She went straight for the kitchen door, twisted the deadbolt, and then rushed to the living room to lock the front door. Her hand was just reaching for the knob when a sharp rapping on the door nearly stopped her heart, prompting her to draw up short with a hand at her chest. She stood there, immobile, for almost half a minute until another loud knock came. She finally found her voice, raspy though it was.

"Who is it?"

No response.

"I said who is it?"

A low, gruff voice finally replied, "Friend of your husband, ma'am."

"What's your name?"

"I just need to talk to you a minute. It's about Glen."

A lump rose in her throat, again stealing her voice. At last, she managed to croak, "Has something happened to him?"

"We better talk face to face."

She pushed herself forward, grasped the doorknob, and gave it a tentative twist, only half-certain she wanted to open it. Before she could make up her mind, the door burst open and the knob smashed into her fingers, sending a blinding jolt of pain up her arm. Stumbling, she threw out her other hand and grasped the stair rail to keep from falling.

An ugly, familiar figure stood in the doorway, small eyes glaring at her from beneath a bony brow, long greasy hair hanging in disarray over his forehead.

"You," she spat. "What do you want? You know you're not welcome here."

"Don't think that matters much, Miz Martin."

In the kitchen, glass shattered, and she heard a heavy thump, as if something large had burst through the window and dropped to the floor. Her eyes widened with dread as Levi Barrow took a step toward her.

"What was that?"

"You're gonna see in a just a minute."

"What do you want, Levi? Glen's not here, and you and I certainly don't have any business."

"Dunno if I'd say that," Barrow said with a dangerous-looking smirk. "The major'll be back soon, I reckon, and then we'll see what business we have."

Click-click-clack...

The sound she had heard from outside, in the house now, in the kitchen, coming this way. What in God's name?

CLICK-CLICK-CLACK...CLICK-CLICK-CLACK...

Barrow's mouth widened to reveal stained, crooked teeth. "Have a look around there, why don't you, Miz Martin."

She could *feel* the other presence in the room. Something was moving behind her; a soft, sliding, scraping sound, slowly drawing nearer. And the smell...acrid, sour. *God!* Unable to stop herself, she turned around and saw the hot golden glow on the hardwood floor, something moving toward her, the size of a good-sized child, but nothing like a child.

Before the scream could burst from her lungs, her consciousness began to flee, and she hit the floor like a sawn branch. She barely felt it when her skull smacked against the stairway rail. The last thing she heard was Levi Barrow's jubilant giggling; then a warm, welcome silence rushed in to replace the loathsome noise, and the world went blessedly dark.

#

Chapter 12

"Mom? Dad?"

Debra's voice echoed eerily through the dead stillness of the Martin house. The moment Copeland had seen the door hanging partway open, he could only fear the worst.

"Major Martin?" he called. "Anyone here?"

"Dad's car is gone. Maybe they're just out somewhere," she said, unable to keep the tremor out of her voice.

Copeland glanced into the living room, the dining room, and then started back toward the kitchen. Debra rushed upstairs. The hideous sense of déjà-vu nearly made him swoon.

The moment he stepped through the door, he stopped in his tracks, and his gorge rose.

"Jesus," he whispered. He heard Debra's footsteps on the stairs, and though knowing it was futile, he forced himself to say, "Debra, don't come in here. Please.".

Her sharp intake of breath broke his heart.

"No," she whispered. "Not them. Please not them."

Glass from the shattered window glittered like jewels on the kitchen floor, on the countertops, on the table. Whatever had come inside had done so with terrific force.

The sharp, acid smell was the same as at Lynette's house.

"There's no blood," she whispered. "They weren't here. They just weren't here."

He wished he could share her hope, but his heart told him otherwise. He saw one dirty dinner dish in the sink and several food containers still on the countertop. If one or both of her parents had escaped, it would be a miracle, he thought. *Better to let her keep hoping.*

But he saw that, as Debra scanned the room, her own hope fled. Her lower lip began to quiver, and before he knew it, she had fallen into his arms, weeping bitterly, her back arching with every wracking sob. He crushed her body to his and felt his own tears beginning to well as his grief for Lynette boiled to the surface again.

He was barely aware of finally taking her hand and all but dragging her to the car. His breath came out in ragged gasps as the Lexus sprang to life, reversed out of the driveway, and screamed into the night, the streetlamps and the lights from the houses blending into a swirling, brilliant blur outside the windows.

When time seemed to return to normal, the headlights were cutting a ghostly path through the darkness, and gnarled, gray trees on either side of the narrow road were bending down to peer curiously, menacingly, into the windows as they sped past.

"What are we going to do, Russ? What are we going to do?"

His hands throttled the steering wheel as his foot pinned the accelerator to the floor. "I'm thinking murder, perhaps."

Debra dug her nails into his right thigh. In a flat, artificially calm voice, she said, "Russ, you don't know that Levi Barrow—or any of them—is responsible. Not for certain."

"Certain enough. Everything goes back to them, doesn't it? Rodney and Zack Baird—up by Barrows. What you saw on their land yesterday. Levi stalking you, and going after your father—just a little while ago."

"It's all circumstantial, at best. What happened tonight wasn't on their land. And that thing you saw on the highway—that wasn't on their land either."

"What—are you defending them? There's nothing circumstantial about Levi being after you. Your father told you as much. You've seen him for yourself."

"Do you have a gun?"

Copeland shook his head. "Not on me. I came here for a funeral."

"A knife? A slingshot?"

He took a deep breath, trying to suppress his rising ire, but the attempt failed. So, for a full minute, he refused to speak for fear of losing his last vestige of restraint. He knew she was in shock, trying to cling to reason, but her parents' unknown fate had sent her emotions over a cliff. That much he understood. Finally, he said, "You want to just hand this over to the sheriff?"

She swallowed hard and shook her head. "No. He's too close to…those people."

"That's what I thought."

She said nothing for a while but watched the trees flash past the windows. "Your mind's made up, isn't it?"

"You know it would be best for me to do this alone."

"Like hell. If you think I'd go home, or anywhere else alone, you're out of your mind."

"Then don't try to stop me."

"I'm just trying to think rationally. Not that it's really working." Her breath caught in her throat.

"I know, I know. But we're running out of alternatives."

"What Lynette had in mind—to get people together. At the church, or maybe the school. Hell, get the mayor involved. He's a friend of Dad's."

"All that will take time. And I don't think we have time. I don't think we have time at all."

They had reached the crest of Yew Line Ridge, and now as they started down the long, curving incline that led through a long, tunnel-like passage of black pines, the reality of where he was going and what he was doing began to temper the heat of his emotions. Beneath the thick boughs, the darkness gathered like an enclave of malevolent ghosts, swallowing his headlights, and Copeland felt as if he were driving into one of his most terrifying juvenile nightmares.

Ahead, he could see a break in the trees, beyond which the Barrow property lay in wait. Not a fleck of light marred the solid black landscape, and anyone watching from the house would soon see his headlights. He slowed down, pulled to the left side of the road, into a half-obscured opening in the trees, and shut off the lights. His hand hovered on the key as a little voice in his ear begged him to reconsider and turn back.

Turn back to what?

He switched off the engine and watched the darkness beyond the windshield for a few seconds to allow his eyes to adjust. When he finally turned to Debra, he saw only the vaguest impression of her face, her features unreadable. But her hand came to rest in his, and he squeezed it with what he hoped was more than empty reassurance. Then he reached into the glove compartment, withdrew his flashlight, and opened the car door. The inside lights blazed like captured daylight; he quickly slid out of his seat, pulled himself to his feet, and closed the door, immediately restoring the darkness, which he hoped would favor him should any searching eyes turn his way. The night air licked at him like a cool, questing tongue, and the profound, unnatural absence of sound set the hair at the back of his scalp to prickling. A few seconds later, with a sharp *click*, the passenger door opened, and again, briefly, light burst in the abyss like a fireball. Then Debra was at his side, the night again as black as the depths of outer space, their breathing and their own heartbeats the only intruders in the endless well of silence.

His one concession to his fear was to open the trunk, dig into the spare tire well, and grab the tire iron, which he slipped into his belt. Hardly the weapon of choice when marching into the enemy's keep, but it beat going empty-handed.

He pushed his way through the low-hanging boughs and stepped onto asphalt, now feeling exposed and vulnerable beneath the glaring onyx sky. No stars, no moon, no clouds—no reflected light. Debra fell in close at his side, and they started walking slowly along the side of the road, his eyes on the coal-black pavement ahead, hers darting back and forth among the trees, their senses almost preternaturally alert for any sign that they were not alone. As they advanced, the trees soon ended, and now they could see a broad, black expanse, which Copeland took to be the grassy meadow that girded the Barrow property. Beyond this dark gulf, an angular silhouette gradually took form, a shade paler than its surroundings; as they drew nearer, he could see that Levi Barrow's truck was gone, and not a glimmer of light shone from any of the windows.

"Russ," Debra whispered pleadingly, "we do not want to go down there."

He nodded, but they walked on, and as they approached the pitted gravel driveway, he led them into the tall grass, picking his steps carefully to avoid any hidden obstacles. Now on Barrow land, he felt cold, nauseating worms squirming in his stomach, and his legs turned more rubbery with every step nearer to the house. He half-expected some lurking guardian to accost them at any second—and he had no doubt that if they were caught, they would be promptly murdered. Yet even that dreadful prospect could not deter him from creeping close to the house, finding the nearest window, and pausing beside it to listen for any hint of movement inside. A faint, repulsive odor wafted from the old wooden structure, a noisome mélange of mothballs, mold, and raw sewage. Moving toward the back of the house, he found all manner of trash and unidentifiable debris in the grass, and his foot dislodged something that clattered noisily as it rolled away. Debra hissed in fright, and he halted until he was certain no one was coming to investigate.

A rickety staircase led to the half-rotted back door, and as he mounted it, his mind zoomed out of his body to view the scene from some distance above. His hand reached out and closed on the rusty doorknob, which rattled hideously, but the door did not budge. *Locked, of course.* Again, he froze, waiting for telltale footfalls inside the structure; none came, and he began to breathe a little easier. Unwilling to be thwarted, he sharply thrust an elbow against one of the dingy glass panes, which popped whole from its frame and splashed into fragments somewhere on the other side. He heard Debra whimper, but he reached in through the new portal, found the handle, and wrestled with the lock. The door sang like a grieving whale as it opened, and as Copeland stepped into the dark entryway, he thought, *you pathetic, arrogant bastards, you would never expect anyone to actually break into your little castle, would you?*

The fact that anyone could actually inhabit such a fetid rat hole only inflamed his contempt for them. He took a few halting steps into the void and then decided to chance his flashlight. He flicked it on for a second—just long enough to get his bearings. He stood in the family's kitchen: a tiny, cluttered room with a wooden table and chairs to his right, the refrigerator, sink, and cabinets to his left. In that moment of illumination, he had glimpsed a number of filthy dishes piled in the sink and on the countertop next to it, and he quickly realized that the sewer-like taint of the air originated in here. Pocketing his flashlight, he reached back and took Debra's hand as she tiptoed in and pressed close to him; then he started walking again, toward the open door he had seen a short distance ahead.

The planks beneath the ratty carpet groaned wearily with each step they took. No one could possibly be home, or they would have come to check out the sound of the break-in—and who would willfully immerse themselves in such complete darkness as this? Once Copeland passed through the doorway into the next room, he reached for his flashlight again, and this time he let it rove freely along the walls and over the furniture. He wanted to know: just who *was* this degenerate, mysterious family whom he suspected of harboring bizarre and almost certainly deadly secrets?

His light revealed a dingy couch with several springs popping through the cushions; a couple of end tables covered with papers, ash trays, and empty bottles of various spirits; a curio cabinet filled with framed photographs, documents, and assorted, unidentifiable objects; a couple of cobweb-laced lamps; and a precariously leaning dining table covered with cast-off clothing, several stacks of unopened mail, and even a few books. A trio of stuffed deer heads and an array of cheap-looking landscape paintings adorned the walls. It was the curio cabinet that most intrigued Copeland, so he made his way toward it and shone the light in through the grimy glass. When Debra came up beside him and peered into the cabinet, she gasped audibly.

Several of the framed photographs pictured a homely young man in an army uniform—some solitary, others with a group. The one that had caught Debra's attention showed a number of men in combat fatigues standing around a tall, hawk-nosed figure with raven hair and narrow, wary-looking eyes.

"My God, it's Dad," she whispered. "This must be Samuel Barrow."

"What is that?" Copeland said, pointing to a tall, ceramic object that almost resembled a crudely molded candle. Then it struck him.

"Oh, no," Debra whispered, before he could utter a word. Do you realize what that is?"

"The tower we've seen. It's that damned tower!"

He focused his light on the object, and his heart began to race again. The miniature pillar stood about eighteen inches tall, its dark surface rough and faceted, like carved graphite. At its apex, several small, narrow stems sprouted toward the heavens almost like the arms of an octopus. It rested on a base shaped like a cluster of boulders, which, at actual size, would have to be gigantic. Copeland noticed a bunch of tiny, etched lines in the ceramic base, which he soon identified as the initials "AHB."

"Amos Hosea Barrow," Debra said. "Levi and Joshua's grand-father. He must have made this."

"Well, well. A nice bit of hard evidence."

Debra nodded and closed her eyes, as if by shutting out the sight of the thing she could deny its existence. But she pressed close to Copeland again as he started up the steep, creaking staircase to the second floor, and here, the narrow, mildewed walls and a thick, almost stomach-turning cloud of masculine body odor made him feel claustrophobic and slightly nauseous. The first door on the left hung open, and after shining his light inside to ascertain it was empty, he reluctantly stepped inside.

They stood in a small room occupied by an unmade single

bed, a wooden desk covered with papers, and—of all things—many shelves of books. On closer inspection, Copeland saw that the volumes consisted of everything from high school textbooks to literature of all varieties. Several of the spines bore no titles or author names; when he pulled one from a shelf and opened it, he found it to be a handwritten journal, its pages yellowed and crumbling. On the frontispiece, he discovered the name of the author: Samuel H. Barrow.

"Not quite the illiterate bunch I would have expected," he said softly, contemplating carrying it with him so he could study it more thoroughly.

"I'm not sure about that," Debra said, pointing to the desk—atop which lay a number of yellow stained magazines of questionable literary merit. "I wouldn't be surprised if there's more porn tucked between the covers of the classics on the shelves."

"I wonder which of the deviants belongs to this room."

"Levi, I believe," Debra said. She held up a small photo in a cracked glass frame. "Here he is with Malachi's mother. Dottie, I think she went by."

The woman in the picture looked like a typical redneck, Copeland thought, caring little about casting aspersions on the Barrow dead. Short, a bit heavy, and definitely homely, wearing threadbare overalls and a ragged-looking checkered shirt, her thin, dark hair pulled back in an untidy bun. Her smile looked almost genuine, and for a second he found himself wondering if that poor creature had ever known a moment of real happiness in her life. He placed the photograph back on the bedside table, and it was then that he noticed something poking out from beneath the mattress on Levi's bed.

The spine of a book.

He slipped the battered-looking, leather-bound volume from its not-so-clever hiding place and aimed his light at its pages. Another journal, this one belonging to Levi Barrow himself.

"Hard to believe the bastard actually knows how to write." Copeland held the book so Debra could see and began to skim the entries, which Levi apparently recorded only sporadically, in an atrocious, barely legible hand. The first entry went back almost four years and recounted the brutal beating of a county taxman who had audaciously attempted to collect his due. As Copeland turned the pages, he found that fights featured prominently in Levi's daily activities—and in none of the accounts did Levi end up for the worst. In situations where the outcome appeared questionable, Joshua generally joined in to shore up the odds. Copeland judged significant the fact that none of their exploits resulted in a run-in between the Barrows and the law.

Even Malachi occasionally bore the brunt of Levi's wrath.

"Jesus, that poor kid," Debra said. "It's no wonder he's ended up the way he is."

Copeland nodded and skipped to the later pages. Then his heart briefly stopped.

The entry upon which his light shone, some eight months old, read:

'I seen her at the school with Malachi, and she treats him kind, not like them teachers hes had all so many years. Major Martin did himself proud with her, cause shes mighty beutiful, and must have a good heart. To see her makes me sad for my own heart, what slipped away from me so long ago its beyond hope. Malachi likes her, not knowing shes the old majors daughter. I cant think of no better mother for Malachi because the boy needs one, not like that hag piece of shit bich I made gone."

Copeland looked at Debra's face. Even in the warm glow of the flashlight beam, it had turned stark white.

He swallowed hard and advanced farther into the book.

"Watched her again through the windows of her class, seen her call on Malachi, obvusly he done wrong because she looked sad with him, but not angry and no kids laghed like them all used to. I reckon it sounds funy but shes like a angel."

Another one, only a month old, read:

"I dont care what the old major done for this family, yeah, I got respect enough for someone whoed help my daddy, and even grandaddy the way he done, but I know hed try and stop me from taken his daughter like I want. Ill have her if I have to kill him, which maybe grandaddy says yes, because Major Martin is up to something but we dont know what. Grandaddy has that keen sight, and hes making it so that soon anything and everthing we want well have, and hes working on it right now. I know he woud be might pleased for me to bring Debra Harington into this family, it would just be she couldnt never know what happen to her daddy.

"Itll be an ajustmet for all us when grandaddy makes the change happen, so I guest first things come first."

From two weeks past:

"Grandaddy makin me his scout he says, to clear the way ahead and test things out and make sure everthing perfet. Got to say, its some werd shit hes bringing down but he knows what hes doing."

The most recent entry came from the day of Rodney's funeral.

"Today they buryid the techers boy what them ones killed. Some new guy, his kin, come to town, staying close to Debra, so theyll get him too. Saw lots of them today, and they be more tomorow. God what a site them things are."

At the very bottom of the page, in large letters, like the scribble of a smitten adolescent:

"I love Debra! I love Debra! I LOVE DEBRA!"

For an endless time, she stood there, her face blank, beyond disbelief. At last, turning away from him, she whispered, "I think I'm going to be sick."

Copeland closed the book and tucked it inside his shirt, no longer caring whether Levi Barrow discovered it missing. Cryptic though it might be, the journal provided a trove of information.

So just what were "them things" that, according to Levi, now had his number?

A low sound rose from another room—a slow, deep, reverberating groan.

In an instant, his finger had snapped off the flashlight, but the light, if not the sound of the break-in, would have already betrayed their presence to anyone in the house. In the new, pitch black, he felt Debra's hand clench his bicep.

Then, as his eyes began to adjust, he discovered that the

darkness was no longer complete. Beyond the door to the narrow hall, a faint, shimmering glow stained the walls like moonlight reflecting off gently flowing water. A pale, luminous blue, it slowly brightened until Copeland could make out the features of Levi Barrow's bedroom—and Debra's taut, terrified face. No further sound reached his ears, so on quivering legs, he crept into the tight passage, Debra's hand clasped tightly in his, and together they made their way toward the source of the radiance: a half-open door at the end of the hall. As they approached, a low, rhythmic rumbling sound crawled out to greet them.

Snoring.

Jesus! At least one of the bastards *was* here—and sleeping the sleep of the dead, if he hadn't heard the glass shattering or seen the flashlight beam roving in the darkness. Copeland's first instinct was to escape with his prize, but an irresistible curiosity compelled him to take that final step and lean into the room, to learn the identity of the sleeper and the origin of the strange light.

He found himself facing a large chamber furnished with age-old relics, all painted a garish, shimmering blue. Bizarre ceramic figures adorned almost every surface, no doubt fashioned by the same hand that had sculpted the tower in cabinet downstairs. A huge lump of a figure occupied a once-plush easy chair at the far end of the bedroom, obviously asleep, his massive, rubbery paws encircling an oblong, sapphire-like crystal the size of a chicken egg that throbbed with electric brilliance. The man's oversized, almost football-shaped head was tilted back, his gaping chasm of a mouth open and issuing an occasional grating roar with the timbre of an injured bear. One of the noisy emissions stirred a movement in a far corner of the room, and Copeland's legs nearly collapsed, for he had not seen the other figure until it shifted. A younger, much thinner man, tucked into a ball on the floor, unfurled like a spider awakening to its prey, grumbling irritably, stretching his gnarled-looking arms with the sound of green wood breaking. Copeland slowly backed up, praying the man's eyes would not open and turn in his direction. To his relief, the younger Barrow—Joshua, he presumed—soon shifted, tucked his limbs back into their original, compact positions, and appeared to drift off again.

At the sight of the homely creature, an unexpected, hot surge of anger and sorrow for Lynette drove Copeland's hand to the tire iron in his belt, and for a terrifying few seconds, he actually started to creep into the room to bash a pair of skulls; if Debra had not gently taken hold of his arm, as if anticipating his feelings, he might have then and there committed cold-blooded murder. In that moment, the personal consequences of acting on his rage meant nothing. Zero.

But the spell passed, and he found his vision blurry with tears. It was time to get out of this place. He had acquired something important, and they had been here too long.

No sooner had they quietly exited the room and started for the stairs than the familiar, arrhythmic rattle of a truck bruised the silence and rapidly grew louder—followed by a second, somewhat less clamorous engine. His breath catching in this throat, Copeland halted at the top of the stairwell, and Debra's hand became a vise around his wrist. Headlights danced off the walls below, the engines went silent, and moments later, a car door squealed and slammed. He glanced at Debra's terror-brightened eyes. Could they make it to the bottom, back to the kitchen, and out the rear door without the new arrivals seeing them? He heard footsteps on the gravel outside—rapid, agitated, and purposeful. *No way.* All they could do now was find a place to hide.

It was definitely Levi coming home; they couldn't go back into his room. Treading as gingerly as he could, the pounding of his heart drowning the groan of the floorboards, he led Debra to another door halfway down the hall, desperately hoping it might offer some kind of sanctuary. He tugged it open and found himself at the bottom of another, even narrower stairwell, which led up to a space blacker than the starless sky above the house, presumably the attic. He all but dragged Debra inside with him, pulled the protesting door closed behind him, and pressed himself against the wall, trying to slow his panicked breathing. His flashlight slipped to the floor with a heavy *thunk,* and the sound stole his breath. He did not move to retrieve it. His lungs had just begun to cooperate again when the downstairs door whined open to admit the newcomers and then banged shut.

For a moment, nothing. Then footsteps on the stairs, tromping heavily upward…more than one pair of lungs heaving in the hallway…and then the footsteps slowing as they reached the stairwell door. Copeland found his arms around Debra, hers around him, their bodies pressed hard together, their lungs paralyzed, one of his hands slithering toward the tire iron hanging from his belt. He resolved that, if they were discovered, he would go out swinging and sure as hell smash the life out of at least one of the enemy.

Then the footsteps began again, this time slower, more furtive. A whispering voice said, "Malachi, get to your room, boy." A pause, and then a lighter tread on the floorboards, moving away in the hall. Then, the heavier footsteps began, obviously heading toward Amos Barrow's chamber of blue light. Several thumps and a scuffling sound followed.

Then the footsteps thumped back into the hall, and Levi Barrow's unmistakable, gruff baritone rolled beneath the door like a muted ocean wave. "What the fuck are you doin' sleepin'? You goddamn moron, you *never* let Granddaddy drift off without watchin' over him. I should break your fuckin' face."

A whimper, then a wet, gurgling noise. Finally, a second voice, pleading: "Levi, stop it, stop it. I *been* watchin' him! I been watchin' him hours and hours. I jest couldn't hold 'em open no more. You try watchin' over him all day and night and not eatin' or sleepin'. So fuck *you*."

Then a third, authoritative but weary-sounding voice spoke. "Levi. Let's get this over with."

Debra sucked in a breath, so sharply that Copeland was sure they would hear her. Her arms crushed his ribs, but then, for a second, he thought she was going to pull away from him. He left his weapon in his belt and wrapped both arms around her again, holding her in an iron embrace, pressing his forehead against hers, willing her to understand the need for absolute silence.

Yet he could barely keep himself from kicking open the door

and confronting those on the other side, even if it meant his death. The third voice had belonged to Debra's father, Glen Martin.

#

Chapter 13

The footsteps resumed, moving in the direction of Amos Barrow's bedroom. A door closed, and muffled voices immediately began haranguing back and forth, now unintelligible. This was their chance to escape, Copeland thought, trying to squelch his new, rising suspicion of Debra's father. But no; even now, behind closed doors, something momentous was happening, and they needed to learn as much as they could—for Debra's sake, if not his. He started to open the door a crack, but then he heard a soft *thump*, just on the other side of the stairwell wall.

Malachi. His room lay between the stairwell and Amos's room.

He didn't dare step out there now. So, he put his ear to the inch-wide gap and listened intently for any discernible bits of conversation. Beyond a few disjointed syllables, he could make out nothing—except what he thought was Debra's name, spoken by her father. She squeezed his arm, trying to position herself where she could listen, but it was no use; neither of them could pick up anything meaningful from the muted exchange. Martin and the Barrow brothers had evidently closed themselves in a room adjacent to Amos's, presumably to keep the volume down.

Then another sound, low and subtle, came from above his head: something moving, sliding slowly along the attic floor. Again, Debra's arms tightened around his body in warning, her body trembling violently. He could see nothing in the pure darkness at the top of the stairs.

Click-click-clack.

A sharp, almost insect-like sound. The same sound he had heard in the woods, just after Lynette had disappeared.

Then a dim, orange glow became visible in the black space above, gradually brightening as the sound of movement drew closer. The light flickered erratically, like roiling flames—or the glowing thing they had seen in the tall grass rushing after Zack Baird the previous day. The clicking sounds came again, and Copeland finally saw a hint of something moving at the top of the stairs.

The thing slid slowly into view around the corner of the stairwell and, without hesitating, began to crawl toward them, its body thudding heavily onto the wooden runners. The stairwell walls brightened with a warm, pulsating light, and the revolting odor of formic acid that Copeland had smelled at Lynette's house now wafted to his nostrils.

Debra gasped loudly, choking back a scream.

It looked like a great worm, its thick, cylindrical body over a yard long, translucent and glowing eerily from within, like an oilskin bag stuffed to bursting with smoldering embers. The thing descended the stairs with a grotesque undulating motion, which stirred several clusters of long, blood-colored barbs that sprouted wickedly from its back—producing the fearsome, insect-like chattering sounds.

But its head! The head resembled nothing so much as a human skull, pitted and bony, its deep eye sockets seemingly hollow and sightless. Now, only a few steps away, the thing paused and reared up, its head swaying cobra-like before them, and Copeland could see, far back in its dark eye cavities, small, crystalline orbs of pale blue.

The very color of the jewel Amos Barrow clasped protectively in his hands.

Blood thundered in Copeland's ears, and all the air in his lungs evaporated. Unable to stop himself, he staggered backward, bumped into the door, and pushed it open. He and Debra spilled out into the hall, their horrified eyes locked on the unnatural monstrosity. It slid down another step, freezing them with its hypnotic gaze; then its knobbed mandible dropped open, spread incredibly wide, and issued a weird, warbling shriek, almost like the cry of a whippoorwill.

Debra's hands had clamped painfully around his bicep. "Oh, Jesus! What the hell is that?"

"That's a Lumera."

Their heads swiveled as young Malachi Barrow appeared in his open doorway, black, impassive eyes regarding them from beneath thick, bony brows.

"Great-Granddaddy calls 'em Lumeras. They come from up yonder." He pointed skyward.

Copeland's hand went for the tire iron and drew it from his belt. The skull-headed thing thudded to the floor at the bottom of the stairs and wriggled slowly toward them.

The door beside Amos's whipped open, and Levi Barrow emerged, a dangerous scowl etched on his craggy face. Joshua followed immediately, and the brothers each took a menacing step forward.

"Wouldn't have expected to find you here, Miz Harrington," Levi said, raising an eyebrow. Then he lifted a beckoning hand to her. "You better just step over here by me, so's that thing don't do to you what it's gonna to do to your friend."

Debra shook her head and took a halting step backward, toward the stairs to the main floor. "Dad!" she called in a tremulous voice. "Dad, where are you?"

Levi gazed at her in disappointment. "Your dad ain't in no position to help you."

Copeland raised the tire iron and whispered to her, "Get down the stairs. Move it."

"But Dad…"

"He's still alive. That has to be enough for now."

The creature, only a yard from Copeland's foot, issued another long, piercing trill. With a last look of longing toward the far end of the hall, Debra spun and bolted like a panicked doe down the stairs. Copeland then wound up and flung his weapon—not at the creature but at Levi Barrow. It whirled through the air straight at his head, but the ugly figure deftly sidestepped; the projectile slammed into the wall behind him and clattered to the floor. But by then, Copeland was hard on Debra's heels, and two seconds later, they had burst through the front door into the chilly night.

Where, in spite of their pursuers, they both stopped and stared, eyes bulging incredulously, hearts leaping to their throats.

The sky, the landscape…the world. All had gone insane.

Overhead, hundreds of swirling and zooming globes of light had set fire to the pitch-black night. The Barrow house, which had nestled in a broad, grassy meadow, now stood amid a forest of very tall, hideously gnarled, ash-colored trees, their crooked limbs arcing over its roof like groping fingers. When Copeland looked toward the ridge off to the north, an icy thrill of terror coursed down his spine, for beyond the inexplicable trees, the alien, but now-familiar tower soared to the heavens like a mile-high arm, its fist puncturing the canopy of sky.

The blazing globes appeared to be emerging from the protrusions at its apex, spewing into space like bees from a hive.

A heavy, rapid thumping from inside the house jolted him back to his senses, so he grabbed Debra's hand and started running at full speed, headed for the road, tugging her behind him as if she weighed no more than a doll.

He wasn't pulling her for long. Before he knew it, she was right beside him, and then in front of him, her legs pumping like pistons on the tar-black asphalt. The limbs of the new, skeletal trees intertwined above their heads, enclosed them like a tunnel that pressed tighter upon them the farther they ran. When Copeland glanced up, he could see the brilliant, gigantic fireflies soaring to and fro just above the branches, occasionally close enough for him to hear faint *whooshing* sounds as they passed. He no longer had any concept of distance, how far away the car was parked—if it was even still there. Endless heartbeats later, though, a fiery glint of metal—a reflection of the airborne horrors on the hood—revealed the Lexus's location to him.

They fought their way through a barricade of entwined branches, which felt unnaturally warm to Copeland's touch. He opened Debra's door first, heaved bodily her inside, and then scrambled over the hood and in through his door, which she had already shoved opened for him.

"Oh, God, oh, God," she whispered, rocking back and forth in her seat. "This can't be real! It can't!"

He shook his head, his mouth too dry to speak. His trembling fingers somehow managed to start the engine, and he jammed the car into gear, praying it could break through the encroaching limbs. When he floored the accelerator, the Lexus leaped obediently forward, but rocked to a halt as the web of branches greedily entrapped it. He threw the gear lever into reverse and the car roared backward, ripping loose some of the groping fingers, stopping just short of smashing into a gigantic black bole. Then, rushing forward again, the vehicle tore through the barricade and leaped onto the road, narrowly missing two running figures that suddenly appeared in the headlights. Smashing the pedal to the floor, Copeland sent the car hurtling back in the direction they had come, back toward town.

"What are we going to do, Russ?" Debra asked in an almost-calm voice. "We've got to find help."

"That might be an issue." He cast a look into the rear-view mirror and caught a brief glimpse of their pursuers standing thwarted in the road. However, evading the Barrows offered not an ounce of consolation, for when he glanced up through windshield at the tangled canopy of branches, the sky swarmed with roving fireballs, and the tower still reached longingly toward outer space. Thankfully, none of the airborne objects appeared to be following the speeding vehicle.

"They're doing this," she said. "Somehow, *they* are responsible."

"There's got to be more to learn from Levi's journal," Copeland said and reached into his shirt—only to hiss in anger when he discovered the book missing. "Damn it! It must have slipped out somewhere back there."

"I can't believe Dad was with them." Debra's eyes had begun to brim with tears. "He can't have anything to do with this. I know him, Russ. He would never cooperate with the Barrows. Not in a million years."

"They must have some kind of hold over him. It's the only thing that makes any sense."

"And Mom. God, what have they done to my mom?"

"We'll get to the bottom of it...somehow," he said, hoping his words rang less hollow to her than they did to him.

He saw her eyes turn somewhere far away—or into herself—but then his attention reverted to the road, for just ahead it veered sharply to the right, and when the car screamed into the curve, he had to work the brakes expertly to keep it from pitching into a yawning black gulf where the trees suddenly ended. For an endless age, the Lexus seemed to hang suspended in midair; then it was again racing through a long, claustrophobic tunnel of foliage, menacing and seemingly sentient. Except for the path cut by the headlights, the night had again become empty darkness. When he looked back up at the sky, he now saw only black.

"Are they gone?" Debra asked softly, turning to peer out the rear glass. "I can't see a thing, not a goddamned thing."

But a moment later, Copeland noticed a warm, gold tint creeping over her features. Then a brilliant glare blinded him, and a miniature sun flashed past the windshield, zooming out in front of the car and veering to the right. The fireball entered the trees at stunning speed, a brightly burning ghost unhindered by the thick, crowded trunks. Eerie gold light bathed the depths of the aberrant forest, and for a few moments, Copeland dared hope the thing would just keep going. Then the light again intensified again, and the fireball came rushing back to keep pace with the car, passing through the trees as if they were shadows.

Debra's eyes locked on the fireball, only a few feet beyond her window. "I can't make out any features," she said slowly, obviously straining to hold her terror in check. "It looks like a solid shape of some sort inside the globe. Jesus, it's something alive, all right."

The road ahead appeared straight, so Copeland stood on the accelerator, winding out the engine, but the fiery ghost continued to pace them. At a loss for anything else to try, he hit the brake, which sent the car into a screaming skid, and thew out one arm to keep Debra from pitching into the windshield.

The brilliant flare shot past the car, veered straight up, and burst through the cover of tree limbs to soar high into the sky, finally becoming the sole star in the vast, black expanse above. Another curve loomed ahead, and Copeland negotiated it at a crawl, fearing what might lurk at the other end.

The sight of the small white church, behind which lay Rodney Lawson's remains, shocked Copeland almost as dramatically as had the onset of the alien landscape. When he looked back, the cavern of trees and the now-distant tower remained visible; but ahead of him, the world seemed to have at least partially regained its senses.

Whatever relief he might have felt evaporated a few seconds later, when Debra turned to look back and the twin beams of distant but rapidly approaching headlights fell upon her face.

With a weak sob, she said, "Jesus. They're coming after us."

Copeland hit the accelerator again, and the car itself seemed to shove them back in their seats as it leaped forward. No way could they go back to her house or to Lynette's. If they drove straight into town, surely there would be people around—somewhere. Were the Barrow brothers brazen enough to move on them in front of God knew how many witnesses?

Why not? The whole town was already witness to their handiwork.

"The sheriff's office," he said at last. When he saw Debra's incredulous look, he added, "Damn it, Sheriff Grayson's not the only law in town. There's got to be deputies—someone—we can convince to listen. They can't very well argue—the evidence is all around us now. We need anyone we can get on our side."

"You don't know these people," she said with a sigh. "When

the sheriff says jump, his people say 'how high?' and all that. They're that tight-knit. If Grayson's in on this and we go to them, we might as well just hand ourselves over to the Barrows."

"So...the Barrows really do run this town?"

Debra gave him a sad look. "Unfortunately, when you're not directly affected by what they're doing—or think you're not—it's easier...safer...to look the other way. Like most people do around here. Like I have...until now. Now, I don't know if I could be any deeper into it."

"No. I don't suppose you could," Copeland said, visualizing Levi Barrow's face and recalling the words he had written into his journal. This was a man devoted heart and soul to fulfilling his desires—one of which was to possess the young woman sitting next to Copeland—and who, as insane as it seemed, literally had the power to change the world at his fingertips.

"They're getting closer."

He sped up as much as he dared. Lynette's and Debra's houses lay just ahead, but neither offered a hope of sanctuary. He passed them at high speed, but the sight of them filled him with a terrible blend of melancholy and fury, and a new longing to avenge his sister's death pushed aside concern for his own safety. Only a sense of responsibility for Debra's well-being stopped him from turning the car to face his pursuers head-on—which would certainly kill them all.

He was not ready to take that step. Not yet. But before all this was over, he thought, he might be.

They passed no other cars on the streets, although here and there a few people had gathered to gaze in obvious awe at the stone monolith towering above the northern ridge, and the magical, fiery sparks that once again danced the onyx sky.

"I can let you out," he told Debra. "You can mingle here, find a place to hide. They'll never know we're not still together."

"Forget it," she said softly. "We've come this far. I'm not going anywhere." She reached for his hand, and when she took it, all his rage and grief fled in an instant, and now he doubted he could willingly part with her even if she wished it.

He made a couple of turns, and the headlights of the trailing vehicle vanished behind other buildings, at least for the time being. Here, the street was deserted, and when he slammed the car to a stop in front of the small, squat brick building, he saw that every official vehicle was gone and not a single light burned in any windows.

No, he was wrong. From within, a brief flash of hot gold illuminated the glass-paned front doors.

"Well." he muttered, "I don't think we need three guesses to figure out what that means."

The car suddenly shook as something heavy thudded into it; startled, Copeland spun his head to see a dark shape pressed against his window. After a moment, he realized it was a man, but darkness obscured his features. The figure awkwardly stumbled back from the car and attempted to walk, only to collapse in a heap on the sidewalk, his head thudding audibly on the concrete. Where the man had pressed against the window, thick streaks of blood painted a revolting, abstract composition on the glass.

Without a second thought, Copeland heaved the door open, climbed out, and rushed to the fallen man, who wore the uniform of a sheriff's deputy. Even in the darkness, there could be no mistaking the hopelessness of his injuries.

"Good God," he groaned, his stomach lurching at the sight.

Half the deputy's face was a black, glistening mass of blood and ruined tissue, and both his wrists ended in jagged, charred stumps. A wet hissing sound issued from a gaping hole above his twisted lower jaw, and one bright eye fixed on Copeland in obvious supplication. A luminous, gel-like substance coated his clothing, but as they watched, it gradually dimmed like moonlight vanishing behind a passing cloud.

So, *this* was what had happened to Rodney.

The passenger door slammed and Debra appeared at his side, only to gasp in horror. Within moments, the poor creature breathed his last, his remaining eye gazing pitiably at the black, mocking sky.

"This had to have just happened," Debra said, glancing at the nearby trees and the low hedge before turning back to the body. "That glowing substance…that's what seems to cause the burning."

"Maybe this fellow didn't jump high enough to suit the sheriff, eh?"

A sudden screeching of tires and blaze of headlights cut off her response. As they stood frozen in the glare, a thrumming motor grew louder, fell to idle, and then a car door thumped shut. Copeland knew right away that this was not Levi Barrow's truck.

"Debra!" came a familiar, plaintive voice. "Debra, don't run, it's me!"

#

Chapter 14

"**D**ad!" she cried, rushing to her father and falling into his embrace. "My God, tell me what's going on? Where is Mom?"

Major Glen Martin shook his head and looked at her sadly. "Get in the car. You're not safe here." He glanced at Copeland. "You're not safe anywhere."

Click-click-clack.

The sound was very close.

"Get in the car—now!" Martin barked. He opened the passenger door for Debra, who slid inside quickly; Copeland hesitated, his mind reeling with uncertainty, his old instinct to preserve his property—his car—briefly asserting itself. Only the intolerable prospect of being separated from Debra finally prompted him to climb into the back seat of the LeSabre.

Martin slammed the car into gear and pulled into the road just as a warm, golden light spilled over the hedge that lined the sidewalk. As the Buick sped away, Copeland saw a hellish, hideous skull-face rise into view and hover above the bushes, grinning wickedly after them.

My God, the thing was huge—twice the size of the one at the Barrow house.

Martin finally said, "Russ, I know you don't trust me. Can't say as I blame you. But thank you for helping Debra. It means a lot to me." Then, after a long pause, the older man nearly lost his composure. "Damn you, going to the Barrows' was the stupidest thing anyone ever did. Don't you know what could have happened?"

"Dad," Debra interjected. "Tell us what's going on."

"First—where are we going?" Copeland asked.

"Going? We're going nowhere, Russ. As fast as we can get there. As I believe you have figured out by now, this town is completely isolated. There's no road, no trail...not even a deer path...that will lead you back to where you came from. As far as the world is concerned, this little corner of it has split off and gone somewhere else. All we can do now is buy time, wherever we can find it."

"The Barrows," Debra said, her eyes begging her father to say she was mistaken. "They're responsible, aren't they? How? How is it possible?"

"They are, and they aren't. The Barrows are a catalyst, I guess you'd say. More specifically, Amos Barrow is the catalyst." With a sigh, he added, "His grandsons are simply opportunists."

"Where is Mom?"

Martin's face appeared corpse-like in the glow of the instrument lights. He shook his head. "I don't know. I don't know if she's still alive."

"You must believe she is," Copeland said. "That's why you were at the Barrows, isn't it?"

He nodded, but for a time his voice eluded him. Finally, he managed, "Levi Barrow wants an exchange, of sorts. Debra for Elise. He's obsessed with you, honey—but you know that too. He told me he would return Elise unharmed if I convinced you to give yourself to him. He's sworn to treat you like royalty, that no harm will come to you. If you refuse, he will offer Elise to those *things*, and then, chances are, he'll just catch up to you anyway."

"And you've thought about doing what he asks, haven't you?" Copeland said. "Is that where we're going now? To hand Debra over to Levi?"

"No!" Martin threw a look of fury back at him. "Do you think I would willingly give my only daughter to someone like him?" His shoulders slumped over the steering wheel. "Of course I thought about it. What would you do? Elise is my wife. And he's threatening to have her killed in the most horrific way possible. Jesus Lord."

Martin drove at a steady speed, heading east, away from the business district, on Hopeman, a sparsely developed, two-lane road. Just trees, empty fields, the occasional mobile home. *Desolate.* For a few minutes, none of them spoke, lost in the enormity of their predicament. Finally, Copeland asked, "What did Amos Barrow do? How did all this happen?"

In a strained voice, Martin said, "*I* am responsible. It all comes back to me, Russ."

"Tell us."

He heaved a long sigh. "Well. Nearly forty years ago, Amos Barrow's son, Samuel—Levi and Joshua's father—served in my outfit. Echo Company, First Battalion, Second Brigade, First Infantry Division. Tay Ninh, South Vietnam. Just a routine patrol one day, and Samuel Barrow found something inside a temple we had raided. A valuable-looking jewel, he thought. *I* thought. But he ended up dead that day, and I ended up with the jewel. Except I didn't keep it. I knew he came from a poor background, and at the time, I had little use for life in general. So, I sent the thing to his family, hoping it would do them some good. And that's how they ended up with it."

"What does that have to do with all this?" Debra asked.

"Pretty much everything. From day one, I could tell there was something odd about that rock. I'll go so far as to say it made me nervous. It seemed to have a kind of *awareness* or something. That's one reason I sent it to the Barrows rather than keep it for myself. Out of sight, out of mind, you know. Except it didn't work out that way. Quite the opposite, actually."

Copeland said, "That glowing blue stone we saw Amos with…"

Martin nodded. "It's called *Zuso Xhan Mat*. That roughly means 'the Blue Terror.' Where it came from, nobody knows. But it interacts with an individual's consciousness. It makes a person dream. Or have nightmares, I should say. The more you dream, the more real they become, until finally they take on physical form. And they begin to alter space." Then, almost to himself: "Which explains some of the things that happened on that day at the temple."

Debra said, "You mean to say these 'Lumeras'—and these *changes* around town—come straight from Amos Barrow's dreams?"

"In a way. The dreams don't actually originate in Amos's subconscious. I guess you'd say they are…implanted. From everything I've been able to gather, they come from some place independent of the Barrows or anyone else. The *Zuso Xhan Mat* is an intermediary. Once activated, it induces the dreams, which are like doorways…or bridges…to what I call the 'Dream Frontier.' The things on the other side cross over, bringing pieces of their reality into ours."

Debra stared at him, aghast. "Dad, if I hadn't seen what's going on for myself, I'd think you were certifiable. How on earth do you know these things?"

"Even after I got rid of the jewel, I couldn't get it out of my mind. Obsessed with it, I suppose. So, for many years I traveled all over Southeast Asia, looking to learn everything I could about the thing, about the place we originally found it. For starters, I discovered that the temple it came from was older than recorded history. No one was ever able to trace its origin." He cracked a grim smile. "And I had it blown up. That day Samuel Barrow died. There was quite the furor over that among…certain people."

"You say the jewel had to be 'activated,'" Copeland said. "What do you mean by that?"

"None of this happens overnight. My understanding is that one must build a rapport with some consciousness that exists on the other side. That part is exceedingly difficult. Hell, it's taken

Amos Barrow nearly forty years."

"This all started before I was born," Debra said. "You settled in this town, where the Barrows lived...why? Did you even understand what *could* happen?"

"Naturally, I was skeptical of the accounts I'd uncovered. They were all very vague, very old. Still, I'd seen enough evidence to know there had to be something to them. Yes, I originally came because the jewel was here. I considered myself something of a watchdog. Back then, though, I had no idea how pervasive the Barrows' influence was in this town." He paused to take a deep breath, to measure Debra's reactions. "For many years, I played nice with them, hoping I might one day have a chance to take that thing from them and somehow do away with it. I had even contemplated killing them, if necessary. Now, I rather wish I had. Because, somewhere along the line, Levi discovered—or figured out—that I wasn't quite the benefactor they originally thought I was."

"How could they even think they'll benefit from what's happening here?" Debra asked.

"You don't understand. Amos believes this is all his own doing. He's actually proud of it. To his mind, he possesses the ultimate power."

"What about Mom? How much does she know?"

Martin shook his head disconsolately. "This has always been my own personal secret. I had hoped to carry it to my grave."

Debra choked back a sob. "Then she has no idea why she was singled out. Why they might kill her."

"No."

"And you never felt you could tell me any of this?"

"What do you think? Even now, with hard proof in front of your eyes, you can barely accept it. But you're right. I should have given you better guidance...some kind of warning. Instead, I sheltered you. Well, I did try to make you see the Barrows for what they are—small, petty people who will take advantage of you the first time you show them any kindness. As you now know all too well."

"What about my sister?" Copeland asked softly. "What happened to her?"

"I don't know for certain," Martin said with a sad shrug. "Lynette was a wonderful person, Russ. Levi probably had her eliminated just to hurt you. To him, you are an obstacle. He intends to kill you."

"So, the Barrows have some control over this dream world?"

"Perhaps. More likely, it's the other way around. If the Barrows' plans do not conflict with those of the others, *they* give the Barrows some latitude."

"The question is...how do we stop them?" Copeland said. "What if we do manage to kill the Barrows? Will that put an end to it?"

"Only if it's done while Amos's dreams still form the bridge the others are using to cross over. That gigantic tower you've seen, which appears intermittently...that's the *true* bridge between worlds. Once it has anchored itself here, Amos and the Barrows become superfluous. Then they will find out how little they mean in the larger scheme. By then, though, it won't matter—to any of us."

"How far will it spread? Beyond Silver Ridge? Everywhere?"

"I have no way of knowing."

"What about destroying the jewel? Is it possible to do that? Would it make any difference at this point?"

Martin looked at Copeland in the rearview mirror and raised an eyebrow. "I have some ideas. But there's no guarantee they will work. This is *the* great unknown, Russ. I need time to figure some things out. Time, though, is in short supply. Look there."

Martin had driven the car up a long hill that overlooked Silver Ridge from the east, and from this vantage point, they could see the monstrous, faintly luminous tower in the distance, its apex hidden by swirling clouds, the black sky speckled with tiny, zigzagging balls of flame. Martin parked beside the road, and the three of them got out, their eyes arrested by the spectacle. The lights of town glowed like embers in a field of darkness, and occasionally, the faint sounds of traffic wafted from far below— the low rumble of engines, sharp blasts from car horns, the shrill screeching of tires. By now, everyone in the community would be aware that they were, in effect, under siege, even if they could not understand by what or by whom.

After a minute or so, Copeland noticed one of the lights above the far-off ridge seemed to be growing brighter. A few seconds later, it swelled distinctly larger, and he realized then that it was coming toward them. He touched Debra's shoulder. "I think we need to get out of here."

"Dad," she said, "Dad, we're in trouble."

He nodded, his eyes on the approaching fireball. "Take the car and go. If Levi still has any control over these things at all, it won't kill you. I'll try to keep it away from you."

"Dad…"

Martin swiveled and glared harshly at her. "Get in the car and go. It doesn't matter where. Back into town. Anywhere you might find help. Just go! That's an order."

A moment later, Russ found himself in the passenger seat, with Debra behind the wheel, her fingers turning the key, her gaze locked on the increasingly bright object in the sky. "That thing saw us," she whispered. "From miles away, it saw us."

"I hope your father was right—that it's not out to kill you." He glanced outside again, the glare of the thing now illuminating the white hood of the car. "Not exactly a sure bet, though. Let us drive. Quickly."

The engine caught on the first turn, and she put her weight on the accelerator, her eyes fearfully scanning on the road. He knew that she ached to look back, to return to her father, but her self-discipline did not waver. Nor did her eyes turn from the road when the brilliant fireball passed over the car and zoomed toward her father, who stood his ground defiantly, as if waiting for an old nemesis.

"One hell of a CO he must have been," he said softly, admiringly. "One hell of a man."

"Yes," Debra said, and he saw tears streaming down her cheeks. "Yes, he is."

In the rearview mirror, Copeland saw the ghostly globe rapidly descending toward Major Martin, bathing his body in stark white radiance. As the car sped around a curve, Copeland lost sight of him, but a vivid blue flash, like an immense electrical spark, briefly lit the sky, and he imagined that, just for a moment, he heard a short, strangled scream.

Then darkness and silence returned to the night, broken only by the hum of the Buick's engine and the soft, heart-wrenching sound of Debra sobbing.

#

Chapter 15

"**G**ood God," Copeland groaned as the headlights fell upon a throng of people gathered at the corner in front of the Allegheny Gas station, some gesticulating in panic toward the sky; others watching the pyrotechnic display above the town with apparent reverence; still others milling about holding food and drinks, their mood festive. "We don't want to get caught up in that. I'm not convinced that Lumeras are terribly selective about their victims."

Debra slowed the car, taking the opportunity to wipe the last tears from her eyes. An unlit residential street branched off to the left just before the gas station, and she made the turn. "I guess we just keep moving. We can't very well go back home. And if what Dad said is true, getting out of town is out of the question."

"After what we've seen, there's no question," he sighed. "Tell me. You know plenty of people around here. Any of them have grudges against the Barrows?"

"Russ, anyone we come in contact with could be in danger. If those things are somehow looking specifically for me..." She shuddered visibly.

"Amos Barrow didn't set them loose to provide a lightshow. No one is safe, with us or otherwise."

She reflected on the point for a few moments, then said, "You know the McAllisters, right? I saw you talking to Doug at the funeral."

"Yeah, he and I go back to Byston Hill."

"His wife, Carolyn, and I are good friends. He's had a few run-ins with the Barrows in his time. Joshua once threatened to kill him for hunting on their property—except that he wasn't on their property. They are no friends of his."

"Doug was up in a deer stand before he could get into a highchair. Well, he wanted me to pay him a visit while I was here. I say we go for it."

"They live a couple of miles from here. Let's just hope we don't run into any surprises on the road."

Debra drove at high speed through an aging, dilapidated neighborhood, of which Copeland had absolutely no recollection. Few lights burned in the windows of the ramshackle houses, and not a soul wandered these streets. From here, the close-pressing woods blocked any view of the distant tower, so he guessed that at least some of the residents remained unaware of the changes taking place around them. Suddenly, though, as Debra turned onto a dark stretch of road, barren but for tall pines on either side, a large, sapphire-tinted globe sailed into view ahead, etching a trail of electric blue light in the black velvet backdrop. A frigid claw gripped the back of his neck, setting his nerves ringing like carillons, for the thing appeared to be moving steadily toward them. Then, to his surprise, it veered sharply into the forest, disappeared, and did not return. He released a pent-up, relieved sigh, but his entire body had begun to ache from the strain of an unrelenting fear. When he lifted a hand to massage his throbbing temples, it trembled uncontrollably.

As they passed a few decrepit mobile homes, a number of unseen dogs began to howl at them, their voices hollow and tremulous. The road was taking them south, away from the nexus of the Dream Frontier—the farther the better, he thought. But how far *could* they go before that vast, misty chasm opened in the darkness to swallow them? He regretted having dismissed the idea of taking Lynette and braving the road when they might have stood a ghost of chance of escaping.

No; he could not dwell on might-have-beens. Lynette was gone, and that was that. For seven years, he had barely kept up with her—rarely given her more than a passing thought, really. They exchanged cards at Christmas and on birthdays. He usually remembered to send something on Rodney's birthday. As kids, they had gotten along as kids did: occasional bickering, a few honest-to-God fights, a heartfelt expression of love for each other once in a blue moon. He remembered the time Dad had driven him to Byston Hill for the first time, at age nine—when she was still two years from entering the exclusive school. She had wanted to accompany them, but Dad had refused her, saying she would just get in the way. She had pitched a pretty good fit, which young Russ had taken for envy, crankiness, or typical childishness; he had even taunted her cruelly, calling her every name in his juvenile catalog of insults. It was only as they were driving away, and he saw her standing in the yard with tears rolling down her cheeks that he realized she didn't want him to go—that she feared loneliness in his absence.

In some ways, that parting had separated them forever.

"Oh, God," he whispered, his blood boiling as if he had personally failed her. His eyes began to burn, and he turned to stare pensively out the window so Debra wouldn't see. Then he found himself choking back a laugh.

Vain, even at the brink of death.

"You all right?" she asked.

"Just wishing I'd done a few things differently in my time."

"Haven't we all." Her eyes were red but resolute, betraying no sign of defeat. One hell of a credit to her father. "Nearly there," she said.

They rounded a long curve, and a small, wood-frame house came into view on the right, set back among the plentiful trees. Lights burned in most of the windows, and as they drew nearer, he made out two figures standing on the front porch, one of which started walking toward them as the car slowed to turn into the driveway. The figure held a shotgun at the ready and leaned down suspiciously to identify the driver, but when he recognized Debra, Doug McAllister lowered his gun.

"God awmighty," he said as she opened her door. "I guess I'm glad to see you. Who's that with you?"

"It's me," Copeland said, getting out of the car, and McAllister did a double-take when he realized who the "me" was.

"Damn, Russ. I didn't know you two even knew each other. I guess you would, though, wouldn't you? Well, come on down. I don't suppose you've got a clue what the hell's going on around here?"

"I'm afraid I might."

He raised an eyebrow, curious. "Then I want to hear it. He started back toward the house, then paused. "Where's Lynette?"

Copeland had already drawn a deep breath to steady himself, knowing the question would come, but saying the words sent a new, constricting pain through his chest. "She...didn't make it."

McAllister froze. "What?"

"My dad too—and probably my mom," Debra said softly. "We just barely made it here alive."

"Oh, my God."

By now, McAllister's wife, Carolyn, had started toward them, obviously alarmed by the gravity of the exchange. As the slim, blonde woman approached, her eyes flew from her husband to Debra. "What's going on? Please tell us what's wrong."

"Carolyn, this is Russ, Lynette's brother," Debra said, her voice a little shaky. "Lynette...and my father...were both killed today. And Mom is missing. I expect she's..."

"Oh, God, no." The younger, blonde woman looked as if she might faint. "All this has got to do with what happened to Rodney, doesn't it?"

Debra nodded. "We're all in danger. There's no way to break it to you easy. And there's more to it than you're likely to swallow. But you have to."

McAllister led them to the small front porch, where a couple of rocking chairs faced the road. "We've seen some mighty strange shit out here tonight. I might swallow more than you'd think. Anyway, come on inside. And you'd both better drink a beer. From the looks of you, I have to insist."

They entered a modest but well-kept living room, dominated by an entertainment center that housed an expensive, wide-screen television. McAllister pointed to it. "Haven't been able to pick up any news for several hours now. Radio, telephone...all out. Can't get anything or anyone."

"You're not going to," Copeland said. "I'm surprised the power is still on. No telling how long it will last."

McAllister disappeared into a back room for a moment, then returned with a couple of cans of Coors, which he handed to his guests. "You're both whiter than ghosts. Steady yourselves for a little. And then let's hear about that clue you might have."

Copeland took a long, gratifying swallow of beer. "First, tell me what's happened here. What have you seen?"

McAllister shook his head as though he doubted his own senses. "I don't know quite how to put it. Carolyn and I both saw them. Lights in the sky...things...spreading outward, from somewhere up north, it looked like. And sounds. Chattering, squalling sounds, coming out of the woods. Like nothing I've ever heard before. We tried to call the sheriff, and that's when we found the phone was dead. Like everything else. So, we've been watching the road for the last hour. Hardly anyone out besides yourselves. And not one car has come from the south, heading toward town. That's beyond unusual."

Copeland and Debra glanced at each other. "If my guess is correct," he said, "a few miles farther south, the world pretty much ends. At least, the world as we know it."

"What do you mean by that?"

"Debra tells me you've had run-ins with certain members of the Barrow family."

"Me and half the town. What of it?"

"Well, the Barrows are behind what's happening. At least in part."

McAllister grimaced. "They would be, wouldn't they? But what is *it?*"

"A bad dream," Debra said softly. "A bad dream come to life."

"Literally."

McAllister and his wife exchanged shaken glances, and then he took a deep breath. "I guess I'm gonna need another beer. Right?"

"Right."

#

"I don't know if I believe it. I *wouldn't* believe it, except for what I've seen. You, I don't know about. But coming from Debra…"

McAllister and Carolyn, both looking pale and haggard, sat across from them at the small kitchen table. Carolyn had set out a bowl of tortilla chips, but despite an achingly empty stomach, Copeland couldn't bring himself to eat.

"We've been right in the thick of it, and I'm still not sure I believe it."

"Somehow, my father was involved," Debra said softly. "He said he had an idea how to stop them, but he never got the chance to explain."

"On top of it all, Levi is bound and determined to get to Debra. Amos may be the Barrow family's brains, but Levi is the muscle."

"Yeah. And don't sell his brother short," McAllister said. "He's one cruel son of bitch. Very nasty with a knife. He tends to wrap up what Levi starts."

"The lot of them ought to have been thrown in jail years ago," Carolyn snapped. "But Sheriff Grayson is hardly any better. He'll come down like a ton of bricks on anyone who crosses him, but the Barrows…he looks the other way while they get away with murder."

"Pretty much literally," McAllister added.

"To think Dad involved himself with them out of compassion—because Samuel was killed," Debra said. "Until today I never knew anything about what happened in Vietnam. But I know my dad tried to do right by those people. He couldn't have realized back then he was doing exactly the *wrong* thing."

"Speaking of the sheriff," Copeland said, "he's been noticeably absent today. You know, those things were at his office...."

Carolyn wrapped her arms around herself and shook her head in disgust. "From the way you describe them, I couldn't wish them on anyone. Even Sheriff Grayson."

"They're awful," Debra said, gazing vacantly into the distance. *"Awful."*

McAllister gave Copeland a long, thoughtful look. "You've seen them. Up close. For real?"

"For real."

"Those lights in the sky. They the same things?"

"I don't know. I don't know what they are. Except that they come from the same place."

"The Dream Frontier."

"Yes," Debra said. "That's what Dad called it. He must have known so much more than he was able to tell us before they... oh, God." She began to weep again. Copeland laid his hand upon hers. "I'm sorry," she whispered at last.

"The way I see it," McAllister said, "if Levi's after you, we need to keep you out of sight. You're welcome to stay here. Of course, I can't offer any guarantees."

"That's appreciated, Candle. We need all the help we can get. But you'd better understand—just by letting us in here, you've opened yourself to greater danger. You say the word, and we're gone. I'd never ask you to risk your family."

"Hey. I am with anybody who'd cross the Barrows. And this is you and me. Sometimes it don't seem that long ago that we were damn close."

"Sometimes."

Debra shifted restlessly in her seat. After a moment, she asked, "May I use your bathroom?"

"This way," Carolyn said, taking her by the arm. "I'll come with you."

Copeland looked after them, and sighed deeply. Debra was a little unsteady on her feet, and for the first time, she looked as if her reserves were beginning to wear thin. As were his own, for that matter.

"She's tough as nails, Candle, but after losing her parents like that…"

"You lost somebody too. I can see it, Russ. You're in shock. You just don't realize it."

"Can't afford to. Things are changing around us. There's no telling what's going on out there, right now. Where's it going to end?"

"It ends where it ends, I reckon. And all we can do is whatever it takes."

"I don't like to think about what it's going to take." He took a deep breath to steady himself. "I'm pretty sure I'm going to have to kill Levi Barrow. Or die trying."

McAllister leaned across the table and said in a low voice, "I'll tell you something, Russ. Just a little while back, I had a bad encounter with his brother, Joshua. I was out deer hunting on Hickory Ridge. Great spot; a good many miles away from their land. But that bastard appeared out of nowhere, told me I was trespassing. When I disagreed, he let his knife fly. Damn thing sliced through my coat sleeve and stuck in a tree. You think he gave a shit I had a rifle in my hands?"

"I'm guessing not."

"He knew up front that I wouldn't shoot him."

"You play by the rules."

"It's more than that. Anybody else had done that, they'd be lucky if I didn't blow 'em to kingdom come. But if I'd shot Joshua, I'd be nailed up like a trophy to a tree. You cross one, you've crossed them all. And they've got old Grayson in their pocket."

"Not to mention a few hordes of Lumeras in the family." He fell silent for a few moments, too stressed, too exhausted to think very clearly. He studied his old friend's face, the decisive firmness of his jaw, the brilliant spark still alight in his amethyst eyes, undimmed after all these years. McAllister had never been much for talking; just action. Finally, Copeland said, "So, Candle. Is it just you and Carolyn? No kids?"

"Got a boy up at Byston Hill. Like father, like son, and all. He's sixteen. Name's Dan. You and what's-her-name never had any kids, did you?"

"No. When you're married to a lunatic, having no kids is a good thing. Megan was my one big mistake in life."

"Sorry to hear it."

"Until I came here, things seemed to be working out for the best." He glanced toward the window that faced the dark backyard, half-afraid he would see something moving—a light in the trees or a pair of sapphire eyes watching them. There was nothing. "Well. Your wife is very nice."

"She's an angel. She puts up with me."

A door in the hallway creaked, and a moment later, Debra and Carolyn reappeared, both looking somewhat more composed. But as Carolyn sat back down next to McAllister, she said, "The wind is picking up outside. Sounds like a storm coming."

They said nothing for several moments, listening. At the edge of his hearing, Copeland detected a faint whisper, and something scraped lightly upon the shingles above their heads. McAllister rose, opened the fridge, and produced another beer, which he handed to Copeland. "Come out to the porch with me."

They went through the living room, and before stepping out, McAllister took his shotgun from its place beside the door. Outside, beyond their little island of light, the night had turned pitch black, and the wind swept down from the mountains in long, wistful sighs. In the distance, a deeper rumbling sound hinted at a powerful gale building. McAllister drew a cigarette from his shirt pocket; his lighter flame danced spastically as he lit it.

"Storm coming, all right," he said. "Way early in the season."

"Yeah. And it's getting cold."

They peered into the darkness for a time, watching the silhouettes of the trees as they began to sway in the increasingly vigorous wind. Finally, McAllister said, "Do you think your Dream Frontier is affecting the weather?"

Copeland shrugged. "Who knows? I suppose it could."

"How many other people know what's going on? Have you talked to anyone?"

He shook his head. "Far as I know, Major Martin was the only one who could have had any inkling."

"So, no one else is in any position to figure out how to stop them."

"Jesus. With all that's happened, we've barely gotten around to thinking about surviving."

McAllister clapped him on the shoulder. "I know, I'm sorry. But now that you're here, we've got to figure out, number one, how to stay alive, and, number two, how to reverse what's happening. If I understand you, Amos is really the one we have to deal with."

"He's the one who opened the door."

"You know, poor and ignorant as they are, the Barrows have always made like they own this town and everyone in it. The idea that Granddaddy Barrow has found some unknown power is, to me, damn scary."

"From what Major Martin said, Amos believes he's creating his own personal kingdom. But this thing is not entirely under his control. I think it's liable to turn on him. By then, though, it could be too late for the rest of us."

"So, the sooner we get to him the better."

With a bleak look, Copeland said, "You know, we can't ignore the possibility that this change is irreversible. Remember, Martin said that once this thing, this tower, has anchored itself—whatever that means—the Barrows are pretty much inconsequential."

"When does this happen?"

"I have no idea."

In the distance—to the north—something flashed in the sky. At first, Copeland thought it was lightning, but then he saw a number of tiny, golden fireflies flitting high over their heads, painting pale yellow streaks on the heavy black backdrop. A few seconds later, the objects disappeared, but Copeland and McAllister peered long and hard into the night sky, wondering if the Dream Frontier were about to unleash some new terror upon them.

"Those are the things we saw earlier tonight," McAllister said.

"A drop in the bucket compared to the ones around that tower."

"Un-freaking-believable."

The wind now howled through the trees, and its chill burrowed into Copeland's bones. The beer can was frigid in his hand, but the alcohol had soothed his nerves, for he no longer felt on the edge of panic. Here, with his old friend, a spreading inner warmth nearly overcame the gale's icy clutches.

"You actually went into the Barrow house, eh? You've got some balls. That's where you saw these things?"

"Originally. They've spread all over the place now."

"What are the chances are of slipping back in there and putting Amos…out of commission?"

He gave McAllister an incredulous stare. "Umm, Candle. It's amazing we got out alive in the first place."

"But that jewel you referred to. That has to be the key, doesn't it? Seems to me we've got to get hold of it."

"Even if we do, I wouldn't begin to know what to do with it. Even Debra doesn't know."

"Destroy it somehow. At least get it out of Amos's reach. For all we know, he has to remain in contact with it."

"Or it might draw those things right down on us."

"You got any better ideas?"

He sighed. "None with a happy ending."

"Think on it. We'll put you up here tonight; hopefully, you can get a good night's sleep. And I propose that, tomorrow, we start actively looking for a way out of this. You're sure we're completely cut off from the outside?"

"Everything I've seen today tells me that Major Martin knew exactly what he was talking about. You said yourself nobody has driven in from out of town."

McAllister gazed into the darkness in the direction of the road. "How far do you suppose one could go till he reaches the limit?"

"I'd guess not very far. Your place is already a ways out of town."

"You know what? It's tempting to go find out."

"But not very wise. Certainly not in the dark, with a storm coming."

"Yeah," he sighed. Then he glanced questioningly at Copeland. "Hey. You didn't know Debra before you got here, did you?"

"I met her right before Rodney's funeral. That seems like forever ago now."

"She and Carolyn—and your sister—have been friends a long time. 'Course, Debra married that Harrington fellow and moved away for a while, which was a damn shame. Hate to say it, but something told me that was never going to work. She's always been one of the few people in this town with any class." He smiled wryly. "Hell, I sometimes wonder what any of us are doing here."

"You seem to have done all right."

"Can't complain. Well, not much. Anyway, I just want you to know. We'll do our best to look out for you. You've both gone through hell today."

"Thanks, Candle." Copeland had to raise his voice as the wind came roaring out of the darkness, its cold fingers slashing his face. "We'd better get back inside. Hell may be just beginning."

McAllister led them back inside, where they found Carolyn and Debra coming toward them from the kitchen.

"Just coming to check on you," Carolyn said. "Sounds like it's getting bad."

"Big wind." He turned to Copeland. "We've got a generator in case the power goes out. Sometimes in the winter, we lose it for days on end. Don't have a whole lot of extra food and supplies, but we can get by for a while if we have to—barring any unexpected trouble."

A heavy gust rattled the window panes, and Copeland felt a little tremor in his gut. Maybe this was just an early storm; maybe it was not. Something clattered heavily over the roof, and his eyes automatically turned to the ceiling. He felt a hand on his shoulder, and looked down to find Debra sliding in close to him, her face again drawn and wan.

"I don't like this," she said in a worried tone.

McAllister gestured to them. "Come with me."

He led them through the kitchen to a small den at the back of the house and a dark wooden cabinet, which he opened to reveal several rifles and shotguns. He selected a hefty-looking rifle and presented it ceremoniously to Copeland.

"This one strikes me as just right for you. Remington Model 7600, thirty-ought-six, pump action. Maybe you'll feel more comfortable keeping that close. I don't know what it takes to kill a Lumera, but if that doesn't perforate one, not much will."

Copeland weighed the weapon in one hand, lifted it, and peered down the barrel. "Haven't fired a rifle in years. I can still ride a bike, though, so I expect I can still shoot."

"It's loaded. Four-round magazine." He reached into a drawer below the cabinet, which was filled with boxes of bullets and shotgun shells; he found the appropriate ammo and handed a box to Copeland. Then he looked at Debra. "We've got something in your size too. A couple of these are Carolyn's. Ruger M77 here. Two-seventy caliber. That'd be perfect for you."

"Whatever," Debra said.

"You shoot?" Copeland asked.

"Everyone in Silver Ridge 'shoots.'"

"Or I've got a 16-gauge, if you prefer."

"The Ruger's fine."

He was just handing the rifle to Debra when his wife's quavering voice beckoned them. "Doug! Doug! Come here!"

They hurried into the living room and found Carolyn peering out the front window. She glanced at them with fear-brightened eyes.

"Something's out there. In the yard."

Copeland's hands tightened on the Remington. "What does it look like? Is it glowing?"

She shook her head. "No. Something dark. Moving fast."

"You want to grab that light there?" McAllister said, pointing to a heavy-duty six-volt flashlight on the mantle above the fireplace. She took it down, and he motioned her to the door. "Russ, come on around here. We'll go out first. As soon as we do, Carolyn, you shine that light out in the yard. Debra, stay inside the door, and be ready with that rifle. Keep an eye on the windows. Everyone got it?"

"Okay," Copeland and Debra said at once. Carolyn nodded, holding her flashlight at the ready.

McAllister reached for the doorknob with his free hand, turned it, then tugged the door open fiercely. In an instant, he was pushing his way through the storm door into the frigid night with Copeland hard on his heels. The moment they set foot on the front porch, Carolyn's flashlight beam swept across the yard, illuminating the swaying oak trees, the stunted dogwoods at the edge of the road, their Durango SUV and Major Martin's LeSabre in the driveway. Copeland's eyes followed the roving beam, but he saw nothing unusual—until something moved at the corner of his eye, drawing his attention to the right side of the house. A dark silhouette, moving rapidly through the yard toward the road.

"Carolyn!" he called. "There, to the right!"

The beam shifted to reveal a pair of huge, golden eyes gleaming back at them. For a second, Copeland's heart stopped; endless moments later, his brain registered the fact that the eyes belonged to a huge, ten-point buck, which stood frozen in mid-stride in the circle of blinding light.

Carolyn lowered the flashlight, and they heard the sound of hooves crunching through the underbrush as the animal fled into the woods. A grim smile spread across McAllister's face. "Now, he would have made for some good eating."

The steady rush of the wind quickly drowned the sound of the deer's passage. But then, from somewhere behind the house, another noise rose out of the deep woods:

Click-click-clack...click-click-clack.

The hair on the back of Copeland's neck rose. He drew his rifle to ready position and called out, "That's it, Candle. That's the sound of a Lumera."

"That's what we heard earlier," McAllister said. "Only there were a lot more than that."

"That's why the deer are running," Carolyn said. "Those things are in the woods."

"And close."

A sudden chirping sound, sharp and shrill, cut through the wind's roar. Copeland heard a heavy scraping sound behind him, and he turned to see a soft, golden glow washing over the eaves of the front porch. A pale, moonlike disc slowly slid into view, from which a pair of glistening, sapphire-colored globes, deep within shadowed sockets, leered at him with distinct curiosity. The thing's gaze—so alien, yet so *sentient*—mesmerized him, rooted him to the spot with an almost morbid fascination. In that long moment, something inside him lurched, and a dark power seemed to grip and then draw the deepest part of himself away from his body, toward some insanely distant, lightless world that teemed with unseen, eerily wailing inhabitants who anticipated his arrival with an almost palpable hunger.

The land of Amos Barrow's dreams.

The shotgun's report shattered the night air, jolting him from stasis, its vivid white flash briefly dispelling the darkness. The grinning visage exploded in a shower of luminous globules, and a long, agonized howl pierced Copeland's already ringing eardrums. The worm-like body convulsed grotesquely, then slid from the roof and fell to the ground with a moist, heavy thud. The six-foot oblong of glowing flesh lay still, thick, amber-colored fluid oozing from the wreckage of its skull-shaped head; then, after a few seconds, it began to scoot erratically forward with the aid of its scrabbling, centipede-like legs, its one remaining jewel-like eye now locking on Copeland's with unambiguous malevolence.

"Oh, God," Carolyn whispered, backing away in horror. Her voice then rose in a shrill cry. "Oh, God!"

McAllister took a few steps toward it, his gun muzzle smoking, his expression more curious than shocked. The Lumera twisted so that its eye fell on its tormentor, and the barbs on its back vibrated violently, producing sharp, whirring, clicking sounds.

"So, this is what Granddaddy Barrow dreamed up? Un... fucking...believable."

"Don't get too close. Those things can burn you somehow."

The front door opened, and Debra stepped out, her eyes wide and focused intently on the wounded monstrosity, her rifle clutched in terror-whitened hands. At the sound of the storm door snapping shut, the ruined skull-head swiveled again, and its eye socket appeared to dilate as it caught sight of its apparent quarry. Its shattered mandible fell crookedly open, and from its gaping chasm of a mouth, a long, piercing wail issued like the cry of a wounded whippoorwill, at such intense volume that the windowpanes shivered. Copeland, McAllister, and Carolyn all stepped away, grimacing from the pain in their ears; but Debra took a few steps forward, lowered the muzzle of her rifle to the Lumera's head, and without hesitation pulled the trigger. The blast silenced the shrieking horror forever, splashing its obscene, misshapen cranium to the four winds.

For countless seconds they stood in tableau, gazing in awe at the monstrous corpse, hardly daring to believe the thing was dead.

"Well, at least we know they're mortal," McAllister said at last. "That's encouraging."

Then, from the darkness around them, a chorus of chirps, wails, and clickings rose steadily into an inhuman aria that drowned the wind and swirled toward the stars. From somewhere to the north, another chorus responded in kind, and the unearthly voices mingled in a ghostly, melancholy dirge that was at the same time terrifying and strangely beautiful.

"That's coming from town," Debra said.

"My God, they must be all over the place," Carolyn said.

"And I get the feeling they are all on their way here," Copeland said, as the sky behind the black tree line began to slowly brighten like a portentous sunrise.

McAllister threw them an astounded glance and then said. "Russ, my friend, you've got to get out of here. Both of you. You've got to get out of here *now*."

#

Chapter 16

Sometimes his own brother scared him.

Of course he did. Levi was headstrong. He was Granddaddy's spoiled one too, but at least they got on better than most brothers did. Had to, cause they didn't have no one else. Levi'd been angrier than a riled lynx, though, ever since he'd caught him sleeping at Granddaddy's feet. But a man could go only so long without rest, and Joshua had gone way past that, what with Granddaddy sleeping most all the time now, and Levi saying somebody always had to watch over him. Hell, though, it wasn't right he was always the one to be that somebody while his brother went out rambling and courting. He could oversee things as well as Levi—like mapping where the land was changing, reporting back what came out of that hellish tower, guarding against trespassers, and all that.

Well, it wouldn't be long, though, before he could do what he wanted to, where he wanted to, and when he wanted to. And Granddaddy, he'd only be sleeping when he felt like it, not cause he had to.

Yeah, them Lumeras scared him a little, but Granddaddy had

said all was well—that them ones were their friends, their "new neighbors." Well, that was all right; everything ugly didn't have to be awful. Hell, look at him. He didn't have no illusions. And Levi wasn't no picture of splendor, but he was well on his way to claiming old Major Martin's little girl as his own. Now *that* was something to carry on about.

Debra Harrington would for damn sure make a better woman for his brother than Malachi's old mom. Dottie had seemed all right at first, but she'd tried to change the whole family, to get them "right" with her God, as she liked to say, and—worst of all—to turn Malachi into something he wasn't. Not a real Barrow, but one of *her* people. Like "her people" weren't the ones who pretended to be meek and proper and God-fearing, but who savored putting the knife into anyone different than they were, and sometimes into each other. Levi would never abide that. He was a Barrow, and a Barrow didn't pretend to be nothing other than what he was. The family did what they had to do to make a place for themselves and keep the rest of the screaming herd out of their business.

Like what Granddaddy was doing now: making a brand-new place in the world, strange to the eye, maybe, but one where *they* were the ones that counted—where nobody'd ever look down on them again. Martin's girl was smart as a whip, that was for sure, so she'd know better than to make trouble for them; once everything was going the family's way, she'd fall right into line. Not to say it wouldn't take a few whippings, and making sure her old man couldn't get to her to mess up her mind—and getting rid of that new fellow that'd been with her. But all that would soon be took care of. The fear was already taking hold of the herd, and death was taking anybody that Granddaddy wanted gone. Like poor old Mr. Mike. Kinda sad about Mr. Mike, cause he'd always been decent enough with them. But when Granddaddy pronounced it his time, it was cause Mr. Mike's heart had turned too far from his kin to ever come back.

He'd let the herd's law get too deep inside him.

Joshua found himself wishing Levi wouldn't stay gone so long. That little girl couldn't go but so far, and they'd catch her soon enough. Despite his family's good relationship with their new neighbors, Joshua didn't feel all that comfortable being so close to any of them.

The Lumera lay in a dimly glowing coil near Granddaddy's feet, the little blue specks in its deep eyeholes following Joshua's every move. Its cold gaze set his nerves on edge, even though it didn't have license to do anything to him. If something went wrong, all Granddaddy had to do was wake up and wish it away, and it'd be gone, just like that. That wouldn't work much longer, though, so they'd told him, and he wondered what Granddaddy had in mind to do when he couldn't get rid of them so easily.

"You needn't worry about such things," the voice in his head said. "You are our hosts, and we are in your debt."

It wasn't really a voice. It was more like thinking—where he didn't hear the words but knew what his brain was telling him. Them ones talked that way. Best he could tell, Lumeras didn't really read minds, but they could pick up impressions, the way a hound could smell fear on a person.

"Sorry, sorry," he said. "I reckon y'all understand that it feels funny bein' trustin' to somebody so different and all. Ain't much used to that."

"We understand," the Lumera told him. "Your grandfather explains your world to us very well. He is kind and patient with us, and we are pleased to have made his acquaintance. He loves you, so we do as well."

"Y'all know about love and feelings and such?"

"Our feelings are not so different than yours. At first, we were surprised that the long-sealed door to your world had opened again, and so we, too, were distrusting. But your grandfather came and explored our world, and proved himself a friend to us. Not all who have come have been so amiable."

"Y'all know people like us?"

"Over the ages, others of your kind have come to us—in what you call dreams. Long ago, certain of them came exploring, and we gave them a means to cross between worlds as they desired. However, unlike your grandfather, they were not truly friends of ours. Thus, we sealed the door, to keep your kind away. Now the door has reopened, and your grandfather has made us understand that some, such as your family, are unlike the multitudes of evil ones who dominate your world. We have decided to offer him—and you—a place such as ours, but upon your own land. It is our gift."

"I reckon that's kind of you."

"For granting us an outpost such as this, it is just."

"Granddaddy says that, to us, y'all are a dream, and we're like a dream to y'all. His gem there makes it so that y'all ain't just a dream anymore."

"That is a concise explanation."

Joshua glanced at his granddaddy, who looked too much like a dead man laid back in his big easy chair but for his chest heaving slowly up and down. His hands lay folded in his lap, his fingers closed around the gleaming, sapphire-like jewel he called the Zeus Jon Mott, or something such. Every now and then, the egg-shaped stone grew bright, and Granddaddy would shift a little in his chair, his brow arching down over his clenched eyes. He hadn't woke up now since he'd sent Mr. Mike away, and his color wasn't looking so good. The brighter that rock got, the paler the old man got—almost like it was taking something out of him.

That jewel was burning like an electric bulb now, causing Granddaddy's hands to glow warm orange. Behind the Lumera, the tangle of barbed cords that covered the walls like wild, twisted vines began to rustle and writhe. They had appeared as if by magic earlier in the evening, and Levi had told him they would help him guard against intruders. But they worried him, too, cause as far as he was concerned, they looked too damn nasty to be inside his own house.

The downstairs door slammed, and he felt a little measure of relief mixed with a new anxiety. Levi was home at last.

"Thanks for telling me what you told me," Joshua said to the cold blue eyes in their dark cavities. "I reckon my brother's come back."

"We will have more opportunities to converse in the future."

"Yeah…okay."

The Lumera's body stopped glowing and became an ugly slab

of gray, wormlike flesh. Joshua heard Levi's distinctive, heavy tread on the stairs, and a moment later, he appeared in the door.

"Granddaddy doin' all right?"

"He just sleepin', like always."

"Ain't nobody come to the house, have they?"

"Hell no, ain't nobody come to the house. Why you think that?"

"I ain't thinkin' it," he said, without further comment, but he gave Joshua a blistering glance. Then he leaned down to study Granddaddy's closed eyes. "He ain't come out of it, has he?"

"Naw, not at all."

Levi glared at his brother. "I want that girl, bro. And I want her tonight."

"I figured that."

"Hey. You'd like to get out of here, wouldn't you?"

"Well, yeah..."

"Awright. I guess we gonna leave Malachi with Granddaddy and you gonna come with me."

Joshua dropped his jaw. "You gonna trust Malachi by hisself with Granddaddy...and them ones?"

"For what we gonna do, I need you more'n Malachi. And Granddaddy...he been doin' okay all this time, ain't he?"

"Well, yeah, if just sleepin's okay."

Levi leaned close to him. "I'm going for Debra Harrington, and I'm aiming to fix that man with her. I ain't leaving him for them ones. It's you and me for him. All right?"

He nodded, and his pulse sped up. "Hell yeah, that's all right. How you gonna find them?"

"You know how them ones kinda talk in your head, right?"

"Sorta."

"They gonna lead me exactly where I want to go. I been makin' some arrangements."

"Okay, then."

Levi went out the door, and returned a minute or so later with Malachi in tow. The boy looked curiously at the Lumera and then said to Joshua, "That one done growed some, ain't it?"

He glanced at the creature and realized Malachi was right.

"Yeah, yeah, kinda looks like it, don't it? Hadn't rightly noticed it before."

"Malachi," Levi said. "I'm gonna leave you in charge for while. Whatcha think?"

"Alone?"

"You and Granddaddy." He swung his head toward the Lumera. "And that one. You gonna have your shotgun, but you don't have to worry about nobody getting in here. Them vine-things'll rip apart anyone comes in here that ain't s'posed to, I guarantee you that."

Malachi looked nervously at the creeping, coiled things crawling like deadly ivy upon the wall. "I don't much like them yonder. How do I know they ain't gonna mistake me for a stranger or something?"

"Don't be stupid. You know them ones ain't gonna hurt any of us, right? Granddaddy says so."

"I reckon," Malachi said, glancing again at the dull, dead-looking Lumera. "That thing asleep or something?"

"Dunno, but don't you worry none. Get the shotgun and sit up here with your Granddaddy. We'll be back after while. And be ready to have some company. You gonna like 'em."

Malachi nodded. "Awright."

As they turned to leave the room, Levi took hold of Joshua's shoulder and said softly, "Take your knife. You may get to do some carving tonight."

Joshua felt his fingers tingling, the way they did when he antici-pated getting to thin the herd. "You gonna let me do it, aren't ya?"

Levi looked at him and grinned. "I'm gonna let you do it all you want to, bro. I'll be havin' plenty else to take care of. Plenty else, yes sir."

#

Chapter 17

"**Y**ou know where the place is, don't you, Debra?" Carolyn asked.

"Yes," she said with a nod, "as long as we can still get there by road."

The McAllisters had all but dragged Copeland and Debra to their SUV with instructions to seek sanctuary in Carolyn's late parents' mountain cabin. "If there's any place they won't find you, that's it," McAllister told them. "It's been empty for a couple of years now. You get your asses up there, in our vehicle, and maybe there's a chance you'll get past them. We'll load up all the supplies we can in my truck and meet you there as soon as we can. But you get going. Go now."

At the best of times, Copeland hated being a passenger, but he reluctantly yielded the keys to Debra, since she knew the treacherous mountain roads far better than he. Besides, if—God forbid—the Lumeras attacked them on the road, he preferred to be able to wield his heavier firepower against them. In addition to the rifles, McAllister had given them both handguns with plenty of ammunition; a Ruger 9mm for him and Smith & Wesson snub-nose

.38 for her. He doubted the smaller arms would so much as dent a Lumera, but they would make a meaningful impact on any human assailant.

He could not forget, though, that the Lumeras might have subtracted the Barrows from the equation by now. That possibility worried him perhaps more than the alternative.

He gave McAllister a long look as he settled into the passenger seat of the Durango. "I don't like this, Candle. If they come in big numbers, you won't stand a chance of getting away alive."

McAllister waved away his concern. "Now, listen. There's nothing up at the cabin to speak of. No food, no firewood, no electricity. There's an old water pump out back, but I don't know if it still works." He jerked a thumb toward the back of the SUV. "There's a case of bottled water and some other stuff in there, and we'll bring everything else we can manage in the truck. It'll be enough for us to hang on for a while. But you need to get this head start. You stay here, and I wager we'll all end up dead."

"Hurry yourself," Debra said to him. "If they converge here…I can't stand to think about what will happen."

"Don't you worry about us. Just go. Go!"

Debra started the engine, threw the vehicle into reverse, and pulled into the yard to go around her father's car. McAllister waved after them, calling, "We'll be up there in a little while. We'll see you."

Copeland waved back, but his entire body throbbed with the dark certainty that he would never see his old friend again. "Where the hell are we going now?" he asked, as Debra turned the Durango onto the road, heading north.

"About five miles up the road. Before they died, Carolyn's mom and dad lived at the top of Mount Hemlock. It's just a little place, and there aren't any close neighbors. I guess you'd say it's pretty well concealed—for whatever that's worth."

"That's the northeast ridge, isn't it? That's closer to town than we are now."

"The terrain's more rugged, though, so it's less accessible. We don't exactly have many choices for shelter, Russ."

"Yeah," he agreed, reluctantly. He glanced at the black, starless sky. "Can you drive without headlights? If those things see as well as they seem to, our lights will be a dead giveaway—especially if there aren't any other cars on the road."

She nodded, slowed the vehicle, and flicked off the lights. The sudden darkness appeared complete for several seconds, until the dim gray pavement gradually re-materialized ahead of them. She maintained a steady twenty miles per hour, which felt too fast, but by now his faith in her was complete. Once they passed the turnoff that led to town—the way they had originally come—the road ascended steadily and curved through long stretches of dense woodland, where houses were virtually nonexistent. A few lights dotted the woods here and there, but they passed no other cars and saw no one on foot. This place was already the end of the world, he thought; civilization could disappear altogether, and nobody here would notice any difference. He liked fleeing to a totally deserted place only slightly more than one filled with people.

The road wound steadily upward, carrying them a couple of thousand feet above the town, the lights of which occasionally sparkled through the trees on the left. They came to a long, dark passage between the towering trees, at the end of which he could see a patch of midnight blue sky, and as the Durango advanced toward it, a little alarm began to clang in his head, steadily intensifying.

"Slow down," he said. "Something up ahead."

She complied without question, and as the vehicle crept forward, he saw that, to the right of the road, a thick gray mist was oozing from the trees, swirling over the road like something alive. She hit the brakes and the tires screeched on the pavement.

"What the hell?"

"That's what I saw out on 201 today."

By an unspoken signal, they both opened their doors and slid out, as silently as possible, into the unnaturally frigid night, Copeland with his rifle in hand. As soon as they began to steal toward the opening in the foliage, he felt exposed and vulnerable, and that sensation of being trapped inside a terrible dream once again overwhelmed him. His feet moved automatically as his mind retreated to some place of perceived safety, just outside his body. He vaguely registered Debra's hand closing on his arm, and he took some comfort in her nearness. If it weren't for her steadying presence, he thought, he might be reduced to cowering impotence in the face of this unimaginable, unpredictable power. But a look at her face told him she felt the same way—that at this moment, only together could they hold onto their wits.

As they stepped out from beneath the trees, Copeland nearly reeled at the sight of the vista that had opened before them, for now they had an unobstructed view down either slope, and he sincerely wished that they did not. Debra's iron grip on his triceps did nothing to diminish the sense of unreality that swept over him in a nauseating wave.

The land to the right of the road dropped off into a vast ocean of swirling, roiling mist, amid which he could discern shifting but clearly malevolent faces with deep, cavernous eye sockets, too like those of the Lumeras to be figments of his imagination. At the extreme range of his vision, he thought he saw mammoth, humped, black shapes leaping above the mist and quickly disappearing, but none remained in view long enough for him to determine whether they were real or illusory products of the rolling gray sea.

If any doubts lingered that Major Martin had spoken a bitter but absolute truth, they now dissolved in the endless vapor, which had swallowed an entire world but for this one tiny, doomed corner.

To the left and below, the lights of Silver Ridge glowed like the smoldering embers of a gigantic bonfire. Above the town, thousands of glimmering fireflies traced erratic patterns against the black backdrop, some brilliant gold, some fiery red, some electric blue. Periodically, one of the fireballs would dive into the geometric patterns of light and create wildly flashing strobe effects; Copeland fancied he could hear the distant, haunting sound of screaming as the Lumeras, with apparent randomness, cruelly obliterated any gatherings of the town's citizens that suited their whim.

Several clouds of the fireflies had gathered into a dense mass and now made their way steadily southward—the direction from which Copeland and Debra had just come.

Far in the distance, looming above the horizon, the tall, fire-crowned spire gazed down on the town like a monolithic sovereign, its black surfaces glittering with the reflected light of countless swirling fireballs. It appeared fixed and unwavering, as solid as the mountains it overlooked.

Had it already anchored itself in this world?

Did the Barrows have any clue what was happening here? Was *this* what old Amos had truly intended to bring forth from the world of dreams?

Copeland's eyes followed the winding road, which dipped below the ridge's summit and veered to the left, where it disappeared into a vast bulwark of towering pines. "Does that road look normal to you?"

She nodded. "I think so."

"How far is the cabin from here?"

"Less than a mile. It *should* be, anyway."

"Do we keep going?"

She pointed to the pulsating congeries of gold and sapphire light that appeared to be drifting in the direction of the McAllisters' home. "We can't go back."

"Then let's do it."

They returned to the SUV, instinctively treading softly, each sensing that the faintest noise might draw unwelcome attention to them. When she turned the key and the engine rumbled smoothly to life, he flinched, half-expecting the sky to brighten suddenly and reveal murderous invaders bearing down on them at frightful speed. But as they started rolling, nothing appeared in their path, and he actually felt a small measure of relief once they reached the concealing darkness of the trees.

After a long silence, Debra glanced at him, her features barely visible. "We don't have much hope of surviving, do we?"

"As far as we know, they still want *you* alive."

She slowly lowered one hand to the .38 on the seat beside her.

"They will never have me alive. Never."

His heart sank, but he nodded. "I understand. But we're going to take as many of them out as we can before we ever go down. You got that?"

She smiled humorlessly. "It's the only way."

"I never thought I would, in this lifetime, ever intend to commit murder. But so help me…if I so much as catch a glimpse of any of the Barrows, I *will* kill them."

"Self-defense isn't murder," Debra said. "They're a clear and present threat."

"I suppose from a legal standpoint, it doesn't really matter anymore. Wherever we are, the law no longer exists."

"If you're concerned, I don't have a moral issue with killing them. Except…"

"What?"

"What about the boy?"

He hesitated, his shaken convictions taking yet another turn. "I don't know," he said at last. "He's already willfully used you so his father could get to you. As far as we know, he's as much a part of this as the others."

"He's only fifteen. Given his background, is he responsible?"

"Maybe more importantly, if they were to come after you, would he be a willing participant? Would that make a difference to you?"

"I don't know," she said, barely above a whisper. "It might."

She began to slow the Durango as they rounded a long curve to the left. A few moments later, on the right, he saw a break in the trees, with only dark, empty space between them. But as Debra pulled into it, he briefly glimpsed the silhouette of a mailbox beside the road. The vehicle ascended at a snail's pace into the pitch-black abyss, bouncing violently on the rutted, uneven surface, Debra surely driving by memory and intuition. On and on they went, and several times, low-hanging branches rattled over the top of the SUV. How they avoided slamming into the close-pressing tree trunks, he could scarcely fathom.

Five minutes later, the darkness ahead changed subtly, becoming somehow heavier and more voluminous. A glimmer of sky appeared behind a canopy of dense, tangled tree limbs, and his eyes gradually made out the angled roof of a small structure just ahead. Debra stopped the Durango and cut the engine. As its rumble faded, Copeland listened carefully before taking hold of the door handle; outside, only a low, eerily whispering wind broke the silence. Finally, he pushed open the door and slid out, his rifle instantly in hand and probing the darkness around him. No other sounds drifted to his ears; not the melancholy songs of night birds nor the chirping of insects. He grabbed the six-volt flashlight McAllister had given him, and with a twinge of apprehension turned it on, shining its beam at their surroundings.

The two-story, chalet-style structure seemed a natural extension of the trees, having been built right into a small clearing. Pine boughs overhung the roof, and smaller maples pressed close against the wooden walls and the railing of the little front porch. The building appeared sound, all the visible windows intact, the solid oak front door tightly closed. The flashlight beam revealed a small outbuilding a short distance behind the house on the left, which he guessed was a work shed.

"So, Carolyn's parents lived here?"

"Ever since she was a little girl. Doug thinks they should have sold it, but she doesn't want to part with it. In a way, I don't blame her. I can't imagine not having Mom and Dad's place..." She suddenly stopped, and Copeland knew her mind had returned to a place they could not afford to have it go just now.

"So, there's no generator here, eh?"

"Where do you think Doug and Carolyn got theirs?"

"Ah."

He stepped up to the front porch, and he could smell the faint, sweet aroma of cedar and perhaps woodsmoke. It was a heady, exhilarating scent, which drew him completely out of the moment and returned him to carefree, innocent times from his youth, when the smell signified warmth and security as cold weather closed in. But then he shook himself, knowing that he, too, could afford only to be here and now, and on guard.

From her pocket, Debra withdrew the keys Carolyn had given her and unlocked the front door. She pushed it open and started to walk in, but Copeland stopped her to shine his light before them. He saw only an empty living room, the few remaining items of furniture covered by dusty white sheets. To the right, there was a broad, stone fireplace, clean but for a couple of years' worth of dust; to the left, a door opened to a hallway and the other rooms. No pictures or other decorations hung on the bare wooden walls. Lots of cobwebs.

"I guess pizza delivery is right out," he said, finally stepping inside, leading with his rifle. She followed closely, peering into the night for a long moment before closing the door. "See something?" he asked.

She shook her head. "No." She reached into her borrowed coat and withdrew a package of Saltine crackers and a handful of plastic-wrapped caramels. "We have these to eat. That's all Carolyn had time to grab for us before we bolted out of there."

He went through the door to the hall, shone the flashlight into each door he passed. The first one was a half bath, but there wouldn't be any running water. Maybe he could pump some water from out back to put in the toilet tank. Also on this floor were two completely empty bedrooms, a small den, and the kitchen. Making his way upstairs, he found a full bath and two more bedrooms, the larger one obviously the master; the bed frame had been removed, but a mattress and set of box springs wrapped in clear plastic leaned against one wall. The room spanned the width of the upstairs, with windows facing both the front and the back of the cabin; beneath the rear window, he could dimly see a shingled canopy above the back kitchen door.

"I say we set ourselves up in here. Only one door, so it's the most easily defensible. If we have to get out in a hurry, we can go through the back window and drop onto the canopy down there."

"Okay," she said. "Plus, it's a tad warmer up here than below."

He realized she was right. During the day, the house would have absorbed the heat from the sunlight, and the cold air had yet to displace it completely. "We'd better sleep in shifts. One of us needs to be awake at all times."

"I don't mind taking the first watch."

"I don't think I could sleep if you put that gun to my head. I'll stay up."

"Whatever," she said with a shrug. "Carolyn said their sleeping bags are in the back of the Durango. At least we'll stay fairly warm. Those two are happy to camp in the bleak midwinter."

"Okay. Let's go get them together. I don't want us to be separated at any time—especially going outside."

She gave him a curt salute. "Yessir."

"Come on then."

They went back out to the Durango and found, in addition to the bottled water and pair of sleeping bags, a couple of Coleman lanterns, extra fuel, three boxes of strike-anywhere matches, and a camping stove. Quickly, they grabbed the goods, closed up the SUV, and in two trips, carried everything inside, grateful for the little warmth it offered.

"That wind's getting colder," she said as they climbed the stairs. "This change is definitely affecting the weather. It's never been this cold at this time of year."

"I expect it's adapting to the Lumeras' climate. It must be."

Once they had placed their gear on the floor, Copeland went to the windows, closed the Venetian blinds that still hung upon them, and lit the lanterns, which painted the dark-stained walls warm gold. Debra began to unroll the sleeping bags, while he lowered the mattress and box springs to the floor and slid them to the rear corner of the room, just beneath the window. As they piled the sleeping bags on the mattress, a pack of Chesterfield cigarettes fell out from one of them. She picked it up.

"Want one?"

"Don't smoke."

"I haven't in ten years or so. You know what? I bet having one now isn't going to kill me." She opened the pack, drew out a cigarette, and looked at it thoughtfully for a moment. "I bitched at your sister for years to quit. She just didn't want to. She enjoyed them too much." Debra struck a match, lit the smoke, and inhaled deeply. Copeland smiled as she made a sick-looking face.

"Laugh all you want to. Smoke one with me."

"That's all right. Really."

"Smoke." She tossed him the pack. Because she wished it, he took one out, put it between his lips, and lit it.

The smoke tasted vile, and he just puffed on it, rather than inhaling it. But for whatever reason, the very act of smoking the thing took the edge off his fear, soothed his jangling nerves as if it were a sedative. He drew in a shallow lungful of smoke and exhaled quickly. It burned his throat a little, but he didn't start coughing.

"Feels better now, doesn't it?" she asked.

"Yeah. A little better."

"You never smoked?"

"Yeah, actually I did. In high school. I didn't enjoy it, though."

"Peer pressure?"

"Well…Candle could be persuasive sometimes."

There was a long silence. "You don't think they're going to get here alive, do you?"

He bit his lip and then shook his head. "I'd say the odds are long." He went to the front window, pulled the blinds aside for a moment, and peered into the darkness. "Black as pitch. Can't even see the lights from town here."

Debra came to his side. "If anyone can make it, they can. You saw him back there. He's fast and just about fearless. And Carolyn's no slouch. A little high-strung, but she's tough as hell. I expect I'd trust my life to her."

He gazed into her deep, liquid brown eyes. *So much life there,* he thought, *even after the day's hellish ordeals.*

"He was always a character in our younger days. Doesn't seem to have changed much. We could be real troublemakers back then. He was the ringleader, of course."

"Of course."

He closed the blinds and tossed his butt into the empty fireplace. "You should get some sleep. I'll see if I can find a chair so I can sit by the window."

She nodded, and he picked up the flashlight, figuring that they were safe enough to leave her alone for just a few moments. Surely, among the sheet-covered furniture in the living room he could locate a chair of some sort. He went down the stairs, but before making his way to the front of the house, he decided to visit the old water pump and see if he might coax some water from it. He went back to the kitchen, which had been stripped of all its appliances, and found a couple of plastic buckets in a storage closet. A rickety-looking door led out to a small back porch. From there, just down the stairs to the dark, half-visible backyard, he found the water pump. To his satisfaction, he discovered that with a few strong pulls on its at-first stubborn lever, it produced a short but powerful stream of cold, clear water. Inside a minute or so, he had filled both buckets.

Back inside, he filled the toilet tanks in both bathrooms and left the buckets with the remaining water beside the fixtures. Then he returned to the living room where, sure enough, he found a warped but sturdy Boston rocker. He awkwardly maneuvered it up the stairs, banging it noisily against the wall a couple of times, which prompted him to mutter "Dammit" a few times under his breath.

"Let's not knock the house down," Debra said as he brought the chair inside and placed it next to the front window. She had removed her coat and was just taking off her shoes; the lantern on the floor cast her shadow, long and tall, on the wall behind her. She was wearing blue jeans and a wine-colored turtleneck sweater, and the golden light flattered her lithe figure.

He forced his eyes to focus on hers. "All right, here it is. We can take care of personal business upstairs and down, we've got drinking water, and this is a very nice fucking chair. Wouldn't you say?"

"Lovely. You sure you want first watch?"

"Yeah. I'll take it."

"Then I guess I'm gonna try to get some sleep, for all the good it'll do."

"Best to try." He turned away from her, pushed aside the blinds again, and peered sightlessly through the glass; behind him, he heard her sliding into the sleeping bag on top of the mattress.

"Hey, I have an idea," he said. Going to the camping stove, he picked it up and carried it to the door to the stairwell. He stood the stove on one end and propped it against the closed door. "We don't have an immediate use for this. This will give us at least a few seconds' alarm if someone—or something—manages to get inside and up here without us knowing it."

"That's good."

"If we survive till tomorrow, we can better fortify this place."

"Yeah." She gave him a weak smile. "You know, so far, you've been almost useful."

"You're too kind. Do you want the lanterns off?"

"No, I don't want them off. It's probably better if they are, though."

He flipped on his flashlight, then extinguished the two lanterns. He knelt next to her, leaned down, and kissed her on the forehead. "I'm sure I'll be awake the rest of the night. You sleep as much as you can. I'm here with the guns, and you're safe. Nothing is going to bother you."

Sadness tinged her smile. "Thank you, Russ. I'm going to try. But I don't know how I'll ever sleep again."

"You'll manage."

"If I do, you'll wake me if Doug and Carolyn get here?"

"You know I will." He rose, went to his chair, and sat down with his rifle propped against the windowsill. He adjusted a few of the slats so he could see out without opening them all the way, then switched off the flashlight. Darkness fell over them like a cerement.

Her voice drifted to his ears. "If you want them, those crackers and caramels are in my coat pocket. You're welcome to them."

His stomach felt horribly empty, but the thought of food still made him slightly queasy. "Maybe later," he said. "Or maybe we can have them for breakfast."

"Okay."

He sat back in the rocker, which creaked slightly. To keep from disturbing her, he sat as still as he could, his eyes locked on the narrow gaps in the blinds. His ears, sensitized by his near-total deprivation of sight, picked up her low, regular breathing, and he thought she might have actually drifted right off to sleep. He found himself remarkably comfortable in the old chair, and a couple of times, his own eyes closed and barely opened again when he willed them to.

Damn, he wanted a drink.

He let himself focus on the annoying absence of good scotch rather than anything else. No way could he contemplate the future; not tomorrow, not even the next hour. He didn't dare think about the lovely young woman lying in the darkness just a few feet away, or about the things that lurked in the evil night, very possibly searching for her, or the fact that their friends had not shown up by now. Only screaming insanity could result from thinking about *anything* other than how very damn badly he wanted a scotch.

Scotch neat. Scotch on the rocks. Scotch with a splash of spring water.

Christ on a bicycle.

Something flashed in the darkness outside the window. Instantly, his heart a jackhammer, he leaned forward, rifle in his hands. He peered desperately through the onyx glass, cocked his ears to catch the faintest noise anywhere in the night. The low breeze still whispered softly past the panes, but not one other sound rose above it.

One of those things in the sky, he thought. A long way off. A long, long way off.

Endless minutes passed, and nothing else appeared. The night remained as empty as the void of outer space, and eventually, he began to relax again. He sat back in his chair, which creaked softly again.

"What's wrong, Russ?"

He glanced into the darkness in her direction. "Nothing. Nothing at all. Sorry if I disturbed you."

"You didn't."

"Okay."

Minutes of silence almost convinced him that she had relaxed and maybe drifted off again.

"Russ?"

"Yes?"

"If they come, you won't be able to stop them."

"Probably not."

"Come hold me."

His heart froze and his stomach fluttered. He propped the rifle against the windowsill again, rose from his chair, and carefully made his way toward her bed. When his foot touched the box springs, he knelt slowly, and he heard her shifting in her sleeping bag. One of her hands touched his arm; he took her hand and let her guide him onto the mattress. He heard her unzipping her sleeping bag, and he took a moment to shed his coat and shoes. Then he carefully maneuvered himself next to her and slipped one arm beneath her head as she made room in the warm sleeping bag. She pressed herself close to him, wrapped an arm around his chest, and one leg around his. He smelled the sweet, citrus scent of her hair and felt the soft caress of her breath on his throat.

They lay in each other's embrace for several minutes, comfortably warm, his heart still pounding but less troubled than it had been for seemingly forever. Finally, she pulled away from him a little, letting a draft of cool air pass between their bodies. Then her lips touched his, delicately and tentatively. She again pressed her body hard against his, and their lips locked together, their tongues exploring each other's with almost desperate intensity.

He rolled so that his body covered hers, and one of his hands closed on her breast, soft and firm beneath the ribbed fabric of her sweater. Their hands roved high and low, first tenderly, then more passionately, one's lips never leaving the other's. As her pelvis began to thrust against his, he felt himself hardening unmercifully behind the constricting denim. One of her hands slipped between their bodies and unfastened her jeans, and she shifted her hips rhythmically back and forth to work her way out of them. Moving her fingers to his belt, she deftly unbuckled it, and then began to work at his fly. He lowered one hand to her rounded rear end and gently massaged it, slipping his fingers beneath her panties and gradually working them farther between her legs. She moaned softly, breathing into his mouth, and he shifted his head, touching his lips to the soft flesh just beneath her ear and tracing the line of her jaw with his tongue. Now she had worked his jeans down over his hips and was pulling him harder against her, again wrapping her legs around his, entrapping him with her body.

Her lips went to his ear, and with cruel coldness, she said, "If they come for us now, the .38 is right beside me."

He looked into the dark space that concealed her eyes. "What if we survive another fifty years?"

Her fierce grip on him relaxed and became tender again. "Then we'll remember this night for as long as we live."

#

Day Four

Chapter 18

It was still pitch dark when Copeland opened his eyes again. He held Debra in a warm, protective embrace, his right hand tucked between her legs. He felt the soft, rhythmic tickle of her breath on his neck. He had no idea how long he'd been asleep, what time it was, or how long since he'd moved; his left arm had gone numb, so he carefully shifted it so that blood could begin flowing to his fingers again. Cold, spiteful air slipped into the new space between them, and she stirred but did not wake. He shivered, his body still enervated from their coupling. He might have been content to lie there with her endlessly but for a low scratching sound on the mattress, which he soon realized was the hair on the back of his neck standing on end.

He held himself perfectly still and listened, but heard only Debra's low breathing and the clamorous thumping of his own heart. Not a speck of light broke the perfect darkness. Except for the insistence of his trusty internal alarm, nothing around them seemed out of place.

The wind. The wind had finally stopped blowing.

Maybe that's all it was.

He tried to make out Debra's face before him, but even that was impossible. In spite of his growing disquiet, he could not help feeling exhilarated after having made love to her so fully and completely. He had never experienced such a bonding with any woman; certainly not the lunatic Megan. And her sharing with him...so deep, so passionate.

Was this really love?

Did it matter anymore?

A rustling sound somewhere outside dragged his attention to the window, just above their bed. For a second, he thought he saw the blinds limned with pale blue, but total darkness quickly returned. A trick of his barely awake eyes? He sat up slowly, trying to avoid disturbing Debra, cocking his head to listen further. No new sound.

Hell, even if he had seen a light, it might have been a reflection from many miles away.

Something scraped the wooden wall, close to the window.

In all the time the wind had been blowing so hard, not a single tree branch had struck that part of the house.

Now, he wished he had taken the time to rig some sort of trap or alarm downstairs in case an intruder managed to get inside. Unable to stop himself, he slid out of the sleeping bag, felt for his flashlight and Ruger until he found them, and then crawled to the window. He lifted one slat of the blinds an inch or so and peered into the darkness, praying to see nothing. And at first, nothing was all he saw.

Then, some distance below, a tiny blue speck appeared and drifted slowly toward him, like a luminous bubble on a lazy current of air. A second bubble winked into existence a short distance from the first; the two jiggled oddly, then gradually expanded as they drew nearer to his window. His finger tightened on the trigger of his gun, but he realized he was mesmerized, rooted to his spot by an expectant dread, wholly incapable of moving his hands or feet. As the pair of luminous globes came to rest on the other side of the glass, he thought he saw strange, swirling shapes within them, as if they were lenses that revealed a view of some other place: a world so dark and distant as to be beyond the view of any mortal eyes before his. An irresistible power had seized his consciousness—his soul—and seemed to drag it from his body. Before he realized what was happening, the Ruger slipped from his fingers and thunked heavily to the floor.

The sound jolted him to his senses, and he tried to withdraw from the window. He only half-succeeded, but in that moment, he found the strength to lift the flashlight, switch it on, and with shaking hands, aim its beam through the gap in the blinds.

The light fell upon an almost human-looking skull, a yard wide, its tooth-studded jaw half-open in a sardonic grin, its eyes—the electric blue bulbs—nestled within a pair of deep, black cavities. At the touch of the beam, the pulsating, wormlike body began to glow like molten gold, revealing its immense size—easily bigger than a horse. It hovered on broad, moth-like wings that beat at dizzying speed, its multitude of long, bony legs twitching erratically beneath the thick, tapered body. In moments, the thing had become a mass of living flame, so brilliant that Copeland's eyes could barely stand it. He fell onto his buttocks, one hand, by chance, coming to rest on the handle of his gun. He snapped it up and aimed it at the window.

Now, Debra sat up, still half-draped in the sleeping bag, her face striped with golden light. "What the..."

He pulled the trigger three times in rapid succession. The Venetian blinds danced, the windowpane exploded, and a shrill, ululating screech rang out, louder than the gunshots. The piercing cry dwindled as the wounded horror fled, and soon, darkness again filled the room, broken only by the quivering beam of his flashlight.

In an instant, Debra had torn herself out of the bed and pulled on her jeans. "God, they've already found us. There's no place we can hide!"

Copeland cautiously moved toward the window and swept the ruined blinds aside. No hint of light marred the darkness, but he heard, in the far distance, the faint suggestion of an insect-like chirping.

"I don't guess there's any point anymore," he said. "They know where we are. We know they're coming. Maybe this is where it all ends."

She was just fastening her pants when her hands froze; her eyes locked on his and began to blaze. "You're proposing we go down fighting?"

He took a deep breath and nodded. "We go down fighting."

She took a few steps toward him, reached out, and clasped his biceps. "Remember what you said. Whatever happens—they can't take me alive. Please."

With a sigh, he nodded. "I'm trying not to think about that. But if it comes down to it...I know what I have to do."

She leaned close to him, and her lips found his, and his arms encircled her body tenderly, protectively. When she drew back, he saw that her eyes were glistening with tears. "We take out as many of them as we can, right?"

"As many as we can."

He found his own clothes and quickly dressed. Knowing it wouldn't matter, he lit the lanterns, then made sure all the guns were fully loaded, with extra ammo close at hand. A low breeze again began to whisper outside the window, and he heard a distinctive *click-click-clack* from somewhere not far away. He went to the window that faced the front of the house, opened the blinds, and tugged the sash up.

Through the trees, perhaps still miles away, a number of brilliant, glowing globes of various colors traced erratic, swirling patterns in the sky.

Incredibly beautiful in their way.

"They're coming, aren't they?"

He nodded. "They're coming."

"What time is it?"

He glanced at his watch. "Four-fifty. Still a good hour to daylight." As he looked at her, he realized he could see tiny, dancing reflections in her dark eyes. The enormity—the terror—of what they were about to face together nearly floored him. His feelings for her, the memory of the warmth they had shared, the unequaled fulfillment he had found with her, seized his body like a tidal surge. If, at the very end, they found themselves at the mercy of those creatures, would he be able to save her by committing the unthinkable?

Something downstairs *thunked* heavily.

"Russ," she said, her face pale, shadowed with sadness. "Thank you for everything you've done for me."

He nodded, barely able to find his voice. At last, he managed to whisper, "I love you." But she did not hear him.

Click-click-clack...click-click-clack...

It was right outside the rear window. He didn't see anything yet, but he could feel the nearby, unearthly presence like a frigid draft. More chattering, chirping sounds clambered in through the front window, and then a pale, golden light danced off the nearby tree trunks. He pressed himself against the wall, rifle at the ready, while Debra positioned herself between the rear window and the door to the downstairs. He had tucked the Ruger into his belt, and he touched its handle, finding it both reassuring and dreadful. She glanced at him, her eyes as defiant and determined as ever, and he knew that their assailants would pay dearly before the end came.

Another heavy *boom* thundered up from the downstairs; Copeland moved to the door and placed his ear against the wood to listen. At first, he heard nothing, but then—overhead—something clattered loudly like hail on shingles, and several streaks of light zoomed past the rear window.

CLICK-CLICK-CLACK!

With a sharp crash, the remaining glass in the rear window shattered and rained over the floor, and both Copeland and Debra swung their gun muzzles toward the dark abyss. He could see nothing, no movement at all, and he swore softly in frustration. Better the creatures should rush in and reveal themselves rather than toy with them.

Another crash, and something smashed the front window, ripping the Venetian blinds, leaving their tattered remains to dangle suggestively in front of the open portal. Now Copeland fired blindly into the darkness; the report hammered his eardrums in the enclosed space. A fiery orange light flickered mockingly on the trees for a few seconds, then all went dark again.

For a full minute, nothing happened. Not a single sound, not a glittering spark outside the house. The stillness grew steadily more burdensome, taunted him like a cruel trickster, and he knew that relaxing his guard would spell instant death. The Lumeras were playing them, preying on their terror with the alacrity of depraved, sadistic human.

Then, his internal alarm shrieked in his brain, and Copeland felt something hot on the back of his neck. Spinning toward the rear window, he saw two glowing blue bubbles within deep black sockets, and something red and frothing came dribbling over the windowsill. As the gooey substance streamed to the floor, smoke curled from the wooden planks. A scrabbling sound alerted him to something at the front window; he spun and saw two bony, clawed appendages grasping the sill. A moment later, a knobby, oversized skull pushed its way through the tattered blinds. He called to Debra, "I've got the one at the front. Shoot the other one!"

The gunshots simultaneously ripped through room, and smoke from the muzzle briefly obscured his view. He thought he heard a sharp, metallic crash, but with the ringing in his ears, he could not be certain. Then, at the corner of his eye, through a veil of smoke, he saw distinct movement; before he could swing the Remington around to meet it, something hit him solidly in the temple, and he staggered backward, watching in disbelief as the room whirled madly around him. He threw out an arm to catch himself, and after a few seconds, his vision began to clear; but as it did, his spirits plummeted, for the door to the stairwell had burst open, and two figures were moving boldly, rapidly toward them.

Levi Barrow held a shotgun, the butt of which he had used to club Copeland in the head. A second hideous figure was trying to wrest Debra's rifle from her hands, using his weight to throw her off balance. With a single turn of his wrists, he ripped the gun away from her, and she sagged to her knees with a bitter sob. Joshua reached down quickly, plucked the .38 from Debra's pocket, and tossed it across the room. Before Copeland could move a finger, he found himself facing the muzzle of Levi's double-barreled 12-gauge.

A glance at the windows showed them vacant, as if the Lumeras had never existed.

"You the sumbitch that likes to come uninvited to where he don't belong," Levi growled, taking a menacing step forward and forcing Copeland to take a step back. "Lessee how you like it, what say? Now, how about you drop that rifle there. Don't do nothing funny cause I'll splatter your head on the wall there before you can move that barrel an inch."

Copeland's first impulse was to accept the challenge—to kill Levi where he stood or die in the attempt. But his preservation instincts won the brief struggle, and he slowly lowered the rifle to the floor, never taking his eyes off his aggressor.

"Okay. Now take that popgun outa your belt and drop it on the floor. You do that real slow. Or maybe I don't just kill you. I let Joshua do what he wants to with the lil girl there. Whatcha think about that, mister?"

"I think you're full of it. You haven't gone through all of this just so your brother can have his way with her."

Levi's eyes narrowed, and he took another step forward, so that Copeland could smell the acrid odor of sweat and cigarette smoke. "You don't know nothing about me, mister smart man. You think you understand someone like me? You don't know nothing. It don't matter to me what he does to that lil girl. Maybe I like her a little more…tame…before I take her *my* way. When Joshua's done, they tame. They always tame."

"You are one sick bastard."

With surprising speed, Levi jabbed him in the cheek with the gun barrel, hard enough to snap his head back. He grimaced as pain shot through his skull and down his neck; but he felt a moment's satisfaction that he had riled the man sufficiently to provoke a reaction. It was a small chance, but if he could incite the other to anger, he might be able to turn it to his advantage.

"You won't face me without your weapons, will you? You're nothing but a little chickenshit, you know that?"

Levi ignored him for the moment and turned briefly to his brother. "Joshua. Bag her."

From behind his back, the ugly man drew a rolled length of material, which Copeland realized was a large burlap sack. Unceremoniously, Joshua placed it over her head, and when she raised her arms to resist, he smacked her solidly in the temple, stunning her long enough for him to tug the bag fully over her upper body. Like a magician, he produced a length of cord, which he deftly wrapped around the open end of the sack and tied it tight, rendering her arms immobile.

"Get her up."

One of his arms encircled Debra's waist, and he heaved her bodily to her feet; then he shoved her against the wall, holding her upright with a hand upon her breast, which drove a blade of fury through Copeland's skull. She exhaled sharply from the blow but then began to breathe deeply but steadily.

Without warning, Levi swung his shotgun around and, with its butt, caught Copeland squarely in the solar plexus. A brilliant starburst exploded before his eyes, his breath whooshed from his lungs as if suctioned by a vacuum, and he pitched heavily to the floor, struggling furiously to draw air into his lungs. The whirling lights slowed and dwindled, but when he could see relatively clearly again, he found that Levi and Joshua had switched places; Levi now pinned Debra against the wall while Joshua stood before him, nimbly twirling in his fingers a wicked-looking hunting knife with a serrated blade.

"Much better," Levi said. He gripped Debra by the back of her neck and sent her lurching toward the door. "Joshua's gonna fix you up real good. Me and Miz Harrington'll say goodbye now." With that, Levi dragged Debra through the door and out of sight. Copeland heard her whimper as she stumbled down the stairs, totally at the other's mercy.

Then the front door slammed and they were gone, leaving Copeland on his knees, dazed and gaping at a murderous, knife-wielding thing with a leering, barely human face.

My God, she was really gone. The Barrow brothers had just

walked in and taken her.

He had failed to keep his promise to her.

"You know," he muttered hoarsely, "those creatures are going to kill you. Levi will probably be dead before he gets back home."

Joshua made an odd creaking sound in his throat, which Copeland realized was a giggle. "You got imagination," he cackled, his eyes shining beneath his brutish, bony brow. "But no damn sense. Stupid sumbitch."

"Why don't you enlighten me?"

Joshua lunged forward with his free hand, drove his fist into Copeland's gut, and knocked him to the floor. Again, all the air burst from his lungs. A strong hand gripped his collar, and he felt himself being dragged toward the front window. Joshua re-sheathed his knife, then with both hands lifted Copeland off the floor. For a panicked moment, he thought the other was going to hurl him to his death, but then his back slammed against the wooden rocking chair, and the strong hands pulled his arms behind his back. Agony arcede through his nearly dislocated shoulders. With no strength to resist, he could do nothing to stop Joshua binding his wrists with a rough length of cord. "I'll enlighten you, mister smart man, yep, yep. I'm gonna enlighten you for a long, long time." Joshua again drew his knife from the leather sheath that hung from his belt.

Copeland tried to ignore the surge of fear that spread rapidly from his chest. "Joshua...what makes you think those things are any friends of yours? They're not. They're going to kill you. You, and your whole family."

The malformed face split into a snaggle-toothed grin. "Yeah? Whatever might give you such a notion?"

The cruel-looking blade gleamed before his eyes; then he felt icy metal touch his cheek, followed by a sudden, searing heat as it cut a deep gash from his cheekbone to his jaw. He cried out, more from shock than pain, but within seconds, the wound began to throb, and warm blood streamed down his neck and over his collarbone.

"I said whatever gives you such a notion?"

Now, Copeland kept his mouth shut, and Joshua leaned close to his ear.

"I'm gonna do that again in just a minute, by the way. And again and again. Until there's nothing left of you but little pieces that I'm gonna feed to our new friends. But they gonna have to wait a while. A long while. You got that?"

"It doesn't matter what you do to me," Copeland spat, strangely bolstered rather than overcome by the pain. "You can't escape what's going to happen to you. If I don't live to see it, well…more's the pity."

"You not going to live to see anything but your own blood spilling all over this floor." To his alarm, Joshua moved behind him, out of his view; then he felt the cold steel touch the back of his neck and slowly glide toward his right ear, as if his tormentor were searching for the most sensitive area to cut. "What say we lose the ears next?" The pressure of the blade increased suddenly at the back of his ear.

"Wait," Copeland hissed, terror now beginning to boil up inside him. "Wait. Let's talk first. You want to know what I know about the Lumeras, right?"

"Well, I dunno," Joshua said, as if he were speaking to a child. "I dunno how much we really got to talk about."

"The Lumeras," he said, trying in vain to swivel his head away from the blade. "It was Major Martin who told me about them. He knew a lot about them."

The knife slipped away from his ear and came to rest on his shoulder. "Old Major Martin done a lot of good for us folks. But he weren't everything he seemed to be. Turns out he was just a liar." He stepped around into Copeland's view again and leaned close to his face. "He's always been a liar. He lied to you, too."

"No. What he told me was no lie. The evidence is everywhere. All around us. They're changing the land itself. You think it's your grandfather doing that?"

"Yeah, yeah, Granddaddy done that. He's making this place into something else. Just for us. Just for us, you got that?"

"Your granddaddy just started these events in motion. But

they're beyond him now. Or soon will be. And then...Joshua... those things are going to rip everyone apart. You, your brother, your granddaddy...everyone."

"Old Major Martin never talked to 'em, did he?"

Copeland shook his head in surprise. "Talked to them?"

Joshua laughed boisterously. "Yeah, talked to 'em. Me, I done that. They told me what they doing here and why. So, anything Major Martin knew, or thought he knew, well, that was just bullshit. I know, mister smart man. *I know.*"

"Joshua...even if you were able to communicate with them... they're not human. They don't think like humans. They kill people. How could you have faith in them?"

The homely creature again leaned into Copeland's face, his eyes hotter than burning embers. "What matters that they kill? Getting rid of pitiful, useless garbage, that's all they doing. You wouldn't know nothing about that, would you? They getting rid of them what took my daddy away and got 'im killed, them what beat down my granddaddy cause he never went to their churches or their schools. He's just as good as any of them—better'n them!—but they hurt him. They hurt him so bad. They hurt all of us. Now, he's just getting a piece of what he always deserved. For his family. All for his family. And for my ma—" Joshua suddenly fell silent and scowled thoughtfully; then he abruptly took the knife and ran its blade along Copeland's jawline, drawing blood. Shocked, Copeland bit back a yelp, the pain hot and jarring, but still manageable. He swallowed hard.

"What about your mother, Joshua?"

"I didn't say nothing about my mama."

He tried to inject some compassion in his voice. "You were treated unfairly, so you're looking to punish the guilty. But what about the innocent, Joshua? What about everyone else who's getting hurt?"

Joshua appeared to calm somewhat. "Ain't no one innocent in this town. So, they gonna die. All of 'em."

"It's not all about your grandfather, is it, Joshua? Tell me about your mother."

"Weren't never anything wrong with my mother. Don't you even talk about her. You say one more word about my mama, and I'm gonna cut out your tongue." He paused and bowed his head for a moment, as if in deep thought. When he looked at Copeland again, his face split into a wide grin, and he said, "Know what? I'm tired of talking to you anyway."

With that, he suddenly gripped the back of Copeland's neck in one hand and began to squeeze, just behind his jaw. He gasped, and as his mouth opened, Joshua quickly slipped the knife between his teeth, nicking his tongue. He began to apply pressure with the blade, using its flat edge to force Copeland's jaw wider.

"No more talking, mister smart man. Yeah, I think I'll just cut your tongue right out. We'll see how you like talking then."

Positioning himself behind him, Joshua slid his arm around Copeland's head and tugged it backward, forcing his mouth open, despite his most valiant effort to lock his jaw. The blade against his teeth prevented him from clamping down, and Joshua began to work the knife inward, its blade biting the inside of his cheek. Realizing with horror there was nothing he could do to thwart his bloodthirsty captor, he thrashed violently, rocking the chair back and forth, hoping now just to buy a few more moments.

"You son of bitch."

For a second, everything went completely still and silent. Then, suddenly, the knife fell from his mouth, and the arm encircling his head drew away quickly. He heard a heavy thud, and Joshua's body struck the chair, nearly upending him. Craning his head around, he saw Doug McAllister clutching a shotgun, which he had obviously just used as a club. The brutish figure on the floor started to scramble toward his attacker, but McAllister brought the butt squarely down on his head, laying him out on the hardwood surface. With a groan, Joshua covered his head with his hands and lay still.

For good measure, McAllister's foot lashed out and connected solidly with Joshua's kidneys. He screeched in anguish, wrapped his arms around his abdomen, and tried to roll away, but the shotgun came down again and whacked him solidly on his bony forehead. This time when he went motionless, blood began to pool on the floor beneath his temple.

"Jesus," McAllister whispered, taking in the sight of his bound friend. "Hold still, I'll untie you."

"Levi took her," Copeland groaned, spitting blood on the floor. "I couldn't stop him."

"We'll get her back. Don't fret. Right now, let's take care of you." He worked at the knots for a time, futilely, and finally said, "I'm gonna have to cut this. Hold still." Retrieving Joshua's knife, he used the bloodstained blade to saw through the cord. When it fell away, Copeland's arms dropped limply to his sides, dead from the shoulders down. He swung his shoulders back and forth for a minute, gradually getting the blood circulating again.

"You're very late."

"Sorry. Couldn't be helped." McAllister leaned close to Copeland's face. "Damn, man. You must've pissed that bastard off right royally. Way to go. But he's cut you good. That cheek could use some stitches. The jaw's not so bad. I got a first-aid kit in the truck we can patch you up with. If there's no bandages, I got duct tape."

"I've always sworn by duct tape."

"Come on, let's get you into the bathroom and cleaned up." He helped Copeland to his feet, bracing his arm to make sure he didn't fall.

"What about him?"

McAllister regarded the fallen figure for several seconds, tossed the knife in the air, and caught it by the haft. "Maybe we should just kill him." He eyed Copeland questioningly. "What do you think?"

He fought down the acid rage that crept up his throat as he gazed at his former tormentor. "He deserves death. A little while ago, I was ready to kill the lot of them. Now, though…I'm not so sure it sits right with me."

"When he comes to, he'll be madder than hell. We can't just let him go free."

"No. That we can't do."

McAllister pondered the point for a moment; then his face

turned rock-hard as he made his decision. Kneeling, he rolled up the fallen man's pants legs, exposing his ankles and lower calves. Then, with the serrated blade, he cut deeply into one of his hamstrings, releasing a rich red flow of blood. Joshua cried out loudly and suddenly began to thrash; undaunted, McAllister deftly cut the tendon of the other leg, then neatly rolled down his trouser legs before stepping away. A whimpering sound came from Joshua's throat, and he rolled onto his back, tears streaming from his eyes. Copeland grimaced and felt an unexpected pang of guilt, despite his satisfaction that this was nothing more than simple justice. "Jesus, Candle," he whispered.

"I suppose he might bleed to death," McAllister said flippantly. "But knowing him, he'll figure out a way to stop it before then. Entirely up to him."

Copeland nodded and put a hand to his throbbing cheek. His fingers came away slick and red, and all traces of guilt vanished. McAllister took up a lantern and led him to the bathroom, where he insisted on cleaning his own cuts with his bottled water.

"Back in a second." McAllister disappeared and soon returned with all the guns. "Wanted to make sure he couldn't get to any of these."

Copeland tilted his bottle, splashed a handful of water onto his cheek, and patted it gingerly with his fingers. "So, what happened to you? We were afraid you'd bought it."

Just then, below, the front door creaked slowly open. McAllister called out, "Carolyn?"

"Yes," came her soft voice.

"Up here."

A moment later, she appeared at the bathroom door, her face ashen, but her eyes relieved to see her husband safe. When they fell on Copeland's face, she gasped. "God, what happened?"

"Joshua Barrow happened."

"Where is he?"

McAllister pointed to the master bedroom. "Do not go in there. I've hurt him, but he may still be dangerous."

She placed a concerned hand on Copeland's shoulder. "I've got some ibuprofen in my purse—in the truck. I can get it for you."

"The first-aid kit should be in the back. Grab it, will you?" She nodded and started down the stairs again. "Watch yourself out there," McAllister called after her.

"I will."

He looked appraisingly at Copeland's cheek. "The cut's pretty clean, so if you don't do anything to make it worse, it'll heal up okay."

"Thanks. So, Candle, what's your story?"

"You know, after all we'd seen tonight, I thought I had prepared myself for what we might run into. Shit." He clicked his tongue. "Everything was completely changed, just north of our house. We drove for hours, got into woods and such that I've never seen before, and kept ending up back at the same place. It was beyond freaky. I've never felt so completely…lost."

"It must have changed after we passed through. It's enough to drive you insane if you think about it."

"At least we didn't see any of those creatures—not up close, anyway. But there were lots of lights in the sky, all rushing back the way they'd come from earlier."

"Really?" Copeland bit his lip. "Interesting."

"Then, out of the blue, everything returned to normal. We were on some strange road, in deep woods, and then…suddenly…I knew where we were again. And that's how we made it here—just in time, by the look of things."

"Another minute, and we wouldn't be talking together now." His stomach quivered at the thought of the cruel torture—and death—he had very narrowly escaped. "By the way…do you know anything about Joshua's mother?"

McAllister raised an eyebrow. "Why do you ask?"

"Seemed to be a sore point with him."

"Well, go figure. Word's always been that his mother was his daddy's sister. She died when he and Levi were kids."

Copeland grimaced. "I see. Well, I guess that fits."

They heard the front door open and close again, and soon Carolyn reappeared, carrying a floral scarf and a small, blue and white plastic box. "Not much in here, but at least there's gauze, tape, and peroxide," she said.

"That'll do nicely," McAllister said. "Now, you mind taking over here? I'd better make sure whosit's not getting into any mischief."

She nodded, opened the kit, and handed a roll of surgical tape to Copeland. "Hold this." He complied, while she knelt to sort through the contents of the box. Taking a small bottle of peroxide, she soaked one end of the scarf, which she used to dab away the blood on Copeland's face. The sudden sting nearly caused him to reel, but he managed to hold still for her. She took a few squares of sterile gauze, pressed them over his wound, and said, "Pull off a couple of pieces of tape, will you? I need to secure these."

Copeland did, and once she had taped the gauze firmly in place, she handed him a handful of pills, which he placed on his tongue. He was just chasing them down with water from his bottle when the shattering report of McAllister's shotgun caused them both to jump nearly out of their skins.

Carolyn leaped toward the bedroom door, but her husband stepped out, his shotgun muzzle dribbling smoke. He laid a reassuring hand on her shoulder. "I'm all right. Everything's all right." To Copeland's questioning glance, he said, "The son of bitch wanted to cut me. Had a nice shard of glass from the window in his hand. Guess he didn't feel at home without a blade of some sort."

"You shot him?" Carolyn asked, her eyes widening.

"Graveyard dead. He made to lunge at me, and damned if I was going to dick around with him any further. Far as I'm concerned, that's one less piece of shit to contend with."

"Oh, Doug," she said with a distraught sigh. "Did you have to?"

"You know I did."

Copeland shook his head in near-disbelief, a little rattled, but unwilling to waste a moment of remorse on that twisted wretch. He pressed the flimsy bandage tight against his throbbing cheek and felt blood dribble down his jaw. "Time's wasting," he said. "I've got to get to Debra. There's no telling what's going on out there now."

"Well, it's a sure bet where she is. There's only one place Levi would take her."

"I can't ask either of you to go there with me. The chances of surviving…" He swallowed hard. "Well, they're not good."

"Debra is my friend too," Carolyn said, somewhat defensively, as she repacked the first-aid kit. "Yeah, your chances are lousy by yourself. I say the more of us the better."

"We all go. That's just how it's going to be," McAllister said. He handed the Remington and the 9mm to Copeland, and Debra's rifle and .38 to Carolyn. "It's probably safe to say they won't be expecting us. So, let's get to it. I'll get the flashlights and the other lantern."

He disappeared into the bedroom for a minute, while Copeland pulled on his heavy coat. As they started down the stairs, McAllister leading, Copeland found his legs barely able to support his weight. He was still in shock, his body exhausted and in pain, his emotions wrung out. "For all we know," he muttered, "by the time we get there, the Lumeras may have finished them all off. Debra too."

"Don't be morbid," Carolyn said.

McAllister glanced back thoughtfully at him. "Major Martin was pretty sure of what he was talking about, wasn't he?"

"Everything he told us has proven true."

As they went out into the dark night, Copeland immediately noticed that the air, though chilly, was distinctly warmer than before. A low breeze still stirred the trees, causing the bare branches to click ominously together—like chattering teeth, he thought. He could vaguely make out the silhouette of the pickup truck parked behind the Durango, and as he walked, he again felt himself somewhere outside his body, his limbs moving automatically, the pain a dull, distant sensation that meant little to him. He felt no hope, no despair; as long as he kept moving forward, continued functioning, he needed no other purpose. Even his fear for Debra seemed a remote, abstract thing, sizzling somewhere deep inside the body to which he barely felt connected.

"Better to take the one vehicle. Don't want to chance getting separated. You can squeeze in up front with us or ride in the back, whichever you prefer."

"I'll take the back."

"If they come after us, you'll be completely exposed."

"That much easier to shoot back." He hauled himself into the back of the pickup, which was loaded with boxes and bundles—the supplies meant to sustain them while they holed up at the cabin. He found a couple of blankets he could sit on, and settled himself behind the cab, his rifle across his lap, the handguns tucked into his belt in easy reach. McAllister opened the sliding panel in the rear window so they could hear each other and cranked the engine. As they started down the rutted drive, Copeland noticed a dull, orange glow behind the cabin—there, next to the little outbuilding—but before his eyes could focus on it, the light vanished.

"Damnation," he said. "I think one of those things is still here. If they really do communicate with each other, we may have just lost the element of surprise."

"Nothing for us but to damn the torpedoes," McAllister replied. "And hope we don't end up on the lunar surface somewhere along the way."

The truck bumped and jolted heavily down the long driveway, and Copeland had to hold onto the side of the truck to keep from bouncing right out of the back. Once they hit pavement, the going became smoother, and he was able to focus his attention on the dark, passing trees, alert for any sign of pursuit. McAllister was driving with his lights on, but that no longer seemed to matter; if the Lumeras desired to find them, they would; simple as that. Despite the rise in temperature, the wind still whipped him with a bone-numbing chill, and he tucked his hands beneath his armpits to keep them warm.

McAllister took the curves at dangerous speeds, but Copeland trusted his friend's skill and good fortune. Hell, they had already surmounted impossible odds to get this far; if there was a chance of getting through this, he was with the right people to do it. Gradually, he began to feel reconnected with his body, and now, for the first time in a long time, he found himself praying earnestly—not for himself and his friends; the worst that could happen to them was death—but for Debra, whose fate lay in the hands of a lovesick madman.

#

Chapter 19

The darkness of the cellar had never particularly frightened Malachi, but with them worm things coming and going as they pleased, you never knew where one might pop up—and he sure didn't like the idea of bumping into one unexpectedly. Nor did he care for the shuddersome, thorny vine-things that seemed to be slowly taking over the house. If them critters didn't take a liking to the house's proper occupants, what was to stop them from just killing everybody and doing as they pleased? That's what was happening everywhere else, wasn't it? Great-Granddaddy had taken to sleeping like the dead now, and Malachi was beginning to have his doubts that he was ever gonna wake up again. The old man kept looking paler and paler, his body wasting away a little more every hour he stayed asleep. His old boastfulness about how good they were gonna have it didn't seem quite so reassuring anymore, not when he wouldn't wake up no matter what was going on around him.

Even his own daddy had gotten worrisome lately, what with his temper getting so short—probably cause he was just as nervous as any of them over their changing circumstances—and his being gone almost all the time. Malachi chafed at the idea of his old man putting Ms. Harrington in the cellar and then telling him to make sure she stayed there—leaving only them Lumeras upstairs with Great-Granddaddy now. His daddy obviously didn't much like that idea either, but he must have figured it was more important for Malachi to watch over Miz Harrington than the sleeping old man. He sure hated to see her tied up like this, since she had always been right kind to him. Well, if not kind, then fair, at least.

But he didn't dare cross his daddy. He'd known that all his young life, but God help him, if he upset Daddy now he might just get fed to them ones. And that was just about the most awful thing he could imagine, cause he'd seen what happened to that little schoolboy when the Lumera got him.

All chewed up and burnt.

"Malachi…are you there?" The faint voice quivered out of the darkness.

"Yeah, I'm still here."

"Where are you?"

"Just sitting on the stairs here."

"Malachi, you know this isn't right. Please…let me go."

"Don't think you understand, Miz Harrington. Can't do that. Sorry you're uncomfortable and everything, but it won't be for much longer. That's what my daddy promises."

"Malachi, your daddy is wrong. You've got to understand that."

"Don't you say that. He ain't, neither."

"Look at what's happening to the world around you, Malachi. Is it the kind of place you want to live in?"

"It's gonna be better for us, Miz Harrington. It'll be better for you too, if you just accept it, like Daddy says."

"Do you really believe it's going to be better? After you've seen what its masters do to people?"

"They not the masters, we are," he said harshly. "My daddy and my great-granddaddy say we ain't got nothing to fear and never will. You calling them liars?"

"Maybe they're just mistaken, Malachi. Think about it."

"You can't do what my great-granddaddy done by mistake, Miz Harrington. Everybody always thought we was all so stupid, but now look at us. You oughta be glad to be where you are, Miz Harrington. Sorry if that sounds ugly and all, but it's true. You show us all respect now, and you'll be just fine, you hear?"

"Do you think it's all right to kill people who don't respect you?"

"Well...I don't know that it's 'right,' Miz Harrington, but you can bet people are getting what they deserve—for being like they been to us all these years. Treating us like dirt and such. Everybody calling me 'Malarkey' all the time. That kinda talk is over now. Hell, a lot of 'em ain't gonna be talking no more at all." He laughed nervously. "I know that worries you some, but Daddy'll make you understand. Just listen to him, and respect him, and you'll see him different than you do now. He thinks you're an angel, you know that?"

"He's got a fine way of showing it."

"Miz Harrington, it ain't *us* killing nobody. Them ones is doing it because they want to repay us for what Great-Granddaddy done for them. Bringing them across from wherever they live, and all."

"Malachi, do you trust me?"

He hesitated. "Well, I reckon so, Miz Harrington. I mean, you always give me a chance where none of them others ever did."

"I know it's been hard for you, and I've tried to treat you fairly. I think you understand that. If you've ever trusted my word about anything, I want you to trust me on this. Those creatures...they're no friends of yours. They're very likely going to turn on you, and you'll be no better off than any of the people they've killed. You have to believe me."

He didn't like to admit it, but Ms. Harrington *seemed* to be making sense. Still...nobody's word could ever mean more to him than his own daddy's, or even Great-Granddaddy's. Then he thought of something. "How would you know anything about them Lumeras, Miz Harrington? Nobody else knows anything about them. Only my folks know."

"That's not entirely true, Malachi."

Just then, the upstairs door creaked open, and a rectangle of light appeared above his head. He stood up as his daddy came down into the darkness, his booted feet clumping heavily on the wooden boards. Levi tugged the little chain hanging over the stairs, and the exposed fortywatt bulb came on, bathing the stairwell in dull, copper-colored light. Malachi could just make out Ms. Harrington huddled in the corner a few feet away, her eyes widening with fear as his daddy reached the bottom.

"You two having a good talk?" Levi asked.

"I reckon so."

"Good, good. It's about time for me and her to have a little talk too." Malachi noticed that his father's face appeared shadowed with concern. "I just checked on Granddaddy, and he still just sleeping away. Your uncle Joshua ain't got home yet, though. I want you to go upstairs and keep an eye out for him. When he gets here, you tell him to get his ass down here."

"Yessir."

"Well, get on, and me and Miz Harrington gonna work on understanding each other a little better."

"'Sir."

Malachi went up the stairs, but something about the way his daddy spoke made him feel anxious. He knew Daddy would never hurt Ms. Harrington; after all, he meant for her to stay with them from here on out. Course, he also knew his daddy loved him, and sometimes the way he showed it weren't too pleasant.

In the kitchen, he closed the door, but instead of going on up to Great-Granddaddy's room, he stayed put, contemplating what Miz Harrington had said to him. She was wrong, simple as that; Daddy'd make her see things right, sure enough. Still, he couldn't help worrying about her, so he slid up beside the door and pressed his ear to the rotting wood, knowing that if he got caught, it would mean big trouble for him. Still…his curiosity burned hotter than his fear.

"So, Miz Harrington," he heard his father said in an uncharacteristically soft, almost meek voice. "I know you uncomfortable, so I'm gonna untie you, okay? I know you know better than to do anything stupid. Anyway, you got nothing to be afraid of here. Don't nobody mean you any harm."

"After what you've done, how could I possibly trust anything you have to say?"

"You just not understanding yet, and I don't fault you for it. It'll take some adjusting and all. I mean, the whole world is changing for all of us. I reckon we'll all have to get used to different things. Hold still now."

A long silence followed, and then his father grunted.

"Watch it now. That's good, you just be calm. Good girl."

Another long silence.

"So, you and Malachi getting along okay?"

"I feel sorry for him."

"You been good to him, and I do appreciate that, I hope you know. Them others…"

"It's not because of the 'others' that I feel for him. You're a bastard, you know that?"

Malachi felt a jab of fear in his gut. It wouldn't do to rile his daddy, not even for her.

But in a placating voice, Levi said, "Let's just be calm, Miz Harrington. You know what…I'm gonna start calling you Debra now, okay? Cause if you gonna be part of the family, we not gonna stand on formality." He chuckled. "Now, let's get back to Malachi. He's a smart boy, as I'm sure you know. He cares about you, and he'll listen to you. That's why it's so important that you tell him the right things. Like I said, there's gonna be some adjustment, so at first, it'll be kinda hard. But it'll get easier as time goes on, and you'll get to caring for him—and for me and Joshua and Granddaddy too. Right now, though, Malachi's most important. You're here for him, and that's because you done proved what kind of heart you have. You got a good heart, Debra, and that boy needs a good heart looking after him. Mine's just…well, it's had to get hard over the years. So, I'm gonna count on you. I *gotta* be able to count on you. Okay?"

"You know what you can count on, Levi? Me slitting your throat at the first opportunity."

Silence.

Finally, Levi said, "That's your frustration talking, and I don't hold that against you. It's natural. But I can't have that kinda thinking last for long. I'm sure you understand."

"Tell me what you've done with my mother."

A pause. "Let's just say that, if you do right, you'll get her back, safe and sound."

"What's about Russ?"

"That fellow that's been with you? We ain't gonna talk about him. Let's just say you don't never have to think about him ever again."

In a steel-edged voice that Malachi had never heard her use, she said, "I *am* going to kill you. You know that, don't you?"

Then he heard her gasp suddenly.

"Jesus, that *hurts...*"

"I can cause you an awful lot of pain without really 'hurting' you, Debra. I don't wanna do this, but sometimes you gotta inflict a little pain to make a loved one understand."

"Stop...please. Please."

"That's better. Being polite is a good first step."

"Levi, look. I tried to explain this to Malachi, and now I'm going to explain it to you. You're living on borrowed time. Those things..."

"You're not gonna start on 'those things' because I know them a lot better than you. Matter of fact, I bet I know 'em better than Granddaddy. I even talk with them, you know that? I understand just what they doing and why. So don't you start trying to turn us against 'em. It's a waste of your breath."

"You don't understand."

"I'm afraid it's the other way around, Debra."

Malachi heard a metallic *clink* and then a rough sliding sound. His breath caught in his throat because he knew that sound all too well.

"I'm gonna start doing a little adjusting of my own here. I know somebody like you knows about what they call tough love. I'm gonna show you some of that, just so you know how important it is to understand everything I've told you."

Malachi's face began to burn, for he could just picture what his daddy was doing down there. He heard her gasp again, and then she suddenly yelped.

"That's better," Levi growled.

After an excruciating silence, Malachi heard a sudden, loud *crack*, followed by a sharp, agonized hiss, as if Ms. Harrington were trying to hold back a scream.

Another *crack* followed, and another, and another. With each blow, Ms. Harrington exhaled harshly, until finally, the pain became too much for her. It came out first as a pitiful sob, then as a long, mournful cry.

Unable to take the sound any longer, tears streaming from his eyes, Malachi turned and fled upstairs, caring little whether his father heard his thudding footsteps. He raced down the hall, past a new tangle of thorn-covered, metal-skinned vines, which writhed violently in recognition of his presence, and then closed himself in Great-Granddaddy's room. With a little sob of empathy for Ms. Harrington, he slid weakly to the floor with his back against the door.

He knew the caress of his father's belt all too well.

The Lumera curled at his great-grandfather's feet began to glow softly and lifted its huge, skull-like head, electric blue eyes within the deep, shadowed cavities studying him coldly.

When the voice that wasn't a voice, like a musical tone ringing somewhere in his head, said to him, "Hello, Malachi," he screamed like a terrified little girl.

\#

Chapter 20

Some distance from the cabin, Carolyn said to Copeland, "I have to wonder. How do you suppose the Barrows get around even when the landscape changes?"

"They must have some foreknowledge of the alterations…or something. Who the hell knows?"

"Or they're able to bypass the changes in some way," McAllister said. "When we were trying to get to the cabin, we drove for miles and miles, and I've got a keen sense of direction. Several times we ended up somewhere that we'd already been, even though there's no way we could have made a loop. It's like we were in a piece of Asher artwork or something."

"I think you mean Escher," Copeland said.

"Whatever. Anyway, maybe they can somehow go straight from place to place, regardless of the alterations."

"Like they have a key or something," Carolyn suggested.

"Or a guide," Copeland said. "I think that's it. Those creatures guide them where they want to go."

"All I know is that, for now, everything looks normal," McAllister said. "Let's hope it stays that way."

Copeland thought for a moment. "I imagine it means Amos is awake. And that tower—their 'gateway'—hasn't fully anchored yet. Which means they still don't have a complete foothold here."

"That's good, right?"

"I hope so."

As they drove down the deserted road, the darkness seemed as tranquil and benign as it would on any cool spring night; but that fact did nothing to assuage the bitter knowledge that Debra remained at Levi's mercy. If anything, with every passing mile, the ache in Copeland's gut grew sharper, exceeding the pain of his wounds. Over and over, he saw Levi and Joshua bursting in and taking them down, virtually without a struggle, their vow to fight to the end rendered meaningless. If only he had bothered to rig the cabin's doors and windows with some sort of alarm—anything that could have given them an additional moment's notice—then both the Barrow brothers would probably be dead now. He should have applied the same thoroughness seeing to their security that he did with the computer systems for which he was responsible, back in his everyday life.

But if he had succeeded, wouldn't the Lumeras have killed both him and Debra? Perhaps they were alive now only because he had failed.

That bleak realization hardly dulled the sting of his failure. Or his guilt.

The truck rolled into a seemingly dead town. Not one vehicle moved on the roads, nor did a single living human being appear on the streets.

However, the Lumeras had left behind profuse, ghastly evidence of their recent passage. At the gas station where he and Debra had encountered the large gathering of people, several blackened, smoldering masses of hideously suggestive size and shape littered the parking lot. He saw more of them near at the grocery store, the bank, on the lawn of the Baptist church. If any doubts lingered in Copeland's mind that the alien creatures were agents of indiscriminate rather than selective destruction, this appalling carnage removed them. He gripped the rifle tighter as the truck made its way to Yew Line Road, his nerves so taut he had to keep his finger outside the trigger guard for fear of accidentally squeezing off a shot.

They were ascending Yew Line and had almost reached the site where Rodney had been killed when the transformation began.

At first, it looked like a searchlight beam climbing slowly into the sky above the dark trees. Gradually, the beam assumed depth and dimension, as if it were solidifying; then, when it resembled a vast spire reaching for the stars, its surface slowly turned black and reflective, as if it were made of onyx. Finally, numerous pinpoints of light ignited at its apex, like flickering candle flames. Almost instantly, the sky exploded with thousands of swirling, spiraling fireballs of many colors, which spread from the tower in every direction, like troops given the order to disperse.

Copeland became aware of a low, almost subliminal vibration—not much more than a subtle change in the atmosphere—which seemed to seep into his body and close around his heart, causing his pulse and respiration to accelerate slightly. Had he not witnessed the night's transition from ordinary to extraordinary, he might never have sensed the strange physiological effect. But he knew that, over time, the insidious vibration might come to wear upon him, dulling his senses—maybe affecting his thinking.

Another weapon in their supernatural arsenal?

"Good God," McAllister said, glancing back through the open panel. "I think we're in for it here."

The trees, already tall and dense, had become huge, monstrous things, hundreds of feet high, gray and metallic-looking, and they now obscured the Dream Frontier's distant, lofty centerpiece. Hordes of flying Lumeras soared into the monolithic forest and swirled among the rafter-like limbs, some settling into the canopy, presumably to watch the lone, tiny intruder determinedly making its way through their midst. To Copeland, they resembled decorative lights on monumental Christmas trees, winking gaily but mockingly at those who dared to trespass in their domain.

To the right, a single ball of fire came drifting toward them, its blazing body painting the giant boles the color of burnished copper. Copeland raised the rifle to fire, but the thing did not attack them; instead, it remained perhaps a hundred yards away, pacing them as McAllister picked up speed. Ahead, the road extended on and on, its sharp, winding curves completely obliterated: it was now a highway leading straight into a bizarrely beautiful, fatally alluring otherworld.

"Can't we go back?" Carolyn cried.

"It wouldn't matter if we could," Copeland said. "Back, forward, it's all the same. Where we are, space is completely different than what we know. You've been there already. You saw it happen earlier tonight."

"Not like this," she said with a shudder. "Not with all those… things…out there!"

"We keep going," McAllister said, shoving the accelerator to the floor. "One way or the other, we've got to finish this."

Copeland hunkered down behind the cab to keep the wind from buffeting him mercilessly. Another airborne Lumera zoomed above the truck and stationed itself directly overhead, just beyond the range of his fire. And now, far to his left, a third one appeared, passing like a brilliant ghost through the trees, keeping pace with the truck. After a minute, he realized that the creatures seemed intent not on stopping them, but on ensuring that they arrived at their destination.

"I guess we've got guides of our own," McAllister quipped, apparently having reached the same conclusion.

"They seem to enjoy toying with us," Copeland said. "I almost wish they'd come at us outright."

"No," Carolyn said, giving him a reproachful frown. "Every minute they give us, that's another minute in our favor."

He nodded to her in acknowledgment; under his breath, he said, "You've been married to that man way too long."

Soon, he saw that the road curved to the left, and the huge trees began to give way to mundane pines. The lay of the land here looked vaguely familiar, and he realized that they were coming out right at the edge of the Barrows' property. He reached in and tapped McAllister on the shoulder.

"Slow down. You know where we are, right?"

"Holy shit, yeah, I do."

The truck emerged from the forest at high speed, but McAllister slowed it to a crawl as the nightmarish hulk of the Barrow house appeared around a curve to the left. A single, murky yellow light burned over the front door, but all the windows were dark.

"I suppose our escort left them no doubt as to our coming."

Copeland shrugged. "Maybe. For all we know, the Lumeras have their own reasons. Maybe they don't involve the Barrows at all."

McAllister gave him a doubtful glance. "Well, there's a hopeful spin for you." He stopped the truck beside the road, not far from the spot where Copeland had hidden his car on his first trip here. A quick inspection of their surroundings revealed that their attendant Lumeras had vanished; in fact, only a few small, distant fireflies continued to swirl around the onyx tower, which they could again see looming vast and ominous above the landscape.

Copeland had just hopped out of the truck when a low, heavy *thrum* seemed to creep through the earth, vibrating faintly beneath his feet. It came again a moment later, and again after that, becoming a slow, rhythmic pulse just at the edge of his hearing.

"Almost like a heartbeat," Carolyn said, gazing thoughtfully at the tower's apex. "Maybe that thing's actually alive."

"Then it needs to die," McAllister said, his voice a little weaker than usual.

Copeland started across the broad, dark field of tall grass that extended to the Barrow's front yard, his companions close behind him. Nothing moved anywhere near the house, and they saw no telltale glowing embers either within or without. Copeland soon made out the shape of Levi's pickup parked in the driveway— so there was no question where they would find Debra. As they drew nearer to the house, they fanned out, moving slowly, guns at the ready. McAllister shifted course and made his way toward the backyard, while Carolyn pressed herself close to the house near the ground-floor window. Copeland crept toward the front door. He glanced toward McAllister, who sent him a thumbs-up, indicating the yard was clear.

But Carolyn held up a hand, and she whispered to him, "I hear something. Music, it sounds like."

Copeland halted and stood listening; at first, he detected only the low, distant whisper of the wind and the steady *thrumming* beneath his feet. Gradually, though, he became aware of a delicate chiming sound, which reminded him of the church bells he had heard from his window on his first morning at Lynette's. The chimes rose and fell with an odd, wandering cadence, now and again joined by other tones ringing in gentle harmony. The music grew steadily louder, and the bell-like sounds gave way to soft, feminine voices; then, like the voice of some great beast, a dark, baritone chorus rose to underscore the sopranos, blending in a kind of dissonant, empyreal fugue. It came not from the house but somewhere beyond it.

The same unearthly music he had heard at Lynette's house the day before.

No telling what it meant, he thought, and he didn't have the time or inclination to speculate. They had to get inside, and quickly; doing it quietly, however, seemed unlikely. Still, he didn't want to betray their presence until the very last second. Where would Levi have taken Debra? Most likely to an upstairs room—perhaps his bedroom. The most direct way was through the front door, so he took a few steps forward, crouching to remain beneath the view of anyone spying from the window. He turned to Carolyn and motioned for her to join him; in turn, she gestured to her husband at the edge of the backyard.

During the brief moment he was facing away from the front door, he realized he felt a presence near him. Turning quickly, raising his rifle as he did, he found a dark silhouette standing directly in front of him—and his heart skipped a beat. Then a solid blow knocked the Remington out of his hands, setting him partially off balance. Though he recovered quickly, as his right hand went to draw the Ruger from his belt, a powerful hand immediately intercepted it, and something hit him in the face like the engine of a freight train. He staggered as new agony exploded through his skull, and an iron hand clutched his throat, dragged him forward, and propelled him through the front door, which now gaped wide like the maw of a ravenous monster. He heard Carolyn cry, "Russ!" but then the door slammed shut behind him, echoing in his brain like a violent thunderclap.

He found himself sprawled on the ratty carpet of the Barrows' living room, stars reeling madly before his eyes. Painfully drawing himself to a sitting position, he saw Levi standing at the front door, a crooked smile etched on his craggy face, his head cocked in an attitude of listening. Outside, both the McAllisters called his name, and he heard several sharp blows on the wooden door.

Levi glared at Copeland. "Since you're here and my brother ain't, I gotta expect he's dead. And since you weren't in no position to do it yourself, I gotta conclude it was them what killed him."

For a second, silence fell beyond the door, and Levi deftly sidestepped just before a portion of the door around the knob exploded inward with a deafening *boom*. Copeland felt a thrill of hope as the door burst open to reveal McAllister standing on the stoop, pumping his shotgun in preparation to fire again. But in the brief second before Levi kicked the ruined wooden slab shut, Copeland saw a brilliant orange glow rising behind his friend, transforming his body into a featureless, backlit silhouette. Now, from beyond the door, a duet of heart-rending screams rose as the Lumeras fell upon the McAllisters. On and on the screams went, gradually diminishing in volume as the monsters dragged away their prey, apparently still struggling.

A moment later, the screams went abruptly silent, only to be replaced by the excited, insect-like chattering of the Lumera horde.

Copeland's heart nearly burst, and as his watering eyes rolled toward Levi, he felt the last threads of his sanity snapping. A rush of adrenaline propelled him forward, and before he realized what he was doing, he found his body flying through the air, which caught Levi unprepared and bulldozed him to the floor. His fists pummeled the other's face, the dull, gratifying *crunch* of his knuckles meeting bone the only thing that registered in his ears. He brought one arm down on Levi's adam's apple, pinning his head to the floor, and his other hand came down with murderous force to smash the fallen man's nose. The blow sent blood spurting from his nostrils. Levi shook his head wildly, choking on his own blood, snorting and huffing as he writhed desperately, trying to dislodge his attacker. One of his hands managed to slither toward Copeland's face, and with a frantic effort, he ripped the bandage from his wound and backhanded Copeland across the cheek.

The pain that arced through his skull, down his neck, and into his back nearly knocked him senseless. His arm involuntarily drew from Levi's neck and went to cover his face. With a sudden thrust of his head, Levi's forehead met Copeland's chin, which snapped his head backward and offered Levi just enough leverage to throw him off. Through his pain, Copeland realized that his adversary was free, and he scrambled backward just in time to avoid the fist that would have shattered his adam's apple. Righting himself quickly, he lowered his head and, with all his weight behind him, rammed it into Levi's gut, which drove the air out of the man's lungs with an explosive "gaah!" Levi flew backward and crashed to the floor, his weight shaking the foundations of the house. As Levi struggled to draw himself up, Copeland again fell upon him and closed his hands around his throat.

Tighter. *Tighter.*

Levi's eyes rolled back in his head as consciousness began to fade, and Copeland knew he had him.

Then he felt a dull thud at the back of his head—barely sufficient to register, or so he thought, until he realized that someone—or something—had taken hold of his collar and was dragging his body backward. His hands jerked away from Levi's throat and flailed madly as he went sailing through the air and crashed in an agonized heap at the bottom of the stairs. The room spun wildly, and all he could do now was try to catch his breath and somehow hold onto consciousness. He heard a vague shuffling sound as Levi pulled himself to his feet with assistance from another figure, which seemed to have magically appeared in the room.

"You hurt my daddy, you sumbitch," a low, quavering voice said. "You gonna die now. You got that, you sumbitch? You gonna die."

Instead of slowing, the room whirled even faster, and the light grew steadily dimmer. He glimpsed Levi's hate-filled eyes glaring down at him, and then everything melted into a meaningless chiaroscuro of gray and black. He realized his head was sinking to the floor, and when his cheek hit the foul-smelling carpet, he swore he heard a violent rattling, as if something inside his skull had been jarred loose.

The world began to fade to black, but not before he heard Levi say, "Naw, Malachi, he ain't gonna die. Not yet. But he's gonna wish he was dead. Yessir, he's gonna wish we'd kill him right here and now."

#

Chapter 21

"**M**r. Copeland?"

The voice was low and masculine, gentle in tone, so unlike the voices he had been hearing in the moments before he lost consciousness. Hearing seemed to be his only functioning sense, for he could see and feel nothing. He sensed he might be lying on his back, but he couldn't tell whether the surface beneath him was a soft bed or a concrete floor. He felt his eyelids creak open, but he perceived only a dull, formless light somewhere nearby; no recognizable objects or shapes. Gradually, he became aware of the pain in his body—primarily in his face. With a supreme effort, he willed one of his fingers to move; he thought he might have succeeded.

"Don't make any sudden movements, Mr. Copeland. Your body's suffered a fair trauma. It's gonna take a little time for you to recover."

The voice sounded concerned, reassuring. Was the nightmare finally over? Everything that had happened up to the point that he blacked out seemed to be coming back to him, perhaps too vivdly. He remembered Debra's abduction and the McAllisters coming to his rescue—only to be taken by the alien things in league with the Barrows. He had fought with Levi and nearly killed him, but someone arrived on the scene to save him.

The boy, Malachi.

Copeland opened his mouth and exhaled, testing the air as it passed over his vocal cords. "Where am I?" he managed to whisper.

"Don't you fret, now. Things will be made clear to you directly. In the meantime, just rest, and don't pain yourself needlessly. Save your strength."

He shifted slightly, and now he could discern a hard, unyielding surface behind his back. *Damn,* he thought, and his spirit plummeted. *So much for being back in a safe, warm bed.* He drew a deep breath, and with supreme effort, raised his upper body until he could prop most of his weight on his elbows. He heard a strange, hollow rustling noise and glimpsed a spontaneous, rapid movement—not in any one place, but seemingly all around him.

Slowly, his eyes began to take in his surroundings. He lay on the floor of a good-sized room, facing a familiar figure seated in a broad, nearly collapsing wing chair. The last time Copeland had seen him, the chair's grotesque occupant had been asleep. And before, the walls of the master bedroom had not been completely covered by writhing, metallic-looking vines covered with long, razor-sharp barbs. The alien vegetation—the only term he could think to apply to it—rustled and shifted nervously, as if cognizant of an unfriendly presence. The seated man's huge, football-shaped head cocked slightly as tiny pig eyes beneath a bony brow studied him intently.

After a time, the lips of the repulsively wide mouth parted, and a paradoxically soft voice came out. "Hello. I'm Amos Barrow."

"So, awake at last," Copeland replied in a measured tone. He managed to pull himself to a sitting position. "And from the looks of this room, I suppose that means there's no sending your 'new neighbors' back where they came from."

"An interesting point," the eldest Barrow said. "In fact, you bringing it up is the reason you're still alive. I want to talk to you."

"Well, I guess I'm not going anywhere."

"Not right away, nope. I guess you know that my grandson—my surviving grandson," he added sharply, "has taken a shine to a young lady of your acquaintance. We had us a nice little talk with her, but we didn't quite get the answers we're looking for. Maybe you can do better."

At the mention of Debra, new apprehension clutched his chest. He stared spitefully at Amos for a long moment and said, "Even if I could, I don't know that I'd be inclined to offer you a thing."

"Mr. Copeland, I been something of a businessman all my life. Maybe not the kind you'd be accustomed to dealing with, but I do know business. And I expect we might be able to come to an arrangement, if you willing to be reasonable."

"Forgive me," Copeland said softly, "but nothing I've seen would give me reason to believe that any of you are 'reasonable.'"

"Let's not be judgmental," Amos said in a paternal tone. "About every soul in this town has been judgmental for as long as the Barrow family has lived here—since long before my day. And that particular failing is pretty much why things have come to what they come to." He stared thoughtfully at Copeland for a minute before continuing, his tiny eyes revealing a surprising depth of intellect behind them. "Some years ago, I lost my boy in a war that he didn't have no business fighting in. But he went, and…well, that was that. Anyway, we come to find that a comrade of his weren't like these people we'd known all our lives. This man was thoughtful…and generous. He knew he couldn't put right what caused me to lose my son, but he wanted to settle up whatever way he could. Least, that's how it seemed, and for a long time, he was a real help to this family. Even saw us through some difficult times, he did. In the end, though, turned out he weren't no different than them others. Maybe even worse, cause he came with false pretenses. Or let's put it this way: I like to think he started out right-headed, but then something went wrong. Whatever it was, we believed in him, and then we was betrayed. You knew old Major Martin, didn't you?"

"Yeah. I did."

"Tell me about how well you knew him."

"Well, what can I say? Only in passing, really. I barely got to spend any time at all with him before he...before *you*..."

"Now, now, Mr. Copeland. I know that he must've shared some of his secrets with you. Otherwise, you wouldn't have known nothing about us. Or our new neighbors."

"All he did was fill in some blanks. Most of what Debra and I learned, we discovered on our own."

"Yeah, I'm told you got into this house a while ago. Damn stupid, Mr. Copeland, but I gotta admire your drive. Anyway. It's them blanks you mention that I'm most interested in. I want to know just how much you know. You may have something that'll help and you don't even realize it. If we talk about it like reasonable people, maybe...like I said...we can come to an arrangement."

"Such as?"

"Such as maybe you won't have to die like your friends out there—them ones that killed my grandson." Amos now leaned forward, his jaw working furiously back and forth, one eye gleaming dangerously. "Levi said it weren't you, which is the only reason you still here to be talking to me. It was *them* that killed my Joshua, weren't it?"

Copeland fixed his glare on the other, unwilling to allow his simmering dread to get the better of him. He finally nodded. "Yeah. But I'll tell you this: if I'd had the chance...I *would* have killed him. I'd have killed Levi, too. You know that, don't you?"

For the first time, Amos looked as if he might rise from his chair and attack him, and Copeland knew there was no way he could fend off even this ungainly old man. But Amos's red-hot eyes slowly cooled, and he relaxed, taking a few deep, noisy breaths. "Looking at you, I reckon you got reason to be angry. What you don't understand, Mr. Copeland, is that *you* got yourself into this mess. You blaming the wrong people."

"Let me tell you something," he said sharply, infused with a new, angry fire. "The reason I'm here is because your 'new neighbors' killed an innocent boy—my nephew. God knows how many others. People who've never done a damned thing to you. Don't tell me about who's to blame for any of this." He spat on the floor. Then he said softly. "You know what, you big, fat piece of shit? Let's forget about any arrangements. Just do what you have to. You're going to get yours anyway."

Amos's face no longer betrayed the slightest hint of emotion. "If you refuse, you know you got nothing to look forward to but a lot of suffering, right? You in a completely different world now. The Lumeras don't just kill you, Mr. Copeland. They slowly consume you, all the way down to your soul. You'll still be screaming long after me and the rest of the world have all passed on." He flashed a sardonic smile and leaned forward. "Is that what you want?"

"Guess what, Amos. I'm afraid that is what *you* have to look forward to. Do you think you are the master of this world? Why would creatures like those even consider sharing power with you? They only let you live as long as you suit their purpose. You're awake, but they haven't vanished. That means you can't get rid of them now. What happens when they decide they don't need you anymore?"

"Is this what Major Martin told you?"

Reluctantly, he nodded. "It was his belief."

Amos grinned broadly. "Of course he would tell you that. *He* wanted the power all along, but it was too late. He handed us the only means to open the door to the dream worlds, and when he discovered what he had given away, he tried to take it back—and he failed. He was simply a bitter old man."

"Then why are you so curious about what he might have told me?"

"Because I want to know if there's another..." The huge figure fell silent suddenly and gave Copeland a thoughtful stare. "No, sir. I don't believe we'll be coming to any arrangement."

"What were you about to say? Are you admitting there's something you don't know? You see, Amos, you are vulnerable. Now let me tell you something. If you know any way to send those things back where they came from, you'd better do it now. Because they're not going to let you to be part of their world for long. They're going to eat you alive."

"Your conclusions are amusing. Mr. Copeland, let me show you just how wrong you are."

Amos held up one hand, a maestro preparing to conduct an orchestra, and suddenly the living mass of creepers exploded into rustling, writhing motion, and some tore away from the wall to slither across the floor toward Copeland. One of the barbed cords whipped at him with a metallic snapping sound, and he backed away just in time to avoid a vicious slash across the chest.

"Because of what I did for them, they've promised me my place here. They got their own rules they abide by, Mr. Copeland, which I've witnessed firsthand over many years. I've walked in their world time and again, and I've learned all their ways. I—and my family—got nothing to fear from them. Do you understand? Nothing! You, on the other hand...got everything to fear. Because your time is up."

The door opened and Levi Barrow stepped inside, blithely disregarding the wicked-looking tendrils that crept within inches of his legs. Amos looked coolly at his grandson and asked, "You still hear it out there?"

Levi nodded. "Yessir, sure do."

Amos drew a long, contemplative breath and looked back at Copeland. "You got one last chance to save yourself. All you got to do is answer me one question."

Knowing he could offer nothing of value, he shrugged. "And what would that be?"

"That music out there. Tell me where it comes from."

Copeland felt his jaw drop. So...Amos did admit he didn't understand everything. He gestured toward the living creepers. "Something of theirs, wouldn't you say?"

"No," Amos said, his eyes turning somewhere far away. "No, it isn't. So...Major Martin gave you no clue?"

"I'm afraid not."

"Well, then." He made a dismissive gesture and said to Levi, "Do what you want with him. Goodbye, Mr. Copeland."

An iron claw fell upon his shoulder. "Get on your feet," Levi said, his voice as sharp as a razor. "Either you walk or I drag you."

With difficulty, he managed to pull himself up, his heart racing. Without looking at Levi, he said, "It doesn't matter what you do to me. It won't change anything, as far as you're concerned."

"It's not *us* you have to worry about," Levi said, tugging him by the collar. "Come on, now."

Copeland didn't have the strength to resist as the other led him out of the master bedroom, down the hall, and to the stairway. He stumbled down the steep, narrow stairs, and when he paused at the bottom, he felt something sharp gouge him in the back; Levi was holding a knife. As he allowed the other to pulled him through the kitchen and to the cellar stairs, he took a quick inventory of his injuries, his remaining strength, his mental clarity. Every muscle in his body ached like hell, but nothing was broken, and his senses seemed to be gradually sharpening. He was still no match for Levi...but if he could trip him on the rickety stairs, he *might* gain some advantage.

Levi shoved him roughly through the door, forcing him to go first, which halfway foiled his plan. He tensed one arm, preparing to drive his elbow hard into Levi's gut, but then the fingers on his shoulder dug in mercilessly, and he again felt the knife press into his back. "I know what you're thinking. You try anything, you won't even get as far as the bottom alive." With a silent curse, he relaxed slightly, and two steps from the bottom, Levi shoved him hard. He landed hard on one foot and tottered for a second, but he managed to keep his balance.

"Russ!"

By the dull orange glow of a huge Lumera nestled in the far corner, he saw Debra a few feet away, cowering from the creature, which appeared to be keeping watch over her. It slowly turned its skull-like head and fixed its deep-set, glistening sapphire eyes on him. The barbs on its back lifted slightly and made a soft clicking sound.

"See, it doesn't like you," Levi said with a harsh laugh. "It and me, though, we understand each other. As you can see, it makes sure she don't do anything foolish while I'm not around."

Copeland gazed at Levi's eyes and, just for a second, caught a flash of uncertainty deep inside them.

Yes...he is still afraid of them.

"You all right, Debra?"

She nodded, and he saw that her cheeks were streaked with tears. "Russ, he doesn't trust those things either. I've tried to reason with him every way I can."

"You're still thinking about things the old way," Levi said to her. "Everything's changed now, and you gonna understand that soon enough. Your friend here, he's gonna help you. In fact, it's gonna be the last thing he ever does."

"Levi…" she began, but he held up a hand.

"I been trying to teach her to look at things in a new light," he said to Copeland, with cunning civility. "Maybe there's something we can do a lil less drastic than what I originally thought."

"The only way I can help you is if you understand that you've got to get out of this. You've got to send them back."

"Well, naw, that ain't quite it. It's like this. The lil girl is having a hard time understanding why she's here and how she's gonna be helping me with Malachi from here on out. Maybe she'll listen to you, though, since you still appeal to her old way of thinking. Here's what we'll aim to do. You make her understand that she's gonna be teaching Malachi, just like she always done, but in the new way, the way things are now. She's gonna stay here, and she'll be safe with me. Now…you help with this, and I'll make you a bargain. I'll cut you loose, and there won't be nothing more against you. You'll have to make your own way out there, and there ain't no guarantees, but I'll see to it that them ones leave you be. You won't have to worry bout them no more. What you say to that, mister smart man?"

Copeland gazed at the other in disbelief. He realized that here, in the cellar, he could feel the deep, rhythmic pulsing beneath his feet. It seemed considerably stronger now. "Let's just say…for argument's sake…that I don't see things your way."

Levi shrugged. "Then the lil girl's gonna get to watch that thing do what it does best. To you. Right here. Which just means I have to go about making her understand things in my own way— which I reckon neither of us will enjoy very much."

With a thoughtful glance at Debra, he drew up his last reserve of courage and said, "Levi, I'd do whatever it takes to see that Debra stays alive and safe. But you know damn well you'd never in a million years let me go free, even if I did exactly what you ask. And again, for argument's sake...let's just say you did. It wouldn't make the slightest difference. As I told Amos upstairs... you're living on borrowed time. I wouldn't be at all surprised if, by sundown tonight, your whole family is dead. You, your grandfather...even your son."

As fast as a bullet, Levi's hand came up and struck him across his cut cheek. The sudden pain floored him, and he didn't even feel it when his head struck concrete. All he knew was another explosion of stars in his vision, an arc of agony from his skull to his toes, and this time, he thought, he wasn't getting up again. He heard Levi mumble something unintelligible, followed by a metallic clicking sound.

Levi was directing the Lumera to attack him.

Beneath his hands, he felt the throbbing pulse in the earth, now so deep and powerful that it felt like something trying to thrust its way up through the concrete floor. When the chattering voice of the Lumera began to rise, he knew it was not in response to Levi's summons, but to something else altogether. He desperately shook his head, trying to clear his vision; and when he finally saw the madman standing before him, face ashen and eyes raised to the ceiling, he knew that something new—and totally unforeseen— was affecting the creature.

The door at the top of the stairs flew open, and Malachi's voice drifted down. "Daddy, you gotta see this. Come up now! Hurry! Hurry!"

Copeland glanced at the Lumera, which had lifted its head toward the ceiling, its focus no longer on any of them. Its mandible hung open, and hot, viscous fluid leaked slowly from its maw and dripped, steaming, to the floor. The barbs on its back had extended fully.

Levi started toward the stairs, scowling disgustedly at the Lumera; but then he stopped, turned to Copeland, and raised his knife. "Know what?" he said softly. "I got no more time to waste on you. The hell with you and everything about you."

Copeland managed to roll onto his back and raise his arms as Levi came at him. The heavy body fell upon him and the knife worked its way through his defenses until it reached his throat. Levi's knees on his shoulders prevented his hands from reaching the weapon, and one arm came down on his forehead, pressing hard to keep his head immobile. The blade began to press against his adam's apple.

"Yeah, I'm gonna cut your head right off. How you like that?"

Then, with a shocked cry, Levi tumbled away as something hit him with great force. The knife went flying and clattered to the floor halfway across the room. Levi's head made a grotesque thudding sound as it struck the concrete.

Debra now lay atop him, her fingers viciously encircling his throat, her long nails digging deeply into his flesh. Realizing the Lumera was no longer watching her, she had launched herself at him and taken him by surprise. Levi tried to throw her off, but as lithe and tenacious as a cat, she clung to him, one leg locked around his. She managed to lift his head once and smash it against the floor; but now, infuriated by the indignity and swearing boisterously, he thrust his torso upward and dislodged her. Then he scrambled back and threw himself on top of her, pinning her beneath his weight.

At the sight of Levi's escape, Copeland somehow found the strength to draw himself to his knees…to his feet…and take a step forward.

Levi raised a hand to strike Debra viciously across the face. Copeland deftly caught it and twisted.

With a roar of surprise, Levi pitched away from her but quickly rose to counterattack. Copeland lunged forward, caught the other in a fierce stranglehold, and with every remaining ounce of energy, hurled him toward the craning Lumera, whose body had begun to glow a bright, fiery crimson. With a shocked cry, Levi crashed into the ten-foot horror, his weight sending the worm-like body toppling heavily to the floor.

The gigantic skull head rose, its eyes flashing like jewels. Then it dove forward, only to rise again with Levi's head clamped firmly between its great jaws. Muffled screams trickled out from the great maw, and Levi's legs thrashed furiously as he fought to disengage himself. But his struggles seemed to spur the creature on, for now it vomited a stream of vile, reddish fluid over his upper body, and his screams grew more intense, his flailing limbs wilder. Levi's clothes began to ooze smoke, and the exposed skin of his arms quickly blackened and swelled, like marshmallow beneath a blowtorch. His struggles gradually weakened, but his cries gurgled forth unabated—and Copeland noticed that, with Levi's every agonized scream, the Lumera's eyes pulsed brightly, as if the thing were deriving pleasure—or nourishment—from his very pain.

"Jesus, God," he whispered in disgust. He took Debra in his arms and pulled her to her feet. "Come on, let's get out of here."

As they struggled up the stairs, he noticed that she moved her legs tentatively. Painfully. "What's wrong? Are you hurt?"

She drew a deep breath. "I'll be all right. The bastard beat me pretty good."

When they reached the top of the stairs, he collapsed on the floor, his energy spent, his eyes burning with tears. Debra knelt next to him and placed a comforting hand on his hammering heart. "Rest, but only for a second. Only for a second."

The awful, ceaseless sound of Levi's death throes drilled cruelly into his ears. He tried to block it out by whispering to himself, "It's only justice. It's only justice." It was what Levi had planned for him. It was how Lynette and her young, innocent son had been killed. The McAllisters. And countless others.

He felt no satisfaction when the screams finally dwindled and died. Nor did he feel an ounce of remorse.

"Let's get out of here," Debra whispered. "That thing could come after us now."

Just as they were pulling themselves to their feet, a figure appeared in front of them and blocked their passage, its eyes blazing accusingly at them.

"Where's my daddy?"

It seemed forever that their eyes remained locked under a pall of expectant silence. At last, Debra said to the boy, "He's gone, Malachi. That thing down there…it killed him. Just as I told you it would."

Malachi's bony jaw dropped and his lower lip began to quiver. He continued to stare blankly at her, and finally a teardrop rolled down one cheek. "You're lying." His voice cracked slightly. "You're lying to me, and you know it."

"It's the truth, Malachi. Now, we're getting out of here. And you'd better come with us because that creature will turn on you, just like it turned on your father."

"Liar!" he cried and swiped a vicious hand across her face. She grimaced but did not sway. As a red patch formed on her cheek in the shape of his hand, his features melted into an expression of pain. "Oh, no, no. Miz Harrington, I—"

"Never mind that. Move!" she cried as a harsh, insect-like chattering sound began to creep from below. She pushed past him, but then grabbed his wrist and attempted to tow him behind her. He pulled free with a sob.

"I ain't going nowhere without my daddy."

"Malachi," Copeland said softly. "It's too late. At least save yourself."

"Fuck you, mister. This is all your damn fault."

Copeland gazed at the boy, trying to suppress the anger that came seething up from his gut. Finally, with a shrug, he said, "Have it your way, son," and took Debra by the arm. "Let's get out of here."

"Russ…"

"Let him go."

Malachi bolted down the stairs, calling, "Daddy! Daddy!" He vanished below, but then he cried, "Oh, no! Oh, GOD!"

Debra turned. "Russ, we can't leave him."

Malachi began to scream, and the Lumera trilled in exultation.

"It's too late."

"No…please no," Debra whispered, but she offered no resistance when Copeland pulled her with him to the back door. He tore it open and tugged her into the cold dawn; then his legs gave way again and they went sprawling onto the brittle grass, where they lay for a long minute, enervated and panting.

The rising sun, just peeping over the ridge to the east, was the color of quicksilver, the sky a uniform, dusky violet. No clouds scudded above them, yet huge, amorphous shadows rushed wildly over the gray-tinted ground, as the lofty, metallic-looking trees clacked noisily together in a gusting wind. Above the onyx tower, which loomed dizzyingly over the landscape, numerous, multicolored fireballs wheeled through the air, leaving trails of smoke like nonsensical skywriting. Just beneath the sound of the wind, the eerie music they had earlier heard resonated like a chorus from a distant, unholy church.

"My God, everything's changed," Debra said, her awestruck eyes blazing. She jerked a thumb at the house. "In there, out here… it makes no difference, does it? We're doomed just the same."

"I'll take my chances anywhere but there," he said. But his gaze could not leave the strange shadows, which slid ominously over the land to gather at a point near the base of the eastern ridge. Slowly, he rose and began to walk, only to discover, to his shock, that he felt remarkably light—as if gravity's pull had decreased by half.

Debra joined him a moment later, her gaze on the steadily merging shadows. "What do you make of that?"

"Not sure we really want to know." He pointed to the road that disappeared into the metallic forest, he said, "Candle's truck is somewhere up that way—if it's even still there. But I'm sure he had the keys with him."

"Even if we could get away…where would we go?"

Copeland shrugged, overwhelmed, lost, helpless. No shelter, no safety. Above the rushing wind and quavering strains of music, he thought he heard a voice calling out. He could not make out any words.

"Hear that?" Debra asked.

"Yeah," he said, his eyes roving. As they fell upon the Barrow house, which no longer appeared menacing but small and vulnerable, he caught sight of a figure framed in an upstairs window. "There. It's Amos."

The eldest and last of the Barrows stood in the open window, shouting something incomprehensible. At first, Copeland thought the voice was directed at them, but then he saw Amos lift a fist and shake it at the sky. Gradually, he began to make out the distorted words.

"I AM the master here! I AM the master!"

Debra glanced at him. "You think he's frustrated?"

"Terminally."

"I banish you!" came the furious voice from the window. "You got no place here, and I order you back! Back, I say!"

At first, Copeland thought he was shouting at the airborne Lumeras, but then he realized that Amos's thrusting fist was aimed at the ridge where the drifting shadows continued to gather. Now, turning to regard the object of the old man's ire, he felt a new thrill of fear as he saw a new, dark shape developing along the crest of the ridge.

"Jesus, look at that."

The shadows had converged and congealed like a massive pool of black blood, which suddenly erupted and hurled hundreds of thin, inky threads across the face of the deep purple canopy. As if alive, the ghostly strands climbed to all corners of the sky, broadening and darkening as they moved, soon becoming thick, fibrous, and jointed. Miles and miles they must extend, Copeland thought, for some of them had reached a zenith above their heads, while others groped toward the horizon in every direction. The filaments flexed, as if gathering strength, and then, arching like spider's legs, began to draw the black, globular nucleus high into the sky.

Amos's voice took on a new, keening pitch as the threadlike arms closed steadily on the tower. From every point of the landscape, the insect trills of Lumeras rose in shrill defiance, and thousands of fireballs materialized in the sky, to rocket like guided projectiles toward the heart of the spreading horror. As they struck the black mass, they exploded like New Year's fireworks, sending earthward a rain of glittering sparks, which struck the ground and blinked out of existence.

Copeland felt the heavy pulse in the earth quickening like a panicked heartbeat. The tips of the groping arms appeared to clutch the very fabric of the sky and, with a sharp, jerking motion, tore it open, releasing from the crevasses an array of black, hazy beams, like negative images of the sun's rays. These fell deliberately upon the tower's onyx surfaces, and everywhere they struck, gray smoke oozed from the stone. Simultaneously, the subterranean throbbing became a maddened pounding, and the ethereal chorale rose in volume and fervor.

Debra's hand closed on his arm. "Something's coming out," she said, and he turned to gaze after her pointing hand.

From the darkness beneath the metallic trees at the edge of the nearby field, a pinpoint of light appeared, which he took to be the eye of a Lumera. But as it drew nearer, he realized it was something else: a small, luminous globe that drifted through the darkness, like yet unlike the glowing, airborne creatures. This one had a pale, jade green hue and was surrounded by a number of smaller, sparkling satellites, which orbited it at dazzling speed. The thing made a beeline straight for them, and Copeland realized then that there could be no escape. No place to run, no weapons to defend themselves. Debra sucked in a frightened breath, and his feet automatically propelled him backward. As the thing drew nearer, it ballooned to massive size—easily larger than the both of them—and swiftly closed over and around their bodies.

He felt Debra's hand fiercely gripping his. Then a wave of pure ice pummeled his face, stole his breath, his eyesight, his hearing. With his final exhalation, all sensation took its leave, though he perceived that his body was dissolving in the jade green sea. Strangely, along with his senses, fear also left. He knew what it felt like to die.

For a brief few moments, he thought he knew the ultimate peace.

#

Chapter 22

It seemed only an instant later that sight, sound, smell, and touch returned to him.

Except he could see and hear nothing. The world had gone dark and silent. But he had returned to the world of the living, that much he felt certain. The air held an odd mélange of scents: the cool tang of mildew, the harsh bite of mothballs, and the sweet, distinctive aroma of cedar.

He could feel Debra's hand still clamped in his.

"Where the hell are we?" she whispered. "How did we get here?"

As his eyes slowly adjusted, he found the darkness not quite complete. Some indeterminate distance ahead, a few tiny slivers of violet dawn cut through the darkness—a window, covered or painted over, he thought. He detected other shapes nearby: stacked boxes and crates, a broken wooden chair, an angled silhouette that resembled a teetering piano.

"Wait," came Debra's voice. "I know where we are. It's the attic of the church. We're in the church!"

Copeland scanned their dim surroundings and discerned no sign of the luminous globe, which by all appearances had delivered them here. For a few seconds, he almost dared to believe he had just roused from a vivid, terrible nightmare. Then a faint, slow, shuffling noise crept from a distant corner, followed a soft intake of breath—human, he thought...he *hoped*. Suddenly, a light flared in the room—an electric, blue-green miniature sun, again familiar, yet different from the *Zuso Xhan Mat* with which Amos Barrow had changed the world.

Something moved near the blocked window, and the glowing gem rose higher into the air. Its gently pulsing glow revealed a crooked figure, which now shambled toward them, bearing the supernal lamp before him in clasped hands.

"Oh, my God," Debra whispered. "Dad. Dad!"

She dashed forward and nearly tackled the older man, who protectively cradled the stone as if it were a precious piece of sculpted glass. His face looked haggard, his eyes dim and exhausted, but he offered his daughter a faint smile as her arms encircled his body.

"Easy, easy," he said, his voice weak and hoarse. "First things first. We've got to stop what's happening."

"I thought you were dead," Debra whispered, tears streaming from her eyes.

"No. I was...protected." He cast his gaze at the glowing stone. To her sudden gape of disbelief, he nodded reassuringly. "I had to keep this a secret from the Barrows at all costs. I didn't dare reveal it, even to you."

"Another one?" Copeland asked dubiously, eyeing the gem warily. "Is...*that*...what brought us here?"

"Yes. I can't explain the details now. But suffice it to say it's how I've come to know about the things we're dealing with." Martin leaned closer to look at his face. "Good God, Russ. The Barrows did that to you, didn't they?"

"I'll be all right. I shouldn't care to shave right away."

"I'm sorry."

He shrugged off the older man's concern. "Tell me. The way we were brought here. That's how the Barrows have been able to go from place to place after the land changed. Isn't it?"

"More or less. Amos is far more expert at manipulating these... openings. With you, I must admit, I was...fortunate."

Copeland blew a long breath. "I'd like to say that's a relief."

"Dad, what is that in the sky—the thing the Lumeras are attacking?"

"That," he said with slow deliberation, "is the product of a new Dream Frontier."

Her jaw dropped again in consternation, but he held up a placating hand.

"There was only one way to counter what Amos Barrow has done, and that was to open a second doorway. Two such spheres cannot exist in the same space."

"My God, Dad. How many of those jewels are there?"

"Whether there are others...I have no idea." His ragged voice was barely audible. "It took me years to find this one. It was in Myanmar—Burma—a few hundred miles from where we found the first."

"Now I know what Amos was trying to get me to tell him," Copeland said.

"Which is why I couldn't possibly reveal it to either of you. He *would* have gotten it out of you, Russ. Or Debra."

"Have you been here since last night?" she asked.

He nodded. "I needed someplace where I could fully attune myself to this thing. Figured it was relatively safe here. Had a close call yesterday afternoon, though. When the stone became active, Levi came to investigate. Bastard killed Loretta Gleasman. Ran her down with his truck, just before I came to see you. God, I wanted to tell you everything then...but I just couldn't."

"Yesterday afternoon." Debra stared into space for a moment. "That's when that music first started, right?"

"Yes. It comes from the new Dream Frontier."

"You activated this thing yourself?" Copeland asked.

"Yes."

"If what you told us before was true, don't you have to be asleep and dreaming to control it?"

The older man did not answer right away. Finally, he said,

"Yes. It functions more or less like the other."

"So, right now it's inactive. But eventually, this one will anchor itself here, just like the other. Am I understanding right?"

"Essentially."

"Then…even if this thing destroys the Lumeras, won't it be just as dangerous?"

"Russ, I had no choice. If I hadn't done this…" Martin's chiseled granite face looked as if it might shatter. "At least I've bought us some time."

Debra stared at him in shock. "At what cost, Dad?"

Rather than face the rising fire in his daughter's eyes, he returned his attention to Copeland. "You were inside the Barrows' house, I take it?"

"We barely got out," he said. "There's at least one Lumera left in there, and God knows what else. But Amos is the only one of them left alive."

Martin held up the glowing stone and gazed into it with haunted eyes. "This has to be taken there. If I'm right, when the two active gems are put together, they will cancel each other out. Annihilate each other. But it's got to be done before the new frontier completely destroys the first. Else you're right—we'll be back where we started."

"But if you have to be dreaming to keep the doorway open… one of us will have to carry the thing. Am I right?"

Martin looked long and hard at him. Then he took Copeland by the shoulder and pulled him away from Debra. Softly, he said, "You're partially right. Once the gem becomes active, it maintains a connection between me and the other side, whether I'm asleep or not. Right now, while I'm awake, it's semi-dormant. Over time, it will start to function independently. But until then, yes…for it to become fully active, I've got to be in dream sleep."

"I see."

Another long silence. Then: "Russ, listen to me. I cannot ask my daughter to undertake this. So, I'm going to ask you. Will you bear this for me?"

His eyes searched Martin's weary, earnest face, then turned to the shining gemstone. Up close, it seemed to burn with a sinister, demonic light, as if its crystalline walls encased something alive and violent, desperately seeking a means to escape. The idea of touching the thing nauseated him. For a moment, hot resentment flooded his veins. He had survived thus far only by the grace of God. His body hurt like hell, and it urgently required rest and rejuvenation. How could anyone expect him to put his life on the line again—this time intentionally?

But Martin was right; no father could ask such a thing of his daughter. And neither would Copeland allow her to walk willingly into what amounted to certain death. If he denied Martin's request, anyone left alive in Silver Ridge—the three of them included—stood to face yet greater horror.

Finally, banishing any thought of the consequences from his mind, he said, "All right. Yeah."

"I can't lie to you, Russ. I don't know what your chances are. They can't be good. The forces you'll be exposed to—they're unimaginable. But you must believe me. This is truly our last, only hope."

He swallowed hard, the first twinges of dread beginning deep in his stomach. "I understand."

Martin stared thoughtfully at him. In a barely audible voice, he said, "It's been a long time since I've sent a man to his death. I never thought I'd have to do it again."

"You haven't issued an order."

"It amounts to the same thing." He glanced at Debra and then looked deeply into Copeland's eyes. He whispered, "Russ, don't tell her this, but...there will be consequences to me, as well. Because of my connection with this thing, I expect..." He swallowed hard. "No...I *know*...that I won't survive this."

Copeland's jaw clenched. He had no words, either for the major or for himself.

Debra's voice drifted to them. "Please, just stop it. I know what you intend to do."

Martin turned to her. "I'm sorry, Debra. What we're attempting is absolutely necessary. You must understand that."

"I do understand. That's why I'm going with Russ."

"Debra..."

"If he doesn't make it to the end, someone will have to finish the job."

For once, Martin appeared defeated, unable to summon the energy or the will to oppose his daughter. "If you do," he said, "at the end of the day, in all likelihood, all three of us will be dead."

Copeland gazed at Debra, suddenly remembering the thrill of her touch, how fervently they had made love. She smiled sadly at him; he made himself turn away.

Martin then gave them both long, searching looks. "Tell me, though. When you were in there, at the Barrows, you didn't learn anything about Elise, did you?"

Debra's eyes glimmered. "Levi told me if I cooperated with him, Mom wouldn't be harmed." After a long pause, she added, "But he was lying. I know it."

The older man lowered his head. "Yes. If she were alive, I would know. I'd know it."

Empathetic grief tugged at Copeland's heart as Debra's shoulders slumped. "So would I," she whispered. "And I don't. I don't know it."

As the silence between them grew longer. Martin nodded to himself, as if coming to grips with his own decision. "It's time we did this. This new one...it moves faster than the Lumeras did. It will anchor itself quickly."

"What do we do? How do we begin?" Debra asked.

"First, I'll have to go to sleep. It won't take long; once that thing has hold of you, it keeps pulling you back." He smiled sardonically. "Then I'll dream a portal for you, like the one that brought you here. Step through it. I know it's disconcerting, but it won't harm you. You'll be back at the point where you left. Then— assuming Amos is still there—you'll have to make your way inside the house. Get as close to the *Zuso Xhan Mat* as you can. I don't know at what point, but as the stones come into proximity, there will be a...reaction."

"What kind of reaction?" Copeland asked.

"At first, just pressure. You know what it's like to try to push the like-charged poles of two magnets together? Not unlike that. Beyond that, though, I can't say. I can only hope the forces destroy each other. They've got to."

"Anything else?"

Martin reached behind him and produced a pistol—an Army-issue Beretta M9—from his belt. He handed it to Copeland. "You may need this to use this against Amos. You can't afford to let him stand in your way. Beyond that, I don't know that it'll do you any good."

He tucked the gun in his waistband. "Thanks. Well, I guess I'd better get started before I change my mind."

"*We*," Debra corrected him. "You mean *we* had better get started."

He gave her a long, wistful look and sighed resignedly. "We."

Taking a deep breath, Martin lifted the softly pulsing gemstone and placed it in Copeland's waiting, trembling hand.

The thing felt frigid, and the throbbing light inside it seemed to change its rhythm. Its surface felt slick, as if coated with oil, and he had to grasp it firmly to prevent it slipping from his fingers. With a scowl of distaste, he slipped the stone into his pocket.

"I gather you don't need to keep this close to you when you're asleep?"

"Now that I'm attuned to it, I could go to China and it wouldn't make any difference."

"China doesn't sound so bad right now."

Martin chuckled wryly. Then he turned, took his daughter in his arms, and held her as if he did not intend to let her go. Finally, he whispered something in her ear and released her, his eyes glistening with tears. He appeared so frail and fatigued that Copeland feared he might collapse before he even lay down to dream. But with heartfelt sincerity, he clasped Copeland's hand and said, "Something tells me that, at the end of it all, we won't even get to see what we've wrought. But good luck, Russ. This is for those we've lost."

"For those we've lost," he said, squeezing the other's hand.

Martin then turned and shuffled back toward the corner by the painted window. "I've got a cot back here. It'll only take a minute or so for me to start dreaming. I can feel that thing's hold on me as we speak."

Debra pressed close to Copeland, watching her father's retreating figure. When he rounded a corner and disappeared in the darkness, a single, soft sob escaped her lips.

Wrapping an arm around her shoulders, he said. "I know I can't talk you out of this. So, I might as well tell you I'm glad you're with me. I don't know how I could do this alone."

She offered him a weak smile. "Scared, are you?"

"A bit."

"Liar."

"A lot."

"I thought so. You know, though…you've done okay in my book. You went through your own hell, but you still managed to come for me."

He squeezed her warmly. "I couldn't bear the idea of losing you. Not after what we went through together."

The look she gave him thrilled him so deeply that, for a few blissful moments, he completely forgot his terror. "You know, back at the cabin—just before the Lumeras attacked—I told you I loved you. You didn't hear me. But looking back, I think you knew it somehow."

She smiled. "I knew it before then."

"Like when?"

"Like the night you got here and watched me through your window."

His jaw went slack and he stared disbelievingly at her. "You've gotta be kidding."

A few feet away from them, a jade-green globe surrounded by whirling, orbiting sparkles winked into existence and hovered a yard or so above the floor. Slowly, it began to drift toward them, gradually expanding like an inflating balloon, soon becoming large enough to swallow them both. From it, they could hear the strains of a dark, distant chorale…ominous, yet alluring.

As the thing began to close over them and Copeland prepared himself for the onslaught of unknown, frigid forces, Debra embraced him and fiercely pressed her lips to his. He lost himself in her kiss, so that when the cold hit him with the force of a tsunami, he neither felt it nor cared about where it might carry his body.

The last thing he heard was Debra's voice whispering, "I love you too."

#

Chapter 23

The second exit from the jade abyss affected Copeland more drastically than the first; this time, the chill didn't leave his bones for a full minute, and his sparse reserve of energy seemed loath to return. But having emerged right in the middle of his worst nightmare, he quickly summoned the strength to scramble to the shelter of a stand of ordinary-looking pine trees at the edge of the Barrow property, with Debra close behind him. They fell behind a cluster of thick boles on the edge of a small hillock, which provided them with a clear view of the Barrow house, a hundred or so yards away. He wasn't sure he possessed the will to cross that open space, though, for doing so would expose him to eyes of the multitudes of luminous things that sailed ceaselessly across the purple sky, or the titanic black globe, which stood miles and miles above the earth on its dozens of arched, buttress-like legs.

Innumerable rents in the sky continuously hurled bolts of black lightning at the smoking tower, which appeared battered and somehow less substantial than before. The new, globe-like thing must be the equivalent of the Lumera's onyx structure, he thought, seeking to anchor itself in the waking world until it formed a permanent bridge to the realm of its nightmarish origin. Each occupied its own opposing corner of the sky, and the dark music had given way to peals of low thunder, which rumbled across the landscape like the threatening voices of monstrous, inhuman adversaries, either of which could crush the life from any mere human with the audacity to challenge them.

Copeland peered intently at the Barrow house and soon spied Amos in his upstairs window, listless and despondent, silently watching the clash of astral forces, neither of which involved him any longer. Totally self-absorbed, he probably still did not realize what had happened inside his own house—that the very things he had called down had wiped out his remaining family. No sympathy from this quarter, Copeland thought; the old man had had every opportunity to choose differently.

"I've got to get across that field," he said softly, fearing that something alien might detect his voice even above the distant thunder. "And there's only one way to do it."

"Yeah. On foot."

"All right. I want you to stay here and keep an eye on me. If I make it as far as the house, then you come. We can't afford for both of us to get caught in the open."

She looked as if she were going to protest, but then thought better of it. "All right. At least that rock of Dad's protected him from the Lumeras. No reason it shouldn't protect you, too."

"No telling what else there is to worry about now." He threw a glance at the vast, black, planet-like shape that dominated the southern sky. "I wonder what your dad learned about *that.*"

"When this is all over, hopefully we can ask him."

He shrugged noncommittally. Then, taking a deep, preparatory breath, he reached into his pocket and withdrew the cold, slick gemstone, radiating pale green, shifting and curdling like a phosphorescent liquid. As he held the object up before him, its inner light coalesced into a small, brilliant orb, like a luminous cat's eye, which peered curiously back at him, as if committing his features to memory. The force within it—or rather, behind and beyond it—was apparently in contact with Debra's father, many miles away. What if Martin should wake up and sever the connection? Or, God forbid, he should die? Would Copeland suddenly be rendered vulnerable, his mission pointless?

No; the thing had shielded Martin from the Lumera's attack even when he was awake.

Such speculation meant nothing, he reminded himself. He either succeeded or he failed; there was no in-between, and close didn't count.

"Well," he said, offering her a look of as much reassurance as he could muster, "I guess I'm off. If I make it all the way, then you come running. Fast as you can."

She nodded her agreement. "I don't guess saying 'be careful' means much. But be careful."

"If something happens to me..." He swallowed hard. "Just remember."

Her voice went weak. "I will."

He turned toward the house. Took a deep breath. And then his legs were pumping fast and hard, the broad field opening up before him, passing beneath his feet, becoming a gray-green blur, the chorus of dark voices roiling around him. As he ran, he again felt as if gravity had released him, leaving him light as a feather, the ground offering little resistance, reducing his traction. It was no illusion; with every step, he sprang higher into the air, yet his forward momentum steadily diminished. Halfway across the field, the ramshackle house seemed just as far away as when he broke from the trees, and he found himself virtually floating above the earth, working his arms against the air as if he were swimming. Conversely, the gemstone had begun to grow heavier, dragging his right hand earthward, interfering with the rhythm of his stride. The contradictory forces threatened to destabilize him—more mentally than physically, he thought, for the sensation was too alien, too suggestive of the unearthly forces he was springing headlong to meet. It was his mind, not his limbs, resisting acclimation.

Just as Martin had intimated, despite the lightness of his body, it felt like pushing against a powerful, opposing magnetic force.

He tried to divert his mind from his objective, to focus on anything other than the doom that awaited him within the next few minutes. He thought back to his childhood, remembering his mom and dad, how deeply they had loved Lynette and him, how proud Dad had been of his academic achievements at Byston Hill, his ambitions to succeed at a life far away from rural West Virginia. If his folks were around today, what would they think of what he was doing now?

No...turn the mind another way. Not back here.

God, it was hard to focus on anything for more than a moment or two. He realized that the gem, which he now had to support with both hands, had become a fiery green star, blazing so brightly that it could not fail to capture any eye that might glance his way.

Debra was still watching him, sending all her hopes with him. Not just for the two of them, but for her father, and the world they had once known.

What an incredible woman, one he wished he had met long ago, instead of crazy Megan, who would surely be in stitches over his current predicament. Rushing to a cliff just to pitch himself over the edge, all the while hoping he could fly; that's what she'd be thinking. That he was on a fool's errand, which could end in nothing less than a fool's death. How could he even think he might deserve the affection—the love—of a woman like Debra Harrington? Or even the respect and trust of her father?

Jesus, how could the wounds from his old breakup still be so raw? Was this just one of the things his mind needed to hash out before he met his final destiny? Could it be that, deep down, he still believed Megan might have been at least partly right? That in spite of whatever success he had achieved, he was still an insecure, immature, West Virginia redneck who had, because of his parents' wherewithal rather than his own, enjoyed better fortune than the rest of his peers—two of whom had met their end, only a few hours earlier?

STOP IT!

Gravity had increased its hold. Still, the house seemed infinitely distant, miles and miles away, but in the upper window, he glimpsed Amos Barrow—who had no doubt noticed the advancing green flame, which to him could herald nothing less than the approach of death itself. He could not yet make out the old man's features; just a pale, bloated face highlighted by a dim, electric blue glow.

Yes. He still held the *Zuso Xhan Mat*.

Suddenly, Copeland's next step did not send him springing almost helplessly into the air but barely propelled him at all. At the edge of his hearing, he detected mumbled words, almost but not quite intelligible. Not a human voice, but articulate thunder. Weight returned with a vengeance, and now the gem was a boulder dragging him into the depths of a vast, unearthly drowning pool. Slowly, he became aware of a hot gaze bearing down on him from above. No mistaking its power, the dark intelligence behind it, even if his own eyes had yet to meet it. It bore deliberately down upon him, a scorching sun on the exposed back of a desert wanderer, sapping his strength, his resolve. It tried to draw his eyes upward, but he somehow resisted, fearing that meeting so potent a gaze would vaporize him on the spot, end his mission before he got far enough for Debra to finish it. Instead, he focused solely on the house, on the figure of Amos Barrow, whose features he could now see, peering back at him with a curious expression, as if he were no more significant than a raccoon or a deer that had wandered out of the woods.

Even now, that idiot didn't realize how precarious his hold on life had become.

Something powerful and fiery, like an arc of electricity, seized his body, gripped his neck, and tugged his head backward, so that his face could not help but lift to the sky. He clenched his eyelids shut, felt the incredible power burn his forehead, his cheeks, and burrow into the knife wounds, which began to throb anew. Then hot, invisible fingers moved to pry open his eyes, and no amount of willpower could fend them off. With a hoarse curse, he stumbled forward, tried to throw himself to the ground, anything to prevent viewing the thing that had singled him out and taken control of his muscles.

The cat's eye in the stone now pulsed rapidly, brilliantly, and that dark, ethereal chorus of inhuman voices roared down from the sky, swept over him, and built to a swirling crescendo that shook his whole body, threatened to scatter it to atoms. He dragged himself a few more steps, his neck on the verge of breaking as invisible puppet strings wrenched his head inexorably upward.

Jesus, God.

The vast black globe, no longer supported by spidery legs but floating free, like a marauding, onyx planet, had expanded in the violet sky and now dominated its entire southern half. The thing appeared to be drifting nearer—on a collision course with the earth. Dizzy and nauseated, he dropped to his knees, his eyes throbbing as if some hideous, invisible force threatened to tear them from their sockets. The pressure of the music mounted in his skull, and a pale green halo formed around the black moon, its glow revealing strange features upon its distant, onyx surface.

No, not *on* but *behind* its surface. The globe gradually became transparent, and now he saw within it a wavering, disembodied face, like a jade-colored death mask suspended inside a liquid-filled crystal ball. It was not human face; maybe not a face at all. Just a flat, two-dimensional lozenge shape with wide, circular openings he took to be eyes, completely empty, yet radiating awareness and…recognition.

This was what Major Martin had called down to destroy the Lumeras?

My God, compared to this nightmare, the Lumeras were angels.

The alien tower, tall and spindly, still pierced the northern sky, but it appeared fragile and innocuous compared to this new horror. Overhead, the vast globe began to distort, the lower end elongating, the other swelling, until it became an inverted pear shape—a head *outside* its depthless, leering face. Its empty eyes studied him, and the hot gaze felt as if it were flaying the skin from his bones, so that it revealed everything inside him down to his heart and soul.

It wondered what he was doing—and why.

Jesus. If this thing determined his true intention, surely it could—and would—obliterate him instantly.

Just don't let it know. Don't let it know.

He tore his eyes away long enough to glance at the Barrow house, now tantalizingly close, its back door still gaping wide. If he could escape the burning gaze, maybe the pressure would subside, allow him to proceed to the bitter end, all thought of which he desperately blocked from his mind—both for his sanity's sake and for fear that the extra-dimensional intelligence might somehow pluck his thoughts directly from his brain.

Amos's mild curiosity turned to concern as Copeland's steps brought him slowly but inevitably nearer to the house. Perhaps the old man's gemstone had begun to react as the second one came within its range, alerting him to the possibility of danger. Still, he made no move to leave his post, and after a few more steps, Copeland found himself in the backyard, no longer in view of Amos's window. His body felt so heavy that he could barely move, and every muscle howled in protest as he lifted one foot and then the other, his only goal to escape the gaze of the monstrous dream entity above.

If he succeeded, anything afterward was gravy.

Another plodding step. Then another. And then he felt a slight cooling of the superheated air, a dimming of the glare from above. His brain vaguely registered that he had stepped under the eaves of the Barrow's back porch, which obscured the face of the horror in the sky. He knew it remained aware of him, that his sense of relief was largely illusory; regardless, he took a few moments to catch his breath and give his aching muscles a respite. He turned to look back at the stand of trees where Debra waited to witness the outcome of his efforts.

An electric jolt nearly tore his legs out from under him.

Instead of a broad field of grass, a jungle of thorny, metallic-looking creepers protruded from the earth, twisted and tangled, some swaying as if stroked by a gentle breeze. Even as he watched, more of them sprouted from the earth and wove their way skyward, some rising twenty feet or more above his head. They rustled and rattled as they moved, and a few of the nearer ones began to creep tentatively toward him.

These things belonged to the Lumera's world. If Amos still had any control over his gemstone, maybe they were his doing. Or perhaps some natural defense, triggered by Copeland's proximity to the *Zuso Xhan Mat*. Whatever the case, the living barrier had completely separated him from Debra.

How could he not have foreseen such a possibility?

No time to indulge in regrets or self-reproach. The task now fell to him alone, and if he failed, there was no one to back him up.

"God help me," he murmured and stepped into the gloom of the Barrow's kitchen. The house's interior wore a surreal violet mask, the shadows all deep purple. The windows admitted only weird, refracted beams of magenta, maroon, and pink. The air here was dank and cool, yet far from refreshing after his torturous trek beneath the alien's hot gaze. In here, however, silence replaced the peals of thunder and the eerie chorale. Not a creak or whisper came from any corner of the house.

Dead silence.

No sign of the Lumera that had killed Levi and Malachi. Probably still in the cellar or upstairs with Amos.

He took a single step into the hallway that led to the living room. Boards groaned beneath his feet, setting his teeth on edge; but Amos already knew he was coming, so there was little point in stealth. Carefully holding the gleaming gem in one hand, he reached for the gun Martin had given him with the other, drew it, and tried to hold it steady. The stone still felt like a piece of lead, so he tucked it tight against his stomach in his right hand, the pistol in his left, and at an excruciating creep made his way toward the front of the house. When he at last reached the stairwell, he halted and peered upward, only to find an impenetrable wall of purple shadow waiting for him, concealing God knew what.

He regarded the thick veil almost with disinterest. "Well, the hell with you," he said. Drawing a deep, bracing breath, he placed his foot on the first step, anticipating a deep, weary groan and a possible attack.

Something rustled and clattered metallically in the darkness above.

The thorny tendrils, which seemed to serve as a living barrier against intruders, he thought. No telling how many of the things up there. Would the green gemstone protect him—perhaps respond automatically to this product of another dream realm? He braved another step, and the rattling noises increased their fervor.

The shadows had become a shifting, dancing mass of half-seen shapes, and as if in response, the gem in his hand throbbed even more brilliantly. Another step up, leading with his gun, though he knew it was useless against anything other than Amos. The scuttling, writhing things upstairs scraped and clattered against the wall, and with a tiny thrill of hope—the first he had known since he set out on this mission—Copeland realized they were not moving to intercept him but retreating.

Still, each step he took required more effort than the last, and finally, with only a couple of steps to go, his knees buckled, his legs too rubbery to support his weight. Then he glimpsed, above the stairs, quick flash of silvery, reflected light, and something slashed the air so close to his head he could feel the rush of wind.

Not all of them had retreated....

A burst of adrenaline sent him moving again, this time on his elbows and knees. To his relief, the thing did not strike at him again.

At last, he found himself facing the violet-shaded, upstairs hallway, which extended before him like a limitless tunnel; a pale blue glow illuminated Amos's open bedroom door, some impossible distance away. Here, he found not a single trace of the Lumeras' defensive tendrils, or other hint of movement.

He pulled himself to his feet and began walking what he prayed would be the final distance before the end.

The gun shook so violently he could barely keep his grip on it, much less aim it, so he let it drop heavily to the floor and used both hands to grip his terrible treasure—which shifted like a snake struggling to escape his clutches. Its surface, which had been so cold and slippery, began to heat up, and its pulsing, internal light intensified, as if to signal alarm.

The thing in the sky...had it finally deduced his intention?

Jarring currents passed through his hands, up his arms, to

his shoulders. Like holding onto a livewire, he thought. God, he wanted this to end—*now!* The strain on his body and nerves was too much; he wasn't even sure whether he was sane any longer, for time stood still, then raced past as he struggled onward. The end of the hallway, infinitely distant, suddenly rushed to meet him. Amos's door gaped wide as if to swallow him. His head reeled as the floor and ceiling switched places, but now, he was beyond fear, beyond reason.

With no thought of the consequences, he took his final step into the room.

Electric blue light exploded in his eyes, ravaged his body, burned like the rays of a sapphire sun. Faint voices began to scream, maybe human, maybe not; hellish, horrifying shrieks that first crept out of the distance and then encircled him, becoming shriller and more potent, drilling relentlessly into his mind.

Through the pain, he felt a small thrill of satisfaction, for these screams belonged to his adversaries.

Something mumbled its way through the unearthly caco-phonies, a low, barely discernible noise that he thought came from something human.

"Mmmisterrr Copelannnd…"

Far, far away, he saw a bulky silhouette limned with sapphire blue—except for the eyes. They blazed in the featureless head like xenon headlights, their beams sweeping over him, transmitting loathing and terror. The last of the Barrow clan stood before his window, through which Copeland could see black shadows racing through a violet sky and clusters of barb-covered, metallic stalks curling and writhing like snakes in mortal agony. The two gemstones flared simultaneously, like dual suns, one blue, one green; Copeland's arms absorbed a sudden shock, and a wave of pressure forced him several steps backward. His entire body went numb, and this time, when he dropped to his knees, he found nothing left inside to draw upon. He wobbled to one side and sagged against the wall, barely keeping himself from toppling to the floor.

"Nottt thisss tttime," came Amos's voice. "Yooou won't tttake thisss from meee."

Outside, the jungle of entwined cords became a whirling blur, then vanished like smoke in a fierce wind. The violet hue of the sky began to shift toward turquoise and then to emerald. A few seconds later, it swirled back to violet.

"It's already been…taken…from…you," Copeland whispered. "You've lost."

Amos, engaged in his own struggle against the monstrous, unearthly forces, shook his head. "Nooo."

Copeland leaned forward and tried to crawl, but even that remained beyond his ability. The green stone lurched in his hands, as if to retreat from the *Zuso Xhan Mat*, but he hugged the thing to his chest, felt its raw power seeping into his body, into his heart. Melting him from the inside out. A quick glance down, and he saw that, in the center of the brilliant jade fire, the stone's heart had turned solid black.

A spent ember.

As spent as his entire body.

He lay on the filthy floor for inestimable ages, his lungs laboring for every breath of hot air, his head spinning, his eyes too heavy to hold open. This had been a battle between the Barrows and Major Martin all along, and he had brought Martin's fight as far as he could. Now, at the last, he had come so close, only to falter beneath the searing forces of opposing dream worlds. Perhaps strangely, he felt no bitterness, no anger; just regret at being separated from Debra here at the end. Still, her chances of surviving much longer were not good, and her father might already be dead or dying. He hardly envied her, alone in a world turned alien and hostile, her inevitable death conceivably far worse than his own.

If anything beyond this life existed, he thought, let it be nothing like the realms of dream now careening madly through his fading reality. If he was lucky, he would be reunited with Lynette, his mom and dad, Doug McAllister…all those he had loved and lost in his lifetime.

And maybe Debra, all too soon.

Something touched his shoulder, and he started. A brilliant, shifting blue and green sea surrounded him, and he could see nothing else, not even Amos. But then he heard a familiar voice, soft but insistent.

Was he dreaming? Or perhaps dead?

"Russ, it's me. Give me the gem. You have to let go of it."

It *was* her!

Gradually, her features took shape in the awry universe of light, her figure ghostly, insubstantial. But he felt her hands on his, solid and firm, prying the gemstone from his pain-locked fingers.

"You made it," he managed to whisper.

"Only just," she said. "Russ, let go of the thing. I've got to hurry."

He tried to relax his hands, but his muscles had little desire to obey his wishes. Finally, he felt her fingers close around the throbbing object and tug it from his own.

Immediately, the vast sea of light dwindled to two separate, small but brilliant flares at opposite ends of Amos's chamber. The old man stood framed against his window, which now revealed a horrifying backdrop: the oblong, crystalline head in the sky, the eyes of the face within it focused deliberately on the window, seeking the source of its unfathomable distress.

Debra now moved slowly toward Amos, brandished the small, flaming globe like a crucifix before the devil. But the old man appeared oblivious, all his attention on the thing in the sky. Amid the constant rumble of thunder, a strange warbling sound crept to his ears, and Copeland realized that it was Amos, sobbing.

Debra moved as if half-submerged in quicksand, her body now subject to the same forces that had assailed him so relentlessly. But she made definite progress, closing on Amos and his precious stone with almost superhuman determination. Copeland could feel, if not see, the electricity crackling between the two alien spheres. The blue glow of the *Zuso Xhan Mat* had diminished discernibly, and the rhythmic pulsating of the other had become erratic, like a heart in the grip of cardiac arrest.

Just a few more steps and she would be there.

Outside, something—a long black shadow—came creeping out of the sky toward the window.

"Hurry," he whispered, his heart picking up steam. "Please."

With a crash, a portion of the wall around the window fell away, leaving a jagged opening from floor to ceiling, some eight feet wide. Outside, a new cluster of metallic ropes came sliding down from above, wriggled through the opening, and quested about like tentative feelers. One of them touched Amos's legs and he cried out shrilly, either in surprise, pain, or both.

Through the opening, Copeland saw, silhouetted against the chaotic, shadow-filled violet sky, the Lumera's onyx tower. It had begun to crumble.

More of the metal fingers curled in and closed around Amos's body. He let out a few hoarse barks of protest, then screeched as the barbs gripped and flayed his skin. It was only as the cords began to drag him toward the opening that Copeland realized what was happening.

"Debra!" he croaked. "They're trying to pull the blue one away from you!"

Spurred on either by his cry or the realization that they stood to lose everything in a matter of seconds, Debra coiled her muscles and launched herself after the old man, heedless of the thorny tendrils entwining themselves around his frantically thrashing body. She collided with him, nearly losing her footing, remaining upright only by gripping the gem in one hand and clutching one of the long barbs with the other. With a cry, she thrust her glowing stone toward the one in Amos's desperately clenched hands, which the cords had rendered immobile.

As the two dreamstones made contact, the entire world seemed to draw a shocked breath.

In the next instant—

Debra fell away from the big man as if she had been kicked. She landed on her backside and threw out her hands—now both empty—to break her fall.

The metallic coils entrapping Amos melted away like wax beneath a flame, but he continued to scream and writhe as if his body were ablaze. His hands—also empty—rose to his throat as if to pull away something that throttled him. But there was nothing there.

Outside, the bruised, purple and black sky brightened and turned cerulean blue. The dark, swirling shadows transitioned to white, gently floating cumulus clouds that caught the rays of a warm golden sun blazing overhead.

The booming, inhuman aria softened, receding steadily into some unimaginable distance, and the last peals of thunder trailed away until the only sound left was the soft whisper of a gentle spring breeze.

No longer weighed down by incalculable forces, Copeland dragged himself to his feet and braced himself against the wall, taking long, deep breaths, barely able to believe that life still lingered in his tortured body. He shuffled toward Debra, who propped herself on her elbows, her eyes still staring past Amos Barrow, locked on something beyond the gaping hole in the wall.

The skeletal remains of Lumera's tower pierced the sky like a twisted, misshapen onyx sculpture—the last remaining trace of either Dream Frontier. As he watched, great pieces of the structure cracked off and hurtled earthward, where they struck like black meteors, splashing earth and rock into the air and leaving huge, yawning craters.

All in total silence. No deafening booms of impact, no groaning of tortured, overstressed stone.

The tall spire slowly melted into the black stone framework, which then collapsed upon itself, throwing up huge clouds of gray dust that billowed into the sky and rolled toward the sun as if summoned by the hands of Helios. Still, no sound rose above the light breeze, and after a few seconds, the dust, the tower's remains, the craters…all had disappeared without a trace.

A few giant fireflies spun wildly in the air, spiraled together as if caught in a huge vortex, and then vanished, drawn back into the outer gulfs from which they sprang.

The nightmare doors had closed.

The old Earth had come home.

#

Copeland had no idea how long he and Debra clung to each other in the corner of Amos's devastated room. The old man had staggered a short distance toward the hallway door and then collapsed, bleeding profusely. Whether alive or dead, Copeland couldn't guess and didn't really care.

Debra appeared to have lost consciousness, so he carefully extricated himself from her arms, which prompted her to stir restlessly, but she did not fully wake. Haltingly, he rose to his feet, testing his muscles, gauging how much movement he could stand before the pain kicked in.

Not much.

In spite of their malodorous surroundings, the air wafting in from outside smelled fresh, purified, invigorating; and after a time, some life began to creep back into his limbs. His chest and stomach ached from the beatings, and his cheek felt as if it had split wide open, but no fresh blood appeared on his fingertips when he gingerly probed the wound. The shallower cut along his jaw was nothing, his nicked inner cheek merely an annoyance. Probably needed a tetanus shot, though; God knew where Joshua's blade had been.

His energy would return. His wounds would heal. Somehow, he and Debra had both survived. But what about her father? Major Martin had anticipated his own death, but he had also predicted Copeland wouldn't survive. Maybe the old man had gotten lucky. For Debra's sake he hoped so.

The sunlit world outside nearly blinded him with its lushness, its vivid spring colors. Its sheer aspect of normality. He had firmly believed he would never see anything like this ever again, and now it seemed too good to be true. The aromatic breeze charged his blood like tonic, and he longed to get away from this decrepit old house and the terrible memories it held for him. They had a long way to go to get back to town—assuming it had not been completely destroyed—but if he had to walk the whole way, then walk he would. First order of business was to get back to Major Martin.

But for Debra's father, none of this would have happened. But without him, none of them would be alive now.

As he reached down to wake Debra, a low, pained groan came

from behind him, and he turned to see Amos stirring on the floor. Bereft of his gemstone and its accompanying power, he seemed little more than an obese, weak, cowardly fool who ought to be locked up for his own good—if he survived.

Pitiful old bastard.

Amos struggled to a sitting position and rubbed his eyes with his bloodstained, grotesquely fat hands. He swiveled to look at Copeland, and as he did, his face contorted into a mask of pure terror and rage, his color going from pallid to purple. He clenched his eyelids shut and began to scream, long and shrill, his vocal cords straining almost to the point of breaking. Then he leaned forward and began beating the floor with his fists, the blows sending up filthy plumes of dust from the ratty carpet, splattering blood across the room, and shaking the wooden walls.

Jesus. He had gone stark, raving mad.

Debra stirred, sighed softly, and opened her eyes, disturbed by Amos's violent fit. She sat up and stared at the old man, her expression betraying disgust. Slowly, she stood, and as Copeland moved to take her in his arms, he halted, realizing that something about her had changed.

They stood at arm's length, each studying the other's face. Copeland felt a sudden tremor in his gut, a little thrill of terror that all was still not exactly as it seemed.

Debra's eyes had changed from deep brown to bright, emerald green.

"Russ," she whispered, pointing to his face. "Oh, my God, your eyes. Your eyes!"

#

Three Days Later

Chapter 24

"There is still no official count of fatalities in Silver Ridge, West Virginia, following what authorities have termed only as 'an unprecedented, unknown catastrophe,' but the number is estimated at well over a thousand. In this community of just under 10,000 people, the loss of life is staggering, and neither scientists nor local citizens have been able to offer any explanation for the events that literally isolated this town from the rest of the world for a period of three days."

Debra's house felt cold and somber, enshrouded by the same deathly pall that had overtaken the town since its reversion to relative normality. Following their return from the Barrow house, Copeland had stayed with her, unable to bring himself to face the emptiness of Lynette's home so soon after losing her. Eventually, he knew, he would need to settle her affairs, but that was the last thing on his mind while he and the rest of the world struggled to come to grips with what had happened here. There would be more affairs to settle in Silver Ridge than his mind could comprehend.

"In addition to the terrible human tragedy, property damage in Silver Ridge has been estimated in the millions. Aerial photographic surveys reveal that roughly two-thirds of the structures in the affected area have been destroyed or damaged. But what has most baffled experts is the fact that, in numerous locations, the lay of the land has been altered significantly, resulting in the destruction or dislocation of many homes and other buildings. According to geologists, these alterations are not typical of any known seismic activity, and none has been detected in the vicinity during the past ten days."

The media had run story after story about the mysterious, impassable "chasm" that had completely encircled Silver Ridge, and while reporters, scientists, clergymen, and everyone's little brother posed questions aplenty, not a soul had offered so much as a reasonable theory to explain the nightmarish events.

And who could? Perhaps only certain inhabitants of shadowy lands halfway around the world, few of whom would likely ever learn of the tragedy suffered by this small Appalachian town. Probably for the best, Copeland thought. And God forbid that any more devices such as those Major Glen Martin possessed should ever see the light of day.

Amos Barrow had been found wandering some distance from his wrecked house, but no one dared approach him, for he had gone completely, violently insane; it had taken four members of the National Guard to subdue him and take him into protective custody. He died the next day without having spoken an intelligible word, so the news reports said. Some witnesses who knew him claimed that his eyes had not always been a brilliant, sapphire blue.

"Russ?" Debra's voice drifted down from her bedroom.

He turned off the television and went to the foot of the stairs. "Yes? You all right?"

"Wanted to make sure you were still here."

"I'm here."

He started up the stairs. Despite how prepared she'd thought she had been to face her parents' deaths, Debra had still suffered a crushing, debilitating blow. Having once believed her father already dead, only to find him alive, she had dared to hope against hope; but this time it was not to be, for at some point during the final conflict, he had apparently suffered a fatal coronary. And no trace of Elise Martin, either living or dead, had yet been found—a sad fact Debra had already anticipated. Her personal losses, along with the shock of all that had happened to the town, to everyone she cared about, had devastated her spirit, and Copeland knew that only time would restore it—assuming the damage was not irreparable.

She sat in front of her dresser, gazing into the mirror. Since their return, she had spent far too much time there, staring deeply into the emerald crystals that she knew did not belong to her. She wanted to understand, he thought, to know how—or how deeply—her experiences had affected her. *Changed* her.

Unlike her, he had avoided mirrors as if the image they reflected might burn out his eyes and sear his brain. He averted his gaze as he came up behind her, leaned down, and gently kissed her cheek.

"You're still planning to go back to Chicago?" she asked, her tone flat.

"I have to," he said. "But not for long. I've got to take care of my business there. Then I'll be back."

"That's right. You told me."

"I wish you'd come with me."

She shook her head. "I can't leave. Not after all this. I have to…help. So many people have lost so much."

"You need to heal first. We both do. No one else was as close to any of this as we were."

A sullen nod, and she continued to stare at her reflection. He caught a glimpse of himself and, almost against his will, glanced at the blazing green jewels where his own gray-blue eyes ought to have been. He turned away quickly.

During the heat of his ordeal, he had erected a veritable wall of numbness, of separation from himself, knowing he *had* to survive and maybe stay sane. After that wall finally crumbled, his grief over Lynette's death came rushing back and dealt a powerful, almost debilitating blow; but as with the physical torture he had suffered,

269

he had rebounded in a short time. So far, neither he nor Debra had spoken a word to any authorities about their experiences, and if he had his way, they never would. What a horror life would become if others should learn what they knew—especially the hawks at the Department of Homeland Security. At best, he and Debra would find themselves spirited away to some secret facility and endlessly tested, interrogated, scrutinized. Caged.

No, he never intended to share his ordeal with another living soul besides Debra.

But he wanted to be able to share them with her forever.

He had no clue what he might do from here. His life lay in Chicago; there was nothing for him in Silver Ridge but Debra. And she would never be happy in the city.

He almost laughed at himself. *Happy.* Neither of them would ever see life with their old eyes again—quite literally. *Happy* now meant looking out the window and seeing a clear blue sky instead of a violet, shadow-filled gulf. But sometimes the sky seemed little more than a thin, fragile mask, perhaps for a monstrous, crystalline face watching them from…somewhere.

The transformation of their irises, surely, was the merest tip of the iceberg. The hours Debra spent in front of the mirror represented her quest to find its underlying heart. He wasn't yet ready to do that—to look that deep inside.

His gravest fear—and most haunting suspicion—was that he would not *need* to go looking.

"Are you hungry?" he asked.

"Yes. Don't know if I can eat, though."

"I'll fix you something. Try."

"Whatever."

As he went down to the kitchen, for an instant, he thought he was on the stairs of the old Barrow house, trying to find a way out. A gust of panic almost swept over him, but it abated before it could mount. Every now and then, he had one of these moments. Probably a natural reaction to his trauma, a delayed stress reaction. It didn't *have* to have anything to do with his body's physiological change; it was just a natural aftereffect, right?

He found himself pouring a glass of scotch rather than fixing any food. But hell, that was no more a result of repressed anxiety or unresolved fear than anything else he did; on an average day he had two drinks, and he had not increased his intake since the demise of the Dream Frontier. He had taken to analyzing his every move, second-guessing any thought in his head, hesitant to trust even his most mundane action—trying to prove to himself he was completely normal, unaffected.

But he wasn't. He *knew* he wasn't. Somehow, he had to accept that he wasn't.

He took a long swig of the scotch, relished its smoky burn, its spreading, fortifying warmth. He opened the refrigerator and rummaged for food, found sandwich fixings of various varieties; he sort of craved a grilled cheese.

"Russell."

There it was again.

He thought he'd heard someone whisper his name a time or two in the last couple of days, each instance when he was alone and everything was quiet. This was the first time it had been so clear, so unmistakable.

It sounded like Lynette.

But it couldn't be Lynette. She was gone. Forever. Dead.

How did he know for certain she was dead?

Just a stirred-up memory, that was all; a pang of repressed grief that had strayed to the forefront of his consciousness. Regret, maybe, for having cared too little about her when she was alive—when caring actually meant something.

He turned on the stove, dug through the cabinets to find a fry pan, and angrily shoved the errant thoughts out of his head. He almost wanted a cigarette.

Okay, I admit it. That's the stress talking.

There were plenty of smokes left in Lynette's house. He could always walk next door and grab a pack.

I will not go into that house. Not now. Not yet.

Not till he had gone home, gotten his ducks in a row at the office, and then returned. By then he would be able to face the task of closing out Lynette's life and getting on with his own. Maybe by then he and Debra would have devised some plan for a future together.

He buttered the bread slices, closed the cheese between them, and dropped them into the fry pan. The aroma immediately reached inside him and tugged the nerves that signaled hunger. At least he could eat again. During the crisis, he had gone a full forty-eight hours without food, and afterward, even when he was almost doubled over with hunger pains, he hadn't been able to choke anything down; not until most of another day had passed.

The sandwiches done, he flipped them onto a plate. Debra liked the flavored bottled water, so he grabbed one from the fridge, balanced his refreshed glass of scotch on the plate, and started back upstairs, this time feeling almost as if he were walking back into a normal, prosaic world, one that had never been altered, where he and the woman he wanted for his new wife could anticipate nothing but a future of hope, health, and happiness.

When he entered her room, he found her still in front of the mirror, but now standing naked, her clothes scattered haphazardly around the floor. She turned slowly to face him, and somehow, the sparkling emeralds in her eyes made her all the more beautiful. *Yet somehow frightening.* He placed the plate and drinks on the dresser as she came to him, and he took her in his arms, lowering his head to press his lips to hers. Her fingers were at the buttons of his shirt in an instant, twisting them open, and then she was leading him to her bed, where she pulled his body over hers like a warm, comforting blanket. He worked himself free of his clothes, and in another minute, he was inside her, meeting her fervently heaving body with forceful, ardent thrusts.

They both opened their eyes at the same time, and the two pairs of emerald crystals met and held each other.

Copeland felt raw power crackling between them, an electric arc that increased in intensity along with his excitement.

Then he closed his eyes again because, far in the depths of hers, he saw shifting black shadows slowly beginning to take shape.

#

"I'll be back in less than a week. But I've got to make sure a number of cases are settled or I'm going to wish we were still facing Lumeras."

"Don't talk like that."

"Sorry. This is important, though. If I can get certain people exactly where I need them, then I'll be free and clear for the foreseeable future. Then we can start making our own plans."

"I understand. I don't like it, but I understand."

"Maybe," he added, a little hesitantly, "getting my mind totally back on ordinary work is just what I need to get grounded again. Maybe then I'll be able to deal with coming back...and handling Lynette's affairs."

"I just don't look forward to being alone. Even for a short time."

"I keep asking you to come with. We couldn't be together all the time, but at least you'd be away from...this. There's nothing for you here but pain."

She shook her head. "That's not true. This is still my home, and I love it...in its way. And I can do some good here, I know I can. I've been trying to do good with these kids for a long time, and they're going to need all the help they can get. Maybe that's what *I* need to do to get grounded again."

He let out a little sigh. "I don't like that, either, but I understand."

"I'll miss you. Even if it's just for a week."

"Yeah. It'll be a long one. But when I get back, we'll figure out what we have to do to make things work for us. You still want that, right?"

"Yes," she said with a solemn nod. "That's exactly what I want."

"Me too."

He looked out the screened door at the Lexus parked in the driveway. Miraculously, or close to it, he had found his car intact, right where he had left it in front of the sheriff's office. *The missing, presumed dead sheriff.* Steeling himself, he pushed the door open and went out into the cool, sunlit morning, which waited for him in silence, except for a few distant, melodious birdsongs. Debra came after him, her pace purposely restrained.

"What are you going to tell people who know you were here?"

He shrugged. "Not a damn thing. Maybe just that I don't remember anything."

"You think they'll believe that?"

"Don't care whether they ido or don't."

She sighed. "You may get some tough questions. I mean, the obvious change…"

"It doesn't matter. There's no one I'd share any of this with. Not there."

"I know. I know what you feel. But maybe we'll need to someday. Maybe we won't be able to keep it just between us."

"We'll worry about it when the time comes. Not before."

She gave him a little smile. "Okay." Then she opened her arms to him, and he took her in a long embrace. He touched his lips to her forehead, and she breathed deeply, contentedly.

"I guess I'm off," he said. "I'll call you when I get home."

"You'd better. You'd better call every day, or…"

"Or what?"

"Or I'll have to keep you after school every day when you get back."

"Yes, teacher."

Their lips came together and parted only reluctantly a long minute later. Then he released her and checked the back seat to make sure he had his bag, which she had retrieved from Lynette's house for him. He opened the door and slid behind the wheel.

Debra stood beside the car, and he saw her eyes glistening. He had nearly grown accustomed to the bright green.

It didn't mean anything. It was just a color. Just a new, unusual color.

"Drive carefully."

He nodded. "You be careful too. I don't want to hear any bad reports about you when I get back."

Her smile was genuine. "I promise."

"I love you."

"Love you too."

He started the engine, gave her house a long last gaze, and shifted into reverse, turning to look behind him rather than watch in the mirror. As he pulled into the street and started toward town, they raised their hands to each other.

Then she was out of sight, and the cold, gray road lay ahead of him.

He drove on autopilot, his mind still with her, the scent of her home still wafting through his mind. He did not see the charred frames of devastated houses and buildings, or the rubble that still closed some of the streets, or the flashing lights and emergency crews that lingered in certain areas. It was time to start thinking of home, of what he had to do to get his company on track for an extended period without him, of the serious choices he would have to make in the not-so-distant future.

"Russell!"

It was in the car with him.

A voice from a dream...from deep in his own memory. That's all it was.

Lynette was dead.

To his right, he saw the diminutive shack called the Chicken House; it was closed but had apparently weathered the cataclysm. Just a few days ago, it had perched on the precipice of the land beyond beyond.

His eyes briefly turned to the mirror, and he saw something.

In the back seat.

A dark, smoky shadow. Just a silhouette. But one he recognized.

"Jesus," he whispered as his heart slammed into high gear. His foot hit the brake, and the car swerved to the side of the road, skidding to a halt just beyond the entrance to the little restaurant.

The back seat was empty now.

He sat there for a good couple of minutes, breathing heavily, trying to slow his heart's jackhammer pounding.

What...was Lynette's ghost haunting him now?

As he turned back to face the road, something flashed brilliantly in the rearview mirror, again startling him. It took him a moment to realize it had been his own eyes, briefly reflected in the glass.

Something was happening in his head; he could feel it, had

been feeling it since the day of their return. His intuition suggested that his senses were retuning themselves, adjusting to some unknown spectrum, a new wavelength, to detect things that his mundane senses could not.

The Dream Frontier's legacy.

He put the car into gear again and pulled back onto the road, anxiously scanning his surroundings with his newly refined eyesight. He did not *want* to see the dead; he had *no business* seeing the dead. Nor should he be able to hear their voices.

A glance upward, and he saw a vague, aqua-tinted shadow crawling slowly across the canopy of blue.

"No!"

The gemstones were gone. There was nothing left to open the way to a new dream realm.

Except for the two people who had borne the second alien object and been subject to its unknown energies. Who had been somehow transformed.

Transformed into what?

"God," he whispered, and hit the brakes again. Without a care for any oncoming traffic, he spun the car around in the middle of the road and sped back in the direction of Silver Ridge, knowing he had to get to Debra. To get back to her and never leave her again because, if he did…

The car screamed to a stop as his foot shoved the brake pedal nearly through the floor.

Stretched out before him, from horizon to horizon, a vast, gaping chasm had opened in the earth and was slowly filling with swirling gray mist even as he watched. Soon, at the farthest reaches of the gulf, strange, mammoth black shapes were swimming through an endless sea of fog, soaring upward like breaching whales, then quickly sounding again.

He slid out of the car on rubbery legs and surveyed his surroundings.

Above, the sun had turned to quicksilver, the sky a luminous turquoise, and from a great distance the eerie strains of dark, inhuman choral music drifted to his ears.

THE NIGHTMARE FRONTIER

Beside his car, Copeland dropped to his knees and wept.

~END~

Meet the Author

Stephen Mark Rainey is author of the novels *Balak, Dark Shadows: Dreams of the Dark* (with Elizabeth Massie), *Blue Devil Island, The Gods of Moab, The House at Black Tooth Pond,* and many others; over 200 published works of short fiction; six short-fiction collections; and a trio of audio dramas for Big Finish Productions based on the *Dark Shadows* TV series, featuring several original cast members. From 1987 to 1997, he edited the award-winning *Deathrealm* magazine and has edited anthologies for Chaosium, Arkham House, Delirium Books, and Shortwave Publishing. Mark lives in Martinsville, VA, with his wife, Kimberly, and a houseful of precocious house cats. He is an avid geocacher and frequently explores "challenging" settings that most sane individuals would avoid. Visit his website at **www.stephenmarkrainey.com**.